For
Stephanie
Enjoy!
Enjoy! Enjoy!

THE WITCH OF AGNESI

ROBERT SPILLER

Bob Spiller

2006

Bronze Imprint
Medallion Press, Inc.
Printed in USA

Dedication:

For my wife, Barbara Spiller.

Published 2006 by Medallion Press, Inc.
The MEDALLION PRESS LOGO
is a registered tradmark of Medallion Press, Inc.

Printed in the United States of America
Typeset in Sabon

10 9 8 7 6 5 4 3 2 1
First Edition

Acknowledgements:

I'd like to thank my critique group for all the hours they put in on my manuscripts:

William Mason
Beth Groundwater
Barb Nickless
Maria Faulconer
Jimmi Butler
Annette Kohlmeister
Shawn Rapjack

CHAPTER 1

THURSDAY WAS SHAPING UP INTO ONE OF those days that made Bonnie Pinkwater wish for a dart gun, the kind used to put rhinos, or in this case teenagers, to sleep. She brushed a gray tendril of hair from her forehead and held up her hands, palms toward her twenty-six student class, the signal for quiet. "One at a time."

Stephanie Templeton shook back her Barbie-doll tresses. "Just explaining to Morticia Addams here that The Witch of Agnesi doesn't have anything to do with witches."

The headache excavating the inside of Bonnie's cranium ratcheted to six on the Richter scale. Her finger twitched at the trigger of her fantasy pistol.

The other girl, Ali Griffith, opened her mouth to speak.

Stephanie cut her off. "It probably got its name because the curves look like witch's hats."

"Play nice, Stephanie. No name calling." Bonnie pointed with her chin toward the other girl. "Your turn."

Ali bristled.

Straight, jet-black, shoulder-length hair, black eye shadow, nail polish and lipstick, Ali—short for Alexandria—bristled better than most. Her dark eyes flashed, and she looked every centimeter the witch she claimed to be. It was easy to believe she might turn a sneering debutant into a spotted salamander.

Ali's ebony lips curled in disgust. "I never claimed The Witch of Agnesi had anything to do with the craft. I just said it seemed a weird name for a curve. Then this, this . . ." Her mouth formed around a B-word.

Bonnie was sure the word in question had nothing to do with Beelzebub. Though she agreed with Ali's unspoken assessment, she gave the girl a warning look nonetheless.

I'm getting too old for this shit.

Red-faced, Ali waved her hand at Stephanie and drew a long breath. "When I told Stephanie, she pulled a Cruella DeVille on me."

Stephanie huffed.

Ali shot her a threatening glare.

Time to take a nap, ladies.

A pair of well-aimed darts from Bonnie's fantasy pistol sent the two arguing girls into the arms of Orpheus. They slumped across their desks, hands dangling each to a side, a look of angelic peace glowing on their unlined faces.

From the hip, no less.

Unfortunately, the real Ali and Stephanie remained painfully awake.

The wall clock showed ten minutes until the end of first period.

Not likely to get more done anyway. "All right, I meant to work with some of the actual math of the curve today and save the story until tomorrow, but what the heck."

Several students settled themselves into their seats, giving Bonnie the vague fear that in her impending senility she'd become one of those teachers who could be distracted into wasting time. To quell a guilty conscience, she wrote both the Cartesian and parametric representations of the Witch of Agnesi equation on the board then drew the corresponding graph.

"As a matter of fact, you two, each of your points is well taken." She pointed to the Cartesian representation. "This implicitly defined equation and its corresponding curve have nothing to do with witchcraft, *per se*. However, how The Witch of Agnesi got its name makes an interesting tale."

The door to her classroom burst open. Edmund Sheridan, a tall Asian boy with blond-tinted spiked hair lurched into the room. "Missus P, Jesse Poole's beating the crap out of Peyton Newlin."

The roar of hallway commotion echoed into the classroom. Bonnie fixed a hand on Edmund's shoulder. "Go get Principal Whittaker."

"He's not in the school."

"Check the Ad-building." She let go of Edmund's shoulder then turned to her class. "Ali, you're in charge until I get back. Call down to the office on the intercom. Tell them what's happening."

When Bonnie saw Edmund still standing in the doorway she shoved him. "Get going. Take the back hallway."

She legged it out of the classroom. At the far end of the gymnasium/library hallway, past yellow lockers lining both sides, a raucous crowd screamed derision and encouragement.

What the hell, don't their teachers wonder where they are?

Opening and closing her mouth like an oxygen-starved goldfish, the new librarian, a twenty-something blonde who looked maybe fifteen, gazed out of her wire-glass window at the chaos in the hall.

Bonnie shook her head and strode toward the uproar. I'm definitely too old for this. Grappling shoulders and pulling herself through, she worked her way into the deafening crowd. "All right!" she bellowed. "Step aside."

Jesse Poole, a bull-necked, teenaged Neanderthal with a glistening bald head sat astride the chest of a bloodied Peyton Newlin.

Bonnie grabbed Jesse's arm.

His meaty paw shoved her back.

She lost her footing and fell into the crowd, her beige wool skirt flying high across her chest. A bolt of pain lanced between her eyes as her headache notched to Richter seven. She rejected assistance and struggled to her feet. Smoothing down her skirt, she shouted, "Mister Poole, stand up immediately!"

A silence fell over the crowd. *All right, that's more like it.*

Jesse stood. Chest heaving, fists balled at his sides, he faced her. Tears poured from his red and swollen eyes. Rivulets of sweat streamed down his shaved head. He locked eyes with Bonnie for an eternal moment then advanced, stopping an arm's length in front of her.

Not liking this much.

"You don't know shit." He brushed past her and pushed through the crowd. "None of you know shit!" he screamed. Waving his hands as if fending off a swarm of gnats only he could see, he lumbered, hunched over for a few more steps. Then with a loping gait, he ran toward the back door and slammed through it.

No way did Bonnie consider challenging him. The satisfaction of control she'd felt moments before gave way to numbed shock. Jesse Poole was a force of nature when angered.

"Back off, people. Let me through." Principal Lloyd Whittaker's nasal voice rose above the crowd murmurs. A white handkerchief in his hand, he knelt and wiped at the blood pouring from Peyton's nose.

As Bonnie approached, Lloyd looked up.

"I was over at Admin speaking with the superintendent. What happened?"

She spread wide her hands. "Jesse Poole—at it

again." With a tilt of her head she pointed back the way Jesse had run.

"What did happen, Peyton?" Lloyd helped the boy to his feet.

"I didn't fight back." Peyton took Lloyd's kerchief and held it under a still bleeding nose. He peered at Bonnie over the cloth's reddening folds.

At four-foot-ten, his blond crew-cut rose only to the height of her chin.

"We'll talk about this in my office." Lloyd took him by the elbow. "Ladies and gentlemen," he shouted. "This is over. Anyone still in the hall when the late bell rings better have a pass."

He hurried the boy toward his office. "What was he doing out of class?"

I'm thinking he spent a portion of his time getting his tiny ass kicked.

Bonnie scurried to catch up. "Peyton and Edmund Sheridan do Calculus independent study in the Library." She followed Lloyd and the boy through the main office and into the principal's smaller one.

Peyton gave his nose a last swipe and set the hand-kerchief onto Lloyd's desk. He fell into a burgundy overstuffed chair and looked up at Bonnie. "Don't let him keep me out of Knowledge Bowl." He thrust out a defiant and split lower lip. "That would be just bunk. I didn't do anything."

Despite his posturing, she saw the pleading in his eyes. But what could she do? If he participated in a fight, a suspension wouldn't be long behind, which in turn would wipe out any possibility of his competing that night. She tried to ignore the selfish voice that whispered—*without Peyton your Knowledge Bowl team will fare pretty much the same as Peyton did a minute ago with Jesse.*

"I'm afraid that's up to Principal Whittaker."

Peyton's face turned red to his hair line. "It wasn't really a fight. I didn't hit back, Mister Whittaker. Jesse, he just pounds on me for no good reason whenever he feels like it."

Lloyd gave the boy a hard stare and poked his head out the office door. "Doris, get the school nurse down here."

He shut the office door and sat behind his battered oak desk.

Bonnie pulled a gray-cushioned folding chair up next to Peyton.

Lloyd leaned toward the boy. "Whether you compete tonight depends on how much I like your answer to my next question. And don't even think of lying to me, son. What did you do to provoke Jesse Poole?"

Peyton folded his pipe-cleaner arms across his chest and slumped back into the deep chair. A storm of emotions played across his freckled face. "He'd been picking on me, taking my books, pushing me in the hall, calling me names. He's a stupid jerk, just jealous because he knows I've got more smarts than he'll ever have." His voice rose with every justification until the final words broke into a squeak.

Lloyd's expression never changed. "You haven't

answered my question."

And you're beginning to annoy me, Bonnie thought.

"I was getting a drink from the fountain when Jesse kicked my feet out from under me. I fell into the fountain, hit my head." He touched a bump on his forehead. "I had water in my face, down the front of my pants. Jesse said I pissed myself."

"How did you respond?" Lloyd asked, not even trying to hide his impatience.

Peyton's glance darted from Lloyd up to Bonnie. "I was mad."

She'd just about had enough of this boy's equivocating. She laid a hand on his thin shoulder. "Stop stalling, Peyton. Tell Principal Whittaker what he wants to know."

"I said I bet his mother would be real proud of him, picking on a thirteen-year old."

Bonnie drew in a long breath.

Lloyd sat back in his chair, tapping the pads of his fingers together.

A knock sounded on the door and Marcie Englehart, the school nurse entered. A gaunt woman with grey-blond hair, she wore a flowered apron over a blue denim jumper. She glanced about the room, nodded to Bonnie and Lloyd and bent over Peyton. After prodding his nose and the bump on his forehead, she pulled a cotton swab from an apron pocket and dabbed at the split lip.

Peyton winced and squirmed beneath her ministrations.

Marcie unclipped a tiny flashlight from a belt loop. She steadied Peyton's head with a heavily veined hand and trained the flashlight first into one eye then the other. "I don't think he has a concussion, but that lip's going to need a stitch or two."

Peyton shook his head. "No stitches."

She shrugged bony shoulders. "Suit yourself."

Looking past the boy to Lloyd, she said, "Stitches are what I'd recommend, but I can rig a butterfly for the lip."

Lloyd stood and stared down at Peyton. "Young man, this is your third altercation in the last month. I'm inclined to pull you from the team just to catch your attention."

Bonnie sat up to speak.

Lloyd quieted her with an upraised hand. "However, unless I find out you lied about your part in this, you can compete tonight. You know I'll have to call your parents?"

Peyton's eyes went momentarily wide and he nodded. "I suppose."

"You suppose right. I know you were angry, but that was an unwise thing you said to Poole. Now go with Nurse Englehart while I talk to Missus Pinkwater."

In an expression which lasted no longer than a second, Marcie articulated the demand that Bonnie fill her in later. Then with a hand to his back, Marcie ushered the boy through the door and shut it behind her.

Lloyd waited until the door clicked shut. Leaning forward, he whispered, "Truth is, Bon, I don't much care for our resident genius. He's sneaky and manipulative. My gut tells me there's a lot more to this business between Poole and him than he's telling."

Bonnie eyed her long-time friend, unsure how she should reply.

On the one hand, she agreed with Lloyd's assessment of Peyton Newlin. The boy was easy to dislike. Aware of his intelligence, he rubbed people's noses in it. On more than one occasion she'd wanted to wipe the smirk from his face and let him know she was unimpressed with his cleverness.

Lately however, she'd developed a grudging affection for the little schmuck. Behind the arrogant posturing she saw an anxious kid hungry for approval.

"I hear you," she said. "And you're probably right. I've never seen Jesse Poole cry before, but he did today. No doubt, Peyton said more than he's admitting to."

Lloyd ran a callused hand down his face. "If I were Jesse I'd have beat the daylights out of Newlin myself. My mother's dying, and this arrogant pipsqueak used the situation to—"

"He's just thirteen, Lloyd."

He waved away her excuse as if it lent a foul smell to the room.

"Bon, this is a bad situation. Poole's going to come after Newlin. You be careful tonight. Everybody in the school knows Knowledge Bowl is at the Interfaith Academy. Jesse Poole's no exception."

$$\triangle$$

BONNIE SQUEEZED PAST PEYTON ON HER WAY INTO THE school infirmary. A white bandage-mustache made the boy's face seem lopsided, like Adolph Hitler after an unfortunate session with a barber.

Looking good, Peyton. "How's the lip?" She worked to keep her expression blank.

Peyton eyed her sullenly and shrugged. "Okay, I guess. Look, I got to get to class. See you tonight." He didn't wait for a reply. In a dozen quick steps, he reached a cross hall and turned out of sight.

Marcie took Bonnie's hand and pulled her into the tiny infirmary, then shut the door with a slam. "Give me the dirt."

Bonnie eyed the door wistfully. *Trapped, trapped like a rat.* "You know as much as I do. Peyton and Jesse exchanged words. Jesse took offense. He beat up Peyton. Pretty much end of story."

Marcie narrowed her eyes. "What did our fearless leader have to say?"

Bonnie glanced up at the infirmary clock. *Thank God, I have only a few minutes left in my planning period.* "He'll talk to other students, try to get the skinny on what really happened. If I were him I'd find out what became of Jesse Poole."

"I guess you heard?"

Bonnie kept her expression blank. "Heard what?"

"Jesse's mother has worsened. How long she lasts is anyone's guess. Jesse spent a sleepless night at the hospital."

How do you learn these things?

She pictured Marcie with her own version of the Baker Street Irregulars. The bell ending planning period rang. "Gotta go. Lots to do before Knowledge Bowl tonight."

Marcie laid a hand on Bonnie's shoulder. "I need to tell you, Bon. I know the boy is a big asset to your team. But for my money, Peyton Newlin, for all his genius, is one oily little creep. The only person likely to give a crap that Peyton got his porch shellacked is Edmund Sheridan."

$$\triangle$$

Turning off Highway Eighty-four, Bonnie stole glimpses of her Knowledge Bowl team in the rearview mirror. Ali Griffith and Stephanie Templeton sat in the seat directly behind her. Heads together conspiratorially, they whispered as if they hadn't been at each other's throats that very morning.

Bonnie smiled. Just another example of why she preferred the company of teenagers. They lived for the moment. And regardless of what most people over twenty-one believed, they rarely held grudges.

On the long seat at the rear of the van, Edmund Sheridan and Peyton Newlin bent over an electronic game. The bandage-mustache on Peyton's lip glowed pale green in the light from the display.

Moments like these were why she refused to even consider retirement—riding to Knowledge Bowl with four of East Plains' brightest students.

Then there was the competition itself. She loved its simplicity; answer the most school-related questions correctly, one point per question, you win. Obviously, a game invented by Mathematicians.

She swung the van into the Interfaith Academy's parking lot. School busses and vans filled almost every available space. Most of their competitors had already arrived. Then again very few of them had to come from as far away as East Plains.

Amid excited chatter her team poised at the van's sliding door like eager soldiers ready for battle. All they needed was a bugle and an American flag.

That's right, cutie pies. You're good. Especially when Peyton's having a killer night.

Inside the combination school and church, she waved to the other coaches but stuck close to her team.

Ali, who had added a silver cobra necklace to her black gothic regalia, strode unselfconsciously through the crowded vestibule. More than a few heads turned in her direction.

When the team reached the tally boards, Bonnie tapped the one titled "East Plains." "Why have we been in first place all season?"

Edmund cocked his spiky blond head. "Our exceptional good looks?"

Ali shoved him. "If that was right, then looking at you I'd say we should be in last place."

He feigned a hurt expression. "You know you love me. Don't hide your feelings behind this pointless hostile façade."

"In your dreams, Samurai."

Stephanie, the team captain, shook her head and regarded her team members as if they were children and she the only adult. "We stay alert. We don't let our energy get down. And?"

"We listen for the magic word," Edmund said.

"And?"

"We kick brain." They high-fived and hip-bumped one another. Even Peyton got involved, although he seemed preoccupied.

Bonnie let the camaraderie envelop her. She loved these children. Right at the moment, she'd rather be here than anywhere else on planet Earth. "We're in the main auditorium." She pointed with her chin down a long hallway.

Stephanie led off, and the others followed.

When Bonnie entered the auditorium, really the Academy's main chapel, Edmund pulled her aside.

"Can I talk with you, Missus P?"

She checked on the rest of the team. Stephanie had the others gathered around the center of three round tables and was handing out paper and pencils. Despite her preoccupation with appearance, or maybe because of it, the girl was a natural leader.

"Certainly, Edmund. What can I do for you?"

Edmund pushed his brushed stainless steel glasses further up his nose. "I'm pretty sure I saw Jesse Poole's red pickup follow us into town."

"You actually saw Jesse Poole?" She tried to keep

her tone casual.

"The inside of the truck was dark, but it looked like Jesse."

She tugged on her ear. "How far did he follow?"

"I looked away to talk to Peyton. When I looked back, the truck was gone. Maybe a couple of blocks from here."

"Did Peyton see the truck?"

"I don't think so."

She draped her arm around the boy. "I'll keep an eye out for Jesse and tell the Academy's principal to do the same. Are you going to be okay?"

Edmund squirmed. "I'm not the one Jesse's looking to kill."

"No one's going to kill anyone."

Stephanie waved from the front of the auditorium, and Edmund hurried to join her.

Bonnie slid into a pew near the front. She didn't want to think of the Jesse Pooles of the world right now. *God damn it, even though the boy has monumental problems, I'd just as soon not deal with him tonight.*

Nigel Jeffers, the Academy's principal, a tall black man wearing an oversized Denver Bronco bow tie, strode up the center aisle.

Bonnie stopped him and tried to explain the situation. Before two sentences escaped her lips the man shook his head.

"I assure you, no one will interfere with this competition while I'm in charge."

"But—"

"I need to begin." With a condescending pat to her hand, he continued up the aisle to a metal podium facing the tables, his back to the meager audience of coaches and a few parents.

Ass.

Jeffers raised a hand for attention. "Fifteen seconds, ladies and gentlemen. Fifteen seconds to buzz in. Fifteen seconds to answer once you're recognized. If the first team answers incorrectly, then the next team to buzz in gets a new fifteen seconds. If that team is wrong, then the third team receives an additional fifteen seconds. Any questions?"

All twelve competitors shook their heads.

"Then I'll read the first question. The category is world capital cities and fruit."

A buzzer sounded.

The timer called, "East Plains."

"I know this," Peyton mouthed to Stephanie.

She nodded.

"Tangiers," he said.

Bonnie couldn't see the reader's expression, but his body language indicated he was both impressed and perplexed. "That's correct, but how?"

Peyton reddened. "Simple. There's only one major world capital named after a fruit."

"Point for East Plains."

All's right in the Milky Way. Bonnie settled into her pew.

"Second question. The category is waterfalls and the rivers that feed them." The reader hesitated and looked to Peyton.

The boy smiled and shook his head.

"Just checking," the reader said. "Name the highest—"

A buzzer sounded.

"East Plains," the timer called.

Ali looked to Stephanie. The team captain nodded.

"Angel Falls on the Rio Churun."

"That's correct. Point for East Plains."

Bonnie noted with satisfaction the other teams' agitation. *Just adding to your freak factor, boys and girls.* As she planned in practice, East Plains would buzz in quickly, rarely hearing all of any one question, but usually preempting the other teams.

A noise behind her made Bonnie turn.

Mrs. Wendy Newlin, an attractive woman with a great mass of red hair flowed up the center aisle. A tube-top blouse revealed more than hid an ample bosom and a wasp-like waist. She excused herself, and sat next to Bonnie.

"Sorry, I'm late," she whispered. Her breath smelled of cigarettes. She waved a multi-ringed, red-nailed hand to her son.

A pained expression on his face, Peyton waved back.

Almost immediately, after their initial success, East Plains went cold. Edmund missed an easy Science question, then another.

The worst was Peyton. He seemed distracted, unfocused. Twice he convinced Stephanie he knew the answer to a question she wanted to answer. Both times, when she deferred to him, he answered wrong.

From the look on Stephanie's face, the girl would have answered correctly.

At the end of the first round, East Plains was tied with the Academy's team, having squandered the five point lead they enjoyed coming into that night.

Bonnie put on a brave face. Before they could rise from their seats, she signaled them back down. "Come on guys. Shake it off. We've only given away five points. We'll get the lead back."

"That's right," Stephanie agreed. "We stunk up the place on that round, but we have two rounds left. What are we going to do?"

Ali and Edmund answered, "Kick brain."

"You bet," Bonnie said, uneasily eyeing Peyton. "Go stretch your legs and be back here in two minutes."

As the team left the auditorium, Peyton approached his mother. Taking his hand, she pulled him aside, behind the baptismal. For the better part of a minute, mother and son whispered furiously one to another, Peyton's face growing red. Just when Bonnie thought the boy might explode, Peyton nodded. He gave his mother a sullen look and retook his seat.

What in hell was that all about? Bonnie stared hard at Peyton, then the mother. *Damn you, woman. Couldn't you have stayed at home for this last meet?* Bonnie could only hope Peyton could shake off whatever weirdness had transpired.

No such luck.

Although Ali and Stephanie rallied, Peyton and Edmund never did recover. Distracted, Peyton played like someone who needed to be somewhere else. Time and again he locked eyes with his mother who returned his gaze like a serene Madonna, nodding approval for her floundering son.

When the final question was read, East Plains had fallen to fourth place. Bonnie sat stunned. For the first time in twelve years an East Plains team finished out of the top three.

Stephanie pushed back her chair, stood, and glowered at Peyton. "Thanks a lot, boy genius." She flounced past Bonnie and out of the auditorium. Ali and Edmund ran after her.

Mrs. Newlin winced, but only momentarily. Her tranquil smile reasserted itself.

Tears glistened on Peyton's freckled cheeks. "I'm sorry, Missus Pinkwater."

Bonnie swallowed her disappointment. "I'm sure you did your best, Peyton. Let's catch up with the others."

The boy blanched. From the look on his face the last thing he wanted was to confront an angry Stephanie Templeton. "I got to go to the bathroom." He shuffled from the auditorium like he carried a sack of bowling balls on his shoulders.

Bonnie had no desire to spend another moment in the company of Wendy Newlin. "Please excuse me. I need to be with the team."

Bonnie resisted the urge to run. No way would she let Stephanie vent her spleen on an already hurting thirteen-year old genius.

At the van, Ali had her arms wrapped around

Stephanie, who was weeping.

The tall blonde looked up. "I'm sorry I let you down, Missus P. And I'm really sorry I was such a bitch to Peyton." She sniffled.

Too taken back at Stephanie's change of heart, Bonnie couldn't bring herself to object to the girl's choice of words. "He'll be relieved to see you're not mad at him. I think he went to the bathroom to avoid seeing you." She handed the girl a tissue.

"It's not his fault. He's not the first team captain in a dozen years to come home without a trophy."

Bonnie took Stephanie in her arms. "East Plains will survive." To Edmund, she said, "Go see what's keeping Peyton."

Edmund left looking relieved to get away from all this womanly grief.

Neither of the girls appeared eager to speak, so Bonnie invited them to sit quietly with her on the back bumper of the van. All around them, busses and vans full of teenagers sped away into the night.

When the last bus left, Bonnie checked her watch. "What's keeping those boys?"

As if in answer to her question, Edmund slammed through the door of the school. Standing in the school's floodlights, he yelled, "I can't find him anywhere. Peyton's gone."

CHAPTER 2

BONNIE LED A HYSTERICAL WENDY NEWLIN into the main office. The red-faced woman sucked air in ragged gasps.

Don't let her pass out, Bonnie prayed.

"Get me a paper bag, maybe yea big." She used her hands to show Principal Jeffers of the orange bow tie the approximate size of a lunch sack. When the man hesitated, she hurried him off.

She pulled a swivel chair from behind a large gray-steel desk and patted the upholstered seat. "Sit here for a moment. Put your head between your knees."

Gasping and shaking, Wendy did as she was told.

"I'll be right back." Bonnie stepped out into the hall.

Stephanie, Ali, and Edmund stood leaning against a wall. They broke off whispering when she approached. Tears glistened on Stephanie Templeton's cheeks.

Bonnie opened her fanny pack, extracted her cell phone, and tossed it to Edmund. "Call your parents, all of you. This could take awhile. Have them come get you."

Stephanie shook her head. "This is all my fault."

Bonnie held up an admonishing hand. "Cut that out. Take Edmund and Ali to the auditorium and make those calls. Can I count on you?"

Stephanie nodded.

"Good girl."

When Bonnie returned to the office, Wendy had her head between her knees. She'd removed her sweater and sat there in a white sleeveless shell. On each of her arms a string of purple bruises stood out like grapes against pale flesh.

The hair on the back of Bonnie's neck bristled. Her jaw tightened.

In the doorway, Jeffers held up a small paper sack. "Will this do?"

She forced herself to smile and took the sack. "Do you have somewhere Missus Newlin can lie down?"

"I'll be fine." Wendy raised her head. "I need to find my boy." She tried to stand and sat down hard.

Jeffers strode past Bonnie to a darkened room and flicked on the light. "Nurse's cubby—the back of my assistant principal's office." He helped Wendy to her feet.

The woman protested, but let Jeffers guide her to a cot behind a mobile canvas screen.

Bonnie handed Wendy the bag. "Just a dozen breaths until your breathing settles."

"I don't think—"

"Humor me."

Wendy sighed but clamped the bag's mouth over her own. Eyes closed, she inflated and deflated the bag like a bellows.

Bonnie signaled Jeffers to accompany her to the door. Once beyond it she whispered, "We need to call the police."

"They may not come. We're talking about a boy who ran away less than half an hour ago. My custodians are still searching."

"We're talking about a missing child, and I'm not so certain he ran away. Remember the red truck you wouldn't let me tell you about?" She gave him an abbreviated version of Peyton's altercation with Jesse Poole.

"And you saw this truck near here?"

"One of my players did."

Jeffers worried a hangnail on his thumb. "I'll call."

As he turned toward the phone on the secretary's gray-steel desk, Bonnie took his elbow. "If you get any kind of runaround, ask for Sergeant Valsecchi. Mention my name. He's a former student of mine."

"Missus P?" Holding the cell phone, Stephanie came into the office. "We've all called."

"That's great, sweetie." She took the phone. "Listen, I've got to see to Peyton's mom. You guys going to be okay?"

Stephanie rolled her eyes. "We're not little kids, Missus P."

Oh good, give me a double scoop of attitude. "Of

course you're not." She left the girl and returned to the back room.

Mrs. Newlin was sitting up. She had the bag in her lap smoothing out wrinkles. "Peyton's run away before."

"He's probably just feeling guilty about the competition." Bonnie shut the door behind her but stayed near it, not wanting to invade the woman's space. "He'll come back when he sorts it out."

"His running away had nothing to do with Knowledge Bowl. It's been building between him and my husband, for weeks—the fights, the getting in trouble." She rubbed her naked arms and winced when her fingers passed over the bruises. Her face reddened. "My husband's not the easiest man in the world to live with."

Bonnie's jaw tightened again. She nodded toward the purple splotches. "Those look new."

Mrs. Newlin cocked her head and eyed Bonnie suspiciously.

I don't blame you, honey, Bonnie thought. *You've got no reason to confide in me.*

"Ralph was waiting when Peyton and I returned from school. We weren't in the house five minutes before he started in."

"Had he been drinking?"

The woman shook her head, red hair falling across her face. She pushed it back with a shaky hand. "Colonel Ralph Newlin doesn't drink."

Her mouth twitched, as if she was forcing down a nervous laugh. "He doesn't relinquish control of anything—his faculties or his family."

"Did he hit you?"

Wendy hesitated then nodded. A knock on the door made her jump.

Jeffers poked in his head. "I called the police."

Wendy crushed the bag in her lap.

Good timing, Jeffers.

The big man crossed the room in three long strides. "Don't worry. I dug out the emergency phone list Missus Pinkwater provided and got a hold of your husband. He's on his way."

"Oh, God!" She locked eyes with Bonnie.

The look demanded an unspoken promise of kept secrets. Bonnie nodded.

Wendy's hand clutching the bag relaxed. She offered the other one to Jeffers, who helped her up. "Thank you for your consideration. If you don't mind, I need a cigarette before my husband arrives." She smiled thinly. "He doesn't approve."

"You want company?" Bonnie asked.

Wendy shook her head. "No. I'm just going out to my car."

At the secretary's desk, she collected her sweater and a beaded handbag. She and Edmund danced around one another, he trying to enter the office.

In frustration, Wendy pushed past the boy and said something Bonnie couldn't hear.

Edmund watched Wendy Newlin walk down the long hall to the stairs. "Stephanie and Ali are gone. Steph's mom was in town, and she took Ali too. My folks won't answer. I'll just ride back with you, if that's okay. My car's still at the school anyway."

Bonnie wanted to follow Wendy, but Edmund blocked her path. "You want to call again?"

"Nah. Is it a problem me hanging here with you?"

Yeah, it's a problem. It was nine-o-clock. The police and an abusive husband were on the way. A thirteen-year old child, who'd been entrusted into her care, might just be in the hands of a maniac. She had no desire to have one more person depending on her.

"Try to stay out of the way."

"Can do."

She pushed past the boy. "I'm going to check on Missus Newlin."

The hall was empty. She took the stairs two at a time, ran across the foyer and burst through the double doors to the parking lot. A silver SUV sped south down Peterson Avenue. In the driver's seat hunched Wendy Newlin, a cigarette glowing in her mouth.

What's with this family and running away?

"Where's she going?" a voice at her elbow asked.

Bonnie yelped.

Edmund Sheridan stood so close he might as well have been in her pocket.

"Good God, Edmund! You liked to give me a heart attack." She moved out onto the concrete steps and watched Wendy's SUV drive out of sight.

Edmund followed her. "Sorry, but wasn't that Missus Newlin?"

"I believe so."

"What's up with—Hey, somebody stuck something

under the van's wipers."

Bonnie squinted trying to see with her fifty-three year old eyes what Edmund had seen with his younger ones. Before she could comment, the boy took off running—long easy strides that carried him across the parking lot.

At the van, he yelled, "It's a note."

He pulled the paper free. "From Missus Newlin. Addressed to you. It's an apology."

"Bring it here."

Edmund took his time re-crossing the lot. He seemed to enjoy her impatience.

She snatched the paper from his hand.

'Mrs. Pinkwater. I know you'll think me the worst mother in the world, but I couldn't face my husband. You have no idea what he can be like. Hopefully, he'll be calmed down by the time he gets back home. Wendy.'

This is dysfunction on a professional level.

Edmund wore a bemused expression. "Crazy, huh? That Mister Newlin must be one mean dude."

Bonnie nodded absently. At parent-teacher meetings last fall, Colonel Ralph Newlin had come alone and in his Air Force Blues. He'd been brusque but not impolite. He seemed genuinely concerned his son do well at a new school, had explained East Plains was the fourth school Peyton had attended in the past seven years.

He didn't come across as abusive.

What did you expect, Bonnie? A sign on his forehead saying "wife-beater"? A chill on the evening breeze had about convinced her to go back into the school when an unmarked car, with its cherry-top flashing, turned onto Peterson road.

"It's the cops," Edmund said.

The young man had always enjoyed a firm grasp on the obvious.

"Go tell Principal Jeffers."

A battered lime-green El Camino pulled up to the steps where she stood. Its lights went off. A solidly built six-foot man in a rumpled suit struggled from the car. With a hand shielding his eyes from the school flood lights, Sergeant Franklin Valsecci squinted up at Bonnie with pale blue eyes.

"You just can't stay out of trouble. Can you Missus P?" He raked his fingers through thinning auburn hair, presented her with a grin, and limped up the concrete steps to the school.

Every time she saw Franklin, she remembered the mischievous boy who bedeviled and delighted her in Algebra One. She felt like mussing his thinning hair. "I didn't expect to see you. What's with the limp, youngster?"

He shook his head.

She knew if she pressed him he'd most likely tell her. She didn't press.

"Caught your name on dispatch and volunteered to take the call," he said, changing the subject. "I was heading home."

Bonnie noticed Jeffers through the wire-glass slits on the double doors. "Let's talk inside."

Jeffers held the door. All were through when a graveled noise from the parking lot made him poke his head back outside. "A classic Stingray, tweety-bird yellow."

"That would be Colonel Ralph Newlin." Bonnie couldn't keep the contempt from her voice.

Franklin gave her a puzzled stare.

"I'll tell you later," she mouthed.

Looking like a press photo from the United States Air Force, Colonel Newlin strode through the open door in his leather flight-jacket. Tall and well muscled, Newlin carried himself like he was used to being admired. He nodded to Principal Jeffers as one would a servant. Newlin removed his flight cap, folded it, and smartly tucked it beneath his epaulet. His hair was silver-white, his face lined and rugged. He held out his hand to Bonnie. "Missus Pinkwater."

Bonnie let the hand hang there a moment before she took it. "Mister, oh, excuse me, Colonel Newlin."

Newlin blinked as if stung. The smile that looked as if it might blossom onto his face faded. "Appears as if you lost my boy."

Bonnie felt her neck hair rise. She bit back a reply she knew she'd regret. "I'm sorry about that."

Franklin hobbled between them. "From what I understand, we'll present a case for an Amber Alert. In a nutshell, we'll involve the media. Does the boy have a cell phone?"

Newlin shook his head. "You kidding? He may be a genius, but he's still just thirteen, too young for his own phone."

"Too bad. Sometimes a runaway will answer his

cell and even tell you where he's at." Franklin checked his watch. "If an Amber Alert is called for, it would be nice to get his picture on the ten o'clock news."

Colonel Newlin fished around in his wallet and handed Franklin a three-by-five glossy. "This was taken just two months ago."

"Thank you. I'm going to need quick statements from each of you. I'll start with you, Missus Pinkwater?"

"Where's my wife?" Newlin demanded.

Bonnie took Franklin by the arm and led him toward the auditorium. From the corner of her eye she saw Edmund walking toward Colonel Newlin. *If Edmund's smart*, she thought, *he'll let Newlin find out on his own his wife is gone.*

"She what?" Newlin howled.

I guess Edmund isn't so smart after all. She kept Franklin walking.

In the auditorium/chapel, she handed Wendy Newlin's note to him. "It was on the windshield of the school van."

Note in hand, Franklin leaned heavily on a pew railing and sat. He read the note then pulled a spiral-bound notepad from his pocket. "When did you get this?"

"Maybe fifteen minutes ago. Missus Newlin took off a few minutes before that." Bonnie relayed the conversation she'd had with Wendy.

He handed back the note. "That explains your attitude toward Colonel Newlin."

"The man's ten pounds of feces in a gold-plated nine pound bag."

"Shucks, Missus P, don't sugar-coat your feelings. What do you really think?"

She slapped Franklin's arm. "Don't mock me, youngster. I knew you when you had zits. Besides, I'm not sure this family upheaval is the reason Peyton Newlin's gone missing." She told him of the fight and Edmund's sighting of Jesse Poole's truck.

Franklin scribbled in the notepad. "The same Asian boy out front?"

She nodded.

"I'll send someone around to Poole's." Franklin struggled to his feet.

"Also check the Saint Francis Hospice. Jesse's mom is in there."

"This thug kidnaps Newlin then goes to visit his mother?"

Out loud, the idea sounded silly to Bonnie, too. "I don't know." A wave of fatigue swept over her. It had been a long day, and it wasn't over yet.

"You look whipped. Why don't you go on home?"

She shook her head. "I've got to wait for Edmund. You're going to want to talk to him. He's the only one who actually saw the truck."

Back in the vestibule, a red-faced Colonel Newlin approached. "Do you really think this Poole character has my boy?"

Before Bonnie could speak, Franklin said, "We can't ignore the possibility. I'm sending out a call on Poole's truck and a sheriff to Poole's home."

He signaled Edmund over. "I'm going to need a

description of the pickup." He led the boy outside through the double doors.

Colonel Newlin watched them leave then turned back to her, his face a rigid mask. "I want to apologize for my wife. She's been under a lot of strain lately. So has Peyton." He obviously wasn't comfortable apologizing.

Thanks to you. She rejected telling this bully just what she thought of him. The best thing she could do for the Newlin family would be to inform Social Services. "I have to get my remaining student home."

When she tried to walk away, Newlin laid hold of her upper arm.

"Don't much like me, do you?"

Bonnie eyed the callused hand on her arm. "It's not my place to like or dislike you. I'm more concerned about your boy." The curt answer was out of her mouth before she could apprehend it.

He raised both of his hands and stepped back, making a show of letting go of her arm. "You've been talking with my wife."

"We talked." She stared him full in the face.

"Now if you'll excuse me." Without a look back, she strode across the vestibule toward the stairs leading up to Jeffers' office.

"You women, you all stick together," Newlin called.

Eat shit and die, you son of a bitch.

In the office, Jeffers and the pair of female custodians who'd searched the building stood praying, holding hands in the center of the room. As she entered, all three supplicants looked in her direction.

Bonnie tugged at her ear, embarrassed to interrupt. "I've got to go. I need to take Edmund home."

The trio made no motion to break their prayer circle. Jeffers lowered his head. "We ask these things in Jesus' name. Amen."

He drew the two women into a group embrace then pulled back. "You ladies talk to the officer then go on home. I'll lock up."

The two women, both in overalls, smiled at Bonnie as they filed past—the smile of folks in the recent company of God.

Jeffers sat on the rim of the gray-steel desk and removed his orange bow tie. "I still think the boy ran away. No one, besides the Chinese boy, saw this red pickup or its occupants."

"Korean."

"What?"

"Edmund's Korean." She sat next to him on the desk. "I want to believe Peyton's just out there being stupid. Certainly, the time constraints bear that out. From the time between when I last saw the boy and when I sent Edmund to find him, the school was packed with students. Someone would have noticed Peyton struggling with his captors. And yet . . ."

"You can't let go of the off chance."

She rubbed her eyes. "Not while there still is an off chance."

He took her arm and led her out of the office. "Go home, Missus Pinkwater."

"Splendid idea."

Edmund stood at the bottom of the stairs. "I can go. I gave my statement to the cop."

Bonnie looked around for Franklin but didn't see him.

As if he read her mind, Edmund said, "The cop and Peyton's dad are in the auditorium. Can we go now?"

She nodded.

By the time she dropped Edmund Sheridan off at the school, it was ten-thirty. The Richter seven headache, which had left her that morning, had returned and now raged at eight.

THE NEXT DAY, BONNIE PASSED THROUGH THE OFFICE on the way to her morning class.

"Bon, can I see you for a moment?" Principal Lloyd Whittaker stood at his office door, only his head poking out.

She wished she'd gone another way, not liking the tone of Lloyd's voice. She came through the swinging gate, around the office counter, and passed Doris, the office secretary.

"Divine," Doris mouthed and pointed with her thumb.

Bonnie's heart sank. She hated Superintendent Xavier Divine and was sure the feeling was mutual. To her, he would always be The Divine Pain in the Ass. It wouldn't surprise her if he knew of his *nom de plume*.

As she came through Lloyd's door she painted a smile onto her face. "Good morning, Lloyd." She fixed a seated Divine with the frozen smile. "Superintendent Divine."

Xavier Divine was an unremarkable little man except for one overriding feature. He possessed an enormous bald head. It was this feature he now wagged in Bonnie's direction. "I received a disturbing phone call this morning from the Newlins."

Bonnie held her breath, waiting for the other shoe to drop.

Divine sat up in the burgundy overstuffed chair. "They claim that in the midst of their agony over their missing child you were rude and impertinent."

Impertinent? What am I, his valet?

Bonnie tried to remember any impertinent behavior. Not only couldn't she recall any, she wasn't certain how anyone beside an underling could even be impertinent. And she didn't consider herself anyone's underling. "Did the call come from Missus or Colonel Newlin?"

"The Colonel."

"I'm not surprised. The man's a sphincter muscle."

Divine's face flushed, increasing the illusion he might be Mr. Potato Head. "The man is a national hero, twice decorated by the President himself."

"Newlin abuses his wife and son. Missus Newlin told me herself Peyton ran away because of him. I intend to report the good Colonel to Social Services the millisecond I leave this office." She chided herself on so blatantly pushing Divine's buttons, but enjoyed watching him struggle with his natural urge to deny her anything she wanted to do.

Fortunately, the Divine Pain in the Ass knew too much school law to do any such thing. If a teacher as much as suspected abuse it was not only correct for her to report it, she was bound by law to do so. Any administrator who even hinted she should cover it up was committing a felony.

She decided she'd throw him a bone. "The competition had ended and Peyton was already in his mother's care when he disappeared."

Divine turned to Lloyd. "Is this true?"

"If Missus Pinkwater says it's true, I believe her."

Divine noticeably relaxed. He sank back into the overstuffed chair, his fingers steepled beneath his double chin. The effect made his head appear like Humpty Dumpty perched atop a finger wall. "This still doesn't excuse a member of East Plains' staff being rude to a parent, but given the extenuating circumstances . . ." He spread wide his hands.

For an agonizing moment, Bonnie thought he might even wink at her. *No, dear God, don't let it happen.*

Mercifully, he stood without winking. "Keep me informed of any progress in locating the boy." To the friction zing of his salmon-pink corduroy pants, the Divine Pain in the Ass waddled from the office.

"Why do you do that?" Lloyd sat down behind his desk.

She fell into the still warm chair. "Do what?"

"Go out of your way to antagonize our mutual straw-boss."

"I didn't start out meaning to make him mad. It

just happened. I think it's a gift."

"It's a gift that's going to get us both fired one of these days."

"I, for one, hope that day is a long time coming. I kind of like working here." She flashed him a toothy grin. "Maybe it's the principal." She got up to leave.

"Hold on." He stayed her with an outstretched palm. "Our local constable, Deputy Fishlock, came by my place this morning."

She sat down. "About Peyton?"

"About Jesse Poole. Sheriffs stopped at his trailer last night, but he wasn't home. I guess some teacher recommended they check Saint Francis Hospice so the Springs' police went there. They found Jesse's truck parked outside and the boy in visiting his mother."

Bonnie pictured Jesse Poole with his hair-trigger temper when the police barged into his mother's hospice room in the middle of the night. "Oh no!"

"Oh, yes. Jesse went ballistic. The staff came to his rescue telling the police he'd been there all evening. That would have been the end of it had it not been for Jesse's bloody shirt."

"He didn't tell them it was Peyton's blood?"

"As a matter of fact he did, claimed it got there when he bloodied the boy's nose earlier that day."

"Did they arrest Jesse?"

Lloyd shook his head. "Not with five members of the hospice staff giving him an alibi. They questioned him and left."

Bonnie checked her watch. "I've got to fly. I need to

report Colonel Newlin to the counselor and get to class."

She left Lloyd's office thinking she should be glad Jesse wasn't involved in Peyton's disappearance. Maybe Peyton did just run off on his own. So why did she have this uneasy feeling the world smelled of fish?

CHAPTER 3

A SEA OF BRAIDED, HALF-SHAVED, AND blue-tinted heads bobbed between Bonnie and the counselor's office. The crowding reminded her just how much East Plains had changed in two years. Time was when she shared these morning halls with about half this many faces, and she knew all their names. Now, strangers stared back at her.

She reached the office of Counselor Freddy Davenport feeling decidedly melancholy. Thank God it was Friday.

Seated in an obviously overburdened desk chair, Freddy Davenport sprawled at the lunch table that served as his desk, fingers laced across his substantial stomach. His double chins rested on a seedy turtleneck pullover which fit him like a sausage skin. Open bowls of Jolly Ranchers and Tootsie Rolls sat on twin beige file cabinets. Discarded candy wrappers littered the floor. Soda-pop cans filled the trash. Across a cookie-crumb covered carpet a dilapidated tan sofa listed.

Lollipop protruding from his face, Freddy hoisted his bulk from the desk chair. "Bonnie, as I live and draw labored breath." He signaled for her to sit and swept a Butterfinger wrapper from the sofa.

She felt the upholstery to see if it was sticky and decided to stand. "Does the janitor know this room exists?"

With a grunt, Freddy lowered his considerable bulk back into the chair. It creaked under the weight. He spread wide his pudgy hands. "What you see here isn't the neglect of our fine custodial staff. I met with my student counselors this morning. Sugar was the order of the day."

He gave her an up-from-under glance. "I'll go out on a limb and predict this isn't the social call I hoped it would be."

Bonnie shook her head. "Sharp as ever. Nothing gets past you."

Despite his slovenliness and his proclivity for sending students into glucose comas, he'd been a find for East Plains. The school went through five counselors in seven years, most of whose back sides she been happy to see in her rearview mirror. Freddy had come to East Plains via law enforcement. After a career as a probation officer, he'd decided he could better serve humanity and himself if he worked with students before they got into trouble.

Bonnie liked his ample back side and the rest of him from the beginning. "I need to report suspected spouse and child abuse."

Freddy's aspect went from jovial host to let's-get-down-to-business. He opened a long file drawer, removed a legal pad and held it out to her. "Give me everything you know or suspect. Include all specifics and everyone you've talked to."

She refused the pad. "It's not much. Can't I just tell you?"

"Certainly." He snatched a pen from under a pile of red licorice and clicked it. "Shoot."

She told him of her evening, ending with the note from Mrs. Newlin.

When he finished writing, he leaned back in his chair and tapped his pen on the lollipop stick protruding from the corner of his mouth. "Peyton's name keeps coming up. I wasn't surprised to hear Jesse Poole thrashed him. Yesterday, Jesse sat on that very couch in a rage because Peyton said unkind things about Jesse's mother."

"What sort of things?"

Freddy bit at his lip and shook his head. "Sorry, Bon. If I started quoting students' private revelations I couldn't convince them to talk to me."

"Have you told Lloyd?"

"Not even Lloyd." He spread wide his sausage fingers. "I live and die by the confidences I keep."

"Can you at least tell me the time Jesse left here?"

"Nine-ten, maybe a little later."

The timing felt out of kilter. Five minutes after

leaving Freddy's office Jesse had already caught up with Peyton and was pounding him. Peyton's mother drove him to school that morning, and Bonnie met the boy getting out of his mother's SUV. They'd walked together to the library. How had Peyton found time to piss off Jesse Poole?

"I know I'm getting dangerously close to confidentiality, but had Peyton insulted Jesse's mother the day before?"

Freddy shook his head, wagging his lollipop stick like a miniature baton. "That morning, in fact, just before Jesse came to see me. We have an agreement, Jesse and I. He comes to me whenever he thinks he might lose his cool. Not a bad boy. He just needs some coping skills."

Don't we all? "Why didn't you inform Lloyd?" She immediately regretted her accusatory tone.

Freddy didn't seem to take offence. "I tried to alert him to the possibility of trouble, but when I called the office Lloyd was gone, and the vice principal was out of the building as well. By the time Lloyd returned, Jesse had already tracked down Peyton and administered instant karma."

Freddy put on an apologetic face. "The rest, as the poet was fond of saying, is history."

The first bell of the day rang.

Freddy walked her to the door. "Do you have Stephanie Templeton, Edmund Sheridan, or Ali Griffith in your first hour class?"

"All three."

"Could you send them to me when it's convenient?"

Bonnie frowned. One of her pet peeves centered on nurses and counselors pulling students out of class, sometimes for trivial matters. "Is this really important?"

"It could be for them."

"Can I get a hint of why?"

He rubbed his hands together. "Do you remember a former student named J. D. Sullivan?"

At first the name didn't ring any bells. Then it came to her. "Must be fifteen years ago. Sure, Josh Sullivan, good Mathematician. A little weak on logic. He went to school somewhere in California."

"That's him. Made a bundle in electronics and is feeling philanthropic. He's interested in funding a scholarship exclusively for East Plains' students. He contacted me last week."

A smile crept up from her belly to her face. "Stephanie, Edmund, and Ali are candidates?"

Freddy nodded. "I got them in here earlier this week, but I need to tell them they made the cut. Out of the baker's dozen of students I sent to Sullivan, he's winnowed it down to four finalists."

"You only mentioned three."

"The remaining finalist was in here yesterday, and I told him the good news." Freddy hesitated, looking uncomfortable. "Our missing genius, Peyton Newlin, is the fourth."

BONNIE ARRIVED FIVE MINUTES LATE TO HER FIRST period, in time to catch her aide dropping the attendance slip into the wire door basket.

Wide eyed, hands on her hips, Carlita Sanchez glared openly at Bonnie.

"What?" she asked, knowing full well what was on the girl's mind.

"You were doing so good. Fourteen days in a row on time. And now." She tapped a non-existent watch.

"Don't start with me, Carlita. I had a bad day yesterday followed by a worse night."

The Junior girl's coffee-colored face darkened. "I heard about the fight. Peyton shouldn't talk trash about Jesse's mom. That ain't right."

"I couldn't agree more." She needed to get past this little Hispanic gatekeeper and start her class. "How many do we have gone today?"

She slipped past the girl into the room.

"A bunch," Carlita whispered, walking behind. "Ali Griffith, Dorry Tomms, Stephanie Templeton, Edmund Sheridan, Billy Quintana."

Bonnie scanned the empty desks. "Have you called the library to see if Edmund's down there?"

"Of course." She gave Bonnie a look that asked if she thought her mentally challenged. "First thing I did."

"All right, have a seat." The entire Knowledge Bowl team gone? That wasn't like them. She took a breath and faced her class. "Take out last night's homework."

Salvador, a serious young man in front-seat-center

raised his hand. "Missus P, you didn't give us any homework."

She remembered the fight. It was fast becoming the gift that kept on giving. "Fair enough. Let's correct that right now." She ignored the groans and wrote the previous night's assignment on the board.

When she turned around, a girl in the back of the room had her hand raised. "How about the story you were going to tell yesterday?"

First Carlita, now this child. When had the inmates gotten control of the asylum?

"Maybe after we've covered the math. I'm not making any promises. Let's concentrate on The Witch of Agnesi and its parametric cousins."

The next hour and ten minutes she put her students through their paces, changing the parameters of the dual equations, noting the corresponding changes in the graphs. When at last they all came up for air, she laid down her chalk. Perhaps Marie Agnesi's story would solidify the Mathematics in their minds.

"Okay, I believe the question was how The Witch of Agnesi got its name."

A knock sounded on her door. Lloyd Whittaker poked his head in the room, his face ashen. "Can I see you in the hall for a moment?"

From the back of the room someone whispered, "Not again."

She didn't even try to identify the whisperer. She excused herself and joined Lloyd outside her door. "What's wrong?"

"I can't go into specifics right now, but Superintendent Divine is going to hold an emergency assembly the last fifteen minutes of fourth period."

Her heart raced. "Is this about Peyton?"

Lloyd wiped his lips with the back of his hand. "Not exactly." He glanced up and down the hallway looking uncomfortable.

He's not going to tell me. She stared impatiently at her long time friend. "Come on, Lloyd, what's this all about?"

He drew a long breath and released it in a sigh. "Bon, don't make me say any more than I have to. Now please go back in your class and inform them of the assembly."

Anger replaced impatience. Her Imp of the Perverse prodded her to push Lloyd. "You're scaring me, Lloyd. Can you at least give me a hint?"

His face grew hard. He took her hands in his. "No, I can't give you a hint. Stop asking me to give you special treatment." He gave her hands a squeeze and walked away.

As she stood staring at his departing back she heard him whisper, "Shit, shit, shit."

$$\triangle$$

BONNIE'S CHEST ACHED.

She stared at her hummus and pinion nut sandwich. Unable to swallow the bite she'd taken, she spit into her napkin and folded it. All around, the voices of her colleagues echoed through the teacher's lounge. Behind her at the other long table, a pair of new teachers laughed. Angry tears clouded her vision. Indistinct noises echoed across her senses but couldn't penetrate her personal fog.

"Mind if I join you?" a voice behind her asked.

Bonnie blinked at her tears trying to put a face to her intruder.

Armen Callahan, the new Science teacher, stood above her, holding a blue plastic tray with both hands. She'd seen him in the halls dozens of times, but since he taught Junior High they hadn't said more than a score of words to one another. As always he wore a sweater vest over a long-sleeved white dress shirt and a tie emblazoned with cartoon characters. This time the sweater was robin egg blue and the cartoon Marvin the Martian. Armen's gray hair and goatee were impeccably groomed. From the patient expression on his tanned face, he looked content to stand there until she gave him permission to sit.

She moved aside her sandwich wrapper. "Not at all."

Armen slid his tray onto the table. "I'm not really sure what this is." He nodded a smiling face toward a mound of mashed potatoes smothered in white gravy. Gray irregular lumps of meat speckled the gravy, giving the mound a vaguely lunar appearance.

"Have you tried this stuff?" He ran a hand through his hair looking as if he might be afraid of the unsavory meal.

She smiled in spite of herself. "I'm a vegetarian."

"A sad one I think." He reached a thumb toward her face and gently brushed away the tear.

He reddened. "Excuse me. I'm not usually so forward."

Heat rose to her cheeks. She let her gaze travel the lounge seeing if anyone noticed. Everyone sat ensconced in their own little worlds.

"I'll be okay. I've got a lot on my mind."

Armen wrinkled his nose then pushed his lunch to the far side of the table. He turned a mischievous face her way. "I thought perhaps it might only be that mud sandwich you've wisely decided not to eat."

She squinted at him trying to decide if she would kick him under the table. "You picked a bad time to disparage hummus and pinion nut sandwiches, mister. They're my favorite. Besides, what are you doing at this lunch? I thought you ate Junior High."

"I usually do, but I'm a free man for this entire period. The seventh grade is on an Art field trip, so I decided to see how the big teachers lived."

"Are you impressed?"

His smile returned, this time crinkling the corners of his blue eyes. "I think I am."

He's flirting with me!

Armen reached out and touched her hand. His fingers were cool to the touch. She thought to pull away but decided not to.

"Do vegetarians drink coffee?" he asked.

The question caught her off guard. "What?"

"Coffee. You know, the brown stuff grown-ups get

to drink."

She sat back to see if he was making fun of her, but his face gave nothing away. "I can't speak for every vegetarian, but I've been known to drink the occasional cup."

"Black, I'll bet."

"Well, yes, how did you know?"

"That's how I like it." He took his hand off hers. "Would you have coffee with me this evening? Black, of course."

A date?

She stared at him, too dumfounded to speak. She hadn't even considered seeing a man socially since her Ben died eighteen months ago. She was fifty-three for heaven's sake, certainly didn't need this complication in her well ordered life. Her brain had already settled the issue but failed to inform her mouth. "Where?"

"I know a place in the Springs, Capulets. Deep up-holstered chairs, antique tables. Can I pick you up at your home?"

She panicked, thinking of a date coming to her door as if she were some school girl—and then taking her home again. "I'll meet you there. What time?"

"Seven?"

"Seven sounds fine." *What in the hell have I done?*

BONNIE FIDGETED UNCOMFORTABLY ON THE STEEL risers of the gymnasium. All around her, the student body of East Plains Junior/Senior High did the same.

The normal rise and fall of five hundred collective voices seemed muted, as if no one dared to speak above a whisper.

Down on the gym floor, an ancient oak podium stood in isolated relief against the purple and yellow paint of the basketball court. The podium sported the screaming image of a Thunder Hawk, the school mascot. Talons extended, the hawk looked as if it had been frozen just moments before it made a kill.

Followed by Principal Whittaker, Superintendent Xavier Divine entered the gym. They both halted at the podium. In contrast to the hawk, Divine appeared docile, almost frightened. He could easily have been the mascot's intended prey.

Divine unwound the microphone from its gooseneck and stepped in front of the podium. "Students and staff of East Plains, I regret the need to inform you of a tragedy."

Bonnie felt her chest tighten.

"Stephanie Templeton, Senior class President, captain of the Knowledge Bowl team, died early this morning."

"What?" Bonnie said louder than she meant to.

Heads turned in her direction. Divine stared at her from the gym floor and frowned.

"Sorry," she mouthed. She'd been expecting news of Peyton Newlin, had steeled herself for the worst. But Stephanie? Bonnie shook her head as if to refute this bolt out of the blue.

"Announcements concerning funeral plans will be

posted in the Gazette and the East Plains Register. The family asks that phone calls be held to a minimum. Please respect their wishes in this hour of sorrow." He handed the microphone to Lloyd.

Islands of grief erupted around Bonnie. Students wept openly, cursed out loud. A trio of girls with Stephanie Templeton blond hair clutched at one another, their faces leaking water. A freshman boy from Bonnie's Algebra One class, his face an empty mask, hammered his fist into the steel seat again and again.

Lloyd's voice insinuated itself into Bonnie's anguish. ". . . are in the building if you need to talk to a counselor. For those of you wanting to go home, the busses have arrived." His eyes met Bonnie's, and he signaled her to join him at the far end of the gym.

As Bonnie made her way down to the gym floor, she came face to face with Diane Wynn, the school librarian. The woman's cheeks were wet, her eyes red-rimmed. "That poor girl. She was like a ray of sunshine, so beautiful. Do you have any idea what happened?"

Bonnie shook her head and pulled the relative stranger into an embrace. They wept together. Students clearing the stands patted their shoulders and backs and moved on.

"I've got to go, Diane," Bonnie whispered into the librarian's hair, and pulled back. "Lloyd's waiting on me. Are you going to be okay?"

The woman sniffled and offered a frenetic nod. "I'll be fine. I'm going to go home and hold my little boy. I might never let him go."

"Give him a hug for me."

Lloyd waited by the wrestling loft stairs. When she approached, he started walking up to the loft.

She followed.

He moved to the back of the loft and sat heavily onto a weight bench. "I've got to get out to the busses, but I have to tell you a few things before I go." He rubbed his eyes with the heels of his hands.

She joined him on the bench.

"Just before dawn a man walking his dog discovered Stephanie's body in a gully near Fulton Hill."

The world suddenly shrank to one isolated weight bench. Bonnie's hands went to her mouth. "Stephanie went home with her mother. What was she doing on Fulton Hill in the middle of the night? That's a good five miles from her house."

Lloyd gripped her hands in his. "I can't answer that question, Bon, but Franklin Valsecci wants you to call him. He's hoping you'll remember anything that might explain the girl's murder."

"Murder? They know that for sure?"

He squeezed her hands until she met his eyes.

"The back of her head was crushed. They found a bloody baseball bat near the body."

$$\triangle$$

BONNIE STRADDLED THE WEIGHT BENCH STARING AT her cell phone. She sat alone in the loft. From the absence of noise below she might be the only one left in the entire gym.

Stephanie's death kept circling in her mind, but not far removed spun Peyton Newlin's disappearance. There had to be a connection.

She punched in Franklin's office number.

He picked up on the second ring. "Valsecci."

"It's Bonnie. You wanted to talk with me?"

"I just need to pick your brain a bit. Tell me what you can of Stephanie Templeton."

Stephanie's face swam in a sea of images—flipping long blond hair over a bare shoulder, the smell of too-much perfume, the valley-girl voice which belied her intelligent mind, the teary girl who blamed herself for not bringing home a Knowledge Bowl trophy.

"East Plains will survive." That's what she told Stephanie. *Damn it, girl, what were you doing on Fulton Hill in the middle of the night?*

And why Fulton Hill? The place was as steep and uninviting as the surface of the moon. More a small mountain, the hill was scarred by dozens of parallel cement-hard erosion gullies, some deep enough to swallow a car—and now a young girl's body.

"Missus P?" Franklin's voice sounded in Bonnie's ear.

"Sorry. I was wool gathering." Bonnie breathed deep. "Stephanie Templeton? A good student, temperamental. Occasionally affected the manner of a ditz but had a practical head on her shoulders. A bit of a prima donna. She was captain of my Knowledge Bowl team. I'll miss her more than I can say."

"What was her relationship with Jesse Poole?"

Bonnie searched her mind for any time she'd seen the two together. "I don't think they had any. They didn't exactly travel in the same circles."

"How about her relationship with Peyton Newlin?"

"Different story. Those two crossed one another's paths constantly. He was in her Math Analysis class, although he did independent study in Calculus."

Franklin whistled. "A thirteen year old doing Calculus? I'll bet a lot of math students resented him. Did Stephanie?"

Bonnie considered the question. "I don't think she did. If anything, Stephanie felt sorry for Peyton."

"Why so?"

"He was like a fish with a moped. He had the equipment but wasn't sure how to use it. She took him under her wing. As much as she could, she tried to shield him from being picked on, which wasn't easy. Peyton Newlin could be a little shit. However—"

"However?"

"It's probably nothing. Last night, Stephanie got upset when we didn't leave with a trophy. She snapped at Peyton and stormed out of the auditorium. She regretted it immediately. The next time I saw her she was crying about it. Called herself a bitch."

"Anything else?"

"This morning the counselor told me Peyton as well as Stephanie, Ali, and Edmund were all finalists for the same scholarship." She told him of J.D. Sullivan.

Papers rustled from Franklin's end. "Edmund

Sheridan? The same Asian boy from last night?"

"The same."

"What can you tell me about him?"

"The Sheridans, a well-to-do couple, adopted Edmund, and his older sister Molly, about ten years ago and brought them over here from Korea. Molly had an accident, developed spinal problems, and has been wheelchair-bound since she was nine. Edmund is very protective of her." Bonnie tugged at her ear trying to think of anything of interest. "Edmund is in Calculus with Peyton. The two are best friends. Edmund's always over at the Newlin place reading comic books, playing electronic or role-playing games."

"And how about this Ali Griffith?"

"She's a witch."

"Come again."

"Ali Griffith and her mother Rhiannon head up a coven. I've known the mother for a good five years, but she's a weird one. We haven't always gotten along. Ali dresses in black, and wears odd jewelry. She's never been anything but a sweetie with me, but I hear she doesn't take crap from anyone who gives her trouble about her beliefs. Even the goat-ropers steer clear of her. Peyton, Edmund, Stephanie, and Ali make up the Knowledge Bowl Team and were all at the church last night."

"This is getting almost incestuous, all on the Knowledge Bowl team, all in the running for a choice scholarship—"

"And all absent from school today."

"Now that is worthy of note. I owe it to myself to

pay the Griffiths and Sheridans a visit."

"Do you think there's a connection between Peyton's disappearance and Stephanie's death?"

"I bet you do."

She felt heat rise to her cheeks. This former student could read her too easily. "It occurred to me."

"It occurred to me, too."

Come on, Franklin, you can do better than that.

After a long awkward silence, he said, "Listen, I've got a lot to do."

Not so fast, youngster. "I've got a few questions of my own."

"Nothing doing, Missus P. We're talking murder here and this is an ongoing investigation."

"And I'm part of it." She went on before he could object further. "About nine last night, Missus Templeton picked up Ali Griffith and Stephanie from the Academy. I assume you talked to the parents. What time did the Templetons get home?"

"They dropped off the Griffith girl and made it home about ten o'clock. Let me save you the trouble of asking. Both the mother and daughter were tired and went to bed right away. Lights off before ten-thirty."

What in hell makes an exhausted girl leave her bed and travel five miles to her death?

"Did Stephanie die at Fulton Hill, or did her killer dump her body there?" She expected him to try to put her off and geared herself up to be good and pissy.

"From the amount of blood found, our people have determined she died at the hill. Now, that's enough. If you think of anything else give me a call." He hung up.

Think of anything else?

Hell, a dozen thoughts flashed across her mind. The last of which was Wendy Newlin racing away down Peterson Avenue in her silver SUV, too scared to confront her husband. What kind of night did that poor woman have? First her son runs off then her son of a bitch husband comes home? Too bad it couldn't be the other way around.

Bonnie checked her watch. Four o'clock straight up. She had three hours until she promised to meet Armen. The thought sent a shiver through her. She certainly wasn't going to sit around and be a nervous ninny until then.

Before she could change her mind, she punched in Wendy Newlin's number.

CHAPTER 4

BONNIE LAID INTO THE GAS. SOMETHING in Wendy Newlin's voice came across unnatural, bordering on creepy.

Not so much what the woman said— "Why sure, honey, come on by. You know the way?"—sounding more like Scarlet O'Hara graciously inviting a poor neighbor to barbeque than a woman whose son was missing.

Yes, definitely creepy.

She slapped the steering wheel. "We would have been there already, Alice, if you hadn't taken so long turning over. I've got no use for a persnickety Subaru. It would serve you right if I just traded you in for something more reliable." She lowered her voice. "And faster, dammit."

An idle threat.

She'd drive Alice until the car's wheels fell off. Hell, longer. A year and a half ago both the front wheels had come off. And yet, here was the old hag, still chugging across the plains.

Ben loved this car. He cursed it—more than once promised to send Alice to that great scrap heap in the sky—but he was the one who named the car Alice after a girl he'd kissed in the second grade.

Bonnie inhaled deeply—a faint reminder of pipe smoke and instant coffee. "I can still smell you, my love." She wrinkled her nose. "Truth is, you kind of stink."

The familiar double row of poplars appeared in the distance. Bonnie slowed.

The Newlin ranch sat close to the southern edge of East Plains. She'd once taken Peyton home after a Knowledge Bowl practice and was surprised at the metamorphosis in the place. The mysterious military family transformed what had once been a working ranch into a palatial estate.

They'd torn down the paddocks, the outbuildings, and the main redwood log cabin and replaced them with a sprawling adobe split level complete with arches and arcades of stucco. A bright green tennis court sat in incongruous decadence against the dull tans and browns of the surrounding desert. Like Twelve Oaks of *Gone with the Wind*, rows of trees lined a half-mile lane leading to the house.

Dim orange light, like banked coals, reflected from multi-paned stained-glass picture windows, spanning fifty of the hundred-sixty foot pueblo style wall. Heavy rough-hewn beams pierced the adobe just beneath a tiled roof. Everything about the place looked clean, brand new, and expensive.

Rumor had it Colonel Newlin's family had money—a brother or maybe an uncle—had been senator in their home state since the invention of rope. Ralph certainly couldn't have afforded the changes on what the Air Force paid him.

Surrounded by what seemed like an acre of flagstone, Wendy Newlin sat cross-legged at a wrought-iron patio set, a cigarette as thin as a darning needle between her lips. Probably the Colonel didn't let her smoke inside.

An open peach-and-lavender cashmere sweater hung across Wendy's knees covering a white tennis top and shorts. She waved then brought a glass to her lips.

Bonnie pulled up next to the patio and came around the Subaru.

Stubbing out her cigarette, Wendy set the drink on a small glass table. She attempted to stand and stumbled. Trying to steady herself with the small table, she sent her drink crashing to the flagstones. The glass shattered. The table toppled. The circular glass top sprang free. By some miracle, it spun like a coin but didn't break.

Wendy lurched upright and stood staring at the devastation, her shoulders heaving.

Bonnie ran, and the woman turned a flushed face her way.

"Oops." Wendy's eyes were full with tears, but they were tears of laughter.

Drunk as a cattleman after branding.

Wendy bent to clean up.

Bonnie restrained her, squeezing her shoulders and pulling her close. "We'll get it later. Can you walk?"

Wendy's head swayed in the approximation of a nod. "Of course, silly." Her breath was heavy with the semi-sweet aroma of whiskey. "Can you?"

Ah yes, drunken comedy. "I'll do my best. Hold on to me."

Luckily, the front door was open. She supported Wendy across an ecru carpet that felt three inches thick and plopped her onto a sofa the size of a small mining town. Wendy scraped a bleeding foot against an ivory-hued ottoman, painting a lightning bolt of blood along its side.

Colonel Ralph Newlin would probably be incensed at the stain, but then again, Colonel Ralph Newlin might possibly have to go screw himself.

Makeup caked the right side of Wendy's face, not quite hiding a massive bruise. Bonnie pinched the woman's chin between thumb and forefinger and tilted Wendy's face to the light of a hanging lamp.

She toppled sidewise on the couch.

Bonnie grabbed the front of Wendy's tennis shirt. "Oh no, you don't." She lifted and jammed the woman into a crook of the couch.

Wendy stared down at the wrinkled front of Bonnie's blouse and giggled. "You're strong."

"And you only smell that way." She swung Wendy's sandaled feet up onto the ottoman. "Stay with me. I'm going to clean up that bloody foot."

The living room opened onto a country kitchen resplendent with hanging copper cookware. A trio of kitchen towels hung from wooden hooks next to an oversized refrigerator. Bonnie snatched all three towels, stepped to the sink, and doused them with cool water.

"Hang in there, sweetie," she yelled from the kitchen.

Bonnie cleaned the foot, removing a sliver of glass then attacked the makeup. Gently, she removed the foundation, revealing a nasty muddy splotch that covered Wendy's face from left ear to cheek.

"You need to get some ice on this. Where's your husband?" She didn't even attempt to hide her anger.

Wendy's hand fluttered to her bruise. "Gone." She cupped her other hand next to her mouth.

"He'll come back with jewelry. Be real sorry." She giggled.

I'd say sorry doesn't cover it by half. "Are you going to be here when the Colonel shows?"

"I have to." The words came out an apology. "What will Peyton do if I'm not here?"

Bonnie sat down on the carpet, her knees wrapped in her arms. She studied the woman. She had to admit to a certain grudging admiration, but her anger splashed it with contempt. "How long have you put up with this?"

Wendy clapped her hands over her ears. "I don't want to talk about it."

With a force she didn't intend, Bonnie snatched the woman's hands into her own. Wendy tried to pull away, twisting and whimpering like a child in full tantrum.

Bonnie held on until Wendy met her eyes. "You're going to have to, if not with me then with Social Services. I reported your husband this morning."

Wendy stopped struggling. Her hands, then her entire body went limp, long red hair falling over her face. "Why?"

"Oh, come off it, Missus Newlin! Some part of you must have known I wouldn't let abuse continue with one of my students. I did what you should have done long ago."

Her eyes hard, her face pulled tight, Wendy lifted a ferocious glare toward Bonnie. "You think you know everything about me. You don't know shit."

That's the second time in as many days someone's told me that. They're probably both right. "Then school me," she challenged.

And it looked as if Wendy might do that very thing when her face went ashen. She sprang from the couch, half ran half crawled past Bonnie, and scuttled down a carpeted hall. She lurched into a side room. The unmistakable sounds of vomiting came from the room.

Bonnie waited a few minutes and followed. She turned on the bathroom light. The rotten fruit smell of liquor vomit hung strong in the air.

Wendy sat in front of the commode, her arms draped along the rim.

Driving the old porcelain bus.

"Think you'll survive?" Bonnie pulled a bathroom towel from an oak rack and tossed it.

Wendy wiped her face and turned an icy stare toward Bonnie. She opened her mouth with the apparent intention of saying something scathing. A burp a stevedore would be proud of exploded from deep in her throat.

Bonnie looked away. She bit her lip trying to keep a straight face. Then she erupted in laughter. She thought of running from the room, but when she turned back Wendy was smiling.

Wendy flushed the toilet and pushed away. "You are one queen asshole." She set her back against the oak paneled wall of a combination bathtub and spa that looked big enough to wash a baby elephant. A laugh turned into a snort. She covered her mouth as if she could retrieve the embarrassing sound then laughed again. "Where the hell did that come from?"

Bonnie stared at the woman, liking her. "I wouldn't worry about it. On you, a snort looks good."

With effort, Wendy scrambled to her feet. "I'll be right back." She returned with a pack of Virginia Slims and sat back down on the floor. "Do you mind?"

Bonnie did mind. She hated cigarette smoke and was certain she would hate it even more in this confined space. "No, go ahead."

The woman's hands shook as she tried to ignite a match.

Bonnie took the matches and lit the cigarette. She lowered the toilet seat and sat.

Wendy inhaled deeply, tilted her head back and blew out a great cloud of smoke. She fisted the cigarette high over her head. "Up yours, Colonel Ralph Newlin, and the jet you rode in on. Look at me, you bastard. I'm smoking in the house." She flicked an ash to the floor.

Wendy's eyes went liquid. "We had a shit bird of a fight. Both said some horrible things. I told him when Peyton returned we were leaving. Ralph stormed out. Gave me something to help me remember him." She laid her fist against her bruise.

Bonnie wanted to embrace the woman, but something hard in Wendy Newlin's face made Bonnie keep her distance. "I'm so sorry."

Wendy's eyes became steel slits. "I'm not. I should have left that dick-head years ago."

She drew on the cigarette. "Almost fourteen years later, here I am." She gave a short laugh—air escaping from a dying balloon. A curtain of smoke poured from her lips and nose.

"Where did he go?" Bonnie tried not to let her distaste for the smoke show on her face.

Wendy shrugged, more of an I-don't-care than an I-don't-know. "Probably woke up one of his pilot buddies. Spent the night calling me a bitch."

Bonnie's heart broke for this damaged family. She wanted to despise Ralph Newlin, but couldn't even work up to disdain. The man would lose everything and likely convince himself it wasn't his fault. Wendy would cobble together a life for her and her genius son. As for Peyton, he'd be a bone his parents would shred between them as they tore at one another. Who could blame him for running away from this train wreck?

"Have you heard any news about Peyton?" Bonnie asked, already knowing the answer.

Wendy shook her head. "I spoke with an Amber Alert representative before I went to bed and again this morning. I gave him Ralph's number at the base. The officer, Keene, I think his name was, said he'd keep me informed."

Bonnie debated telling this already overburdened woman the news of Stephanie Templeton's death and decided against it. Wendy didn't look like she had room on her plate for another tragedy.

A clock sounded from the family room, and Bonnie absently let the gongs wash over her. Not until the sixth did she realize the truth. She sprang out of her seat. "Is that time right?"

Wendy squinted up at her through a smoky haze. "I suppose, why?"

"I promised to meet someone in the Springs at seven."

Wendy lifted the toilet lid and dropped in her cigarette. "We'd better get you on the road."

Bonnie offered Wendy a hand, but she refused.

"I feel a lot better." Shakily, she used the spa's wall to stand. "I can see why Peyton likes you. Come back, please. I'm going to need a friend over the next couple of months."

"I can always use a friend." Bonnie led the way through the house and onto the flagstone patio. "I promised I'd help you clean up this mess."

Wendy waved away the offer. "I don't even want to think about cleaning right now."

Bonnie thought to argue, but let herself be persuaded. She climbed into the Subaru. "I'll give you a call this evening."

Wendy nodded.

The ancient car wheezed as if it might self-destruct and finally turned over. Bonnie offered an embarrassed smile. Alice lurched back toward the poplar lane, now in deep shadow. In her rearview mirror Bonnie watched Wendy Newlin open her front door and be swallowed by her giant home.

$$\bigwedge$$

SIX MILES OUT, BONNIE REACHED A RIGHT-ANGLED crook on Coyote Road, the major dirt artery that earlier took her to the Newlin place. The Subaru shuddered. Bonnie patted the cracked dashboard. "Don't do this, Alice. I'm already running late."

The car decelerated, slowing to less than twenty miles an hour. Bonnie jammed the accelerator to the floor, but the pedal felt spongy. The Subaru continued its decline. Bonnie tried fluttering the pedal, something which worked in the past, but to no avail. Alice drifted to a stop.

"Damn, damn, damn." Bonnie banged her fists on the steering wheel. "I wasn't serious about trading you in. You know I'd never do that."

Alice gave a final shudder and died.

"Thank you very much." Bonnie slumped back in her seat. She stared out her window. The sun hung low over Pike's Peak, promising a glorious sunset. She was in no mood to enjoy it.

Bonnie reached for her fanny pack and the cell phone within. Her hand froze in mid-air then came to rest on the empty passenger seat. An image of the pack sitting on her desk at school appeared in her mind. "Well, Alice, I picked a fine time to forget my purse. Double damn."

Six miles back and down a half mile of lane, she wouldn't reach the Newlin place until well past dark. The idea of the trek made her body ache. She wished she'd paid more attention to the houses she passed on the way. In the back of her mind she remembered Rhiannon Griffith, Ali's mom, had a ranch out this way. If memory served, it couldn't be more than a few miles, just over the next rise to the north.

If I leave right now, I could make the ranch and call Capulets Cafe. Leave a message for Armen.

Cursing, she pushed the Subaru off the road into a sandy ditch which bordered Coyote. With any luck, she'd get a tow truck to move Alice out of harm's way before some drunken cowboy slammed into the car.

Bonnie debated walking along the dirt road, but the curve up ahead changed her mind. For the next two miles, it perversely headed east, away from where she pictured the Griffith ranch. She'd reach the ranch quicker cutting diagonally across the desert. She struggled over a wire-mesh fence and set off across scrub grass and sand.

By the time Bonnie reached the crest of the rise,

she knew she'd been deluding herself. Stretched out before her was more of the same gray-brown landscape she'd just hiked across. Another rise beckoned a half mile north. A sensible voice whispered she should turn around right now and go back to Newlin's, but she ignored it.

No way. The damn place is even farther now. And surely she couldn't be wrong a second time.

A massive bramble of cactus sat between her and the rise, but she didn't let it deter her. She skirted toward the mountains, thinking she needed to go west eventually. By the time she cleared the cactus, the sun swam in an ocean of pink and orange. She checked her watch. Already past seven. Armen would be sitting in Capulets wondering where she was.

She reached the top of the rise, and her heart sank—more sand and scrub-grass as far as the eye could see. To make matters worse, in the distance an arroyo sliced east to west interposing itself in her path, beyond that an even steeper rise. She looked wistfully back the way she came but couldn't spot her car.

"Griffith's can't be too much further." Now her saner self argued that this was madness. If she was really honest she'd admit she was wrong and turn around.

"I'm not wrong." She picked up the pace.

The sun slipped behind Pike's Peak. Grays and purples replaced the muted browns. Night comes quickly on the desert plains. Once the sun sets behind the mountains, deep shadows race across the sand.

She hadn't reached the arroyo before she found herself walking in darkness.

Bonnie promised herself henceforth she'd keep a flashlight in the trunk. "Especially, Alice, if you insist on stranding me in the middle of nowhere," she bellowed.

The sound of a car engine startled her. From the west, a set of headlights bounced in her direction. Someone, maybe even Wendy Newlin, had seen her broken down car and was coming to her rescue. Bonnie waved, ignoring a nagging voice which insisted Wendy's hacienda lay south, not west.

Standing there, she played with the notion Alice had repented and in a fit of automotive remorse was coming to make amends. The ridiculous thought brought back a cartoon memory from her childhood—Beanie and Cecil, the seasick sea-serpent. In Beanie's darkest hour, Cecil would come charging in yelling, "I'm comin', Beanie Boy!"

"I'm waiting, Alice girl," she whispered. She waved again.

The car's high beams blazed on, pinning her in blinding light.

Bonnie shielded her eyes. *What was this idiot up to?*

Too soon came her answer. The sound of an engine revving higher screamed out of the light. In panic, Bonnie pitched herself to one side.

A red pickup truck whipped past, spraying her with gravel. It spun into a hard turn. Her heart wanted to stop with the realization it was Jesse Poole's truck.

"Oh, shit!" She picked herself up and ran.

The squeal of protesting metal grew louder. Light enveloped her. Her bleeding knees burned. Sensing the truck closing on her, she hurled herself to the side.

The bumper clipped her foot. A stab of pain shot through her ankle. Screaming, she fell.

Surrounded by a halo of light, the truck crashed through a patch of yucca.

Bonnie struggled to her feet. Her ankle shrieked in protest. A wave of nausea swept over her. Any moment, she expected the truck door to open. Jesse Poole, the little bastard, would chase her down.

Gravel churned behind her.

The truck reversed hard and spun to face her, pinning her again in the high beams.

Gears ground, and the truck crept forward.

"Leave me alone, you little asshole." She limped backward unable to take her eyes off the truck. The truck closed the gap. Then the ground vanished beneath her feet. She flailed through the air. The back of her head smacked something hard. The world exploded in fireworks and faded to black velvet.

$$\bigwedge$$

BONNIE WOKE TO A HEADACHE THAT PROMISED TO sever skull from shoulders. Her hand came away sticky from her scalp. A hard something poked her spine. She shifted, and her ankle screamed. Nausea punched her stomach.

She vomited. Wave after wave of convulsions

gripped and shook her. Minutes later, she rolled away from the vomit, her throat raw, mouth tasting of bile.

She lay back, exhausted. Overhead, a full moon shined down from a strip of sky. A corridor of stars winked.

Where the hell am I?

She remembered the truck and sat bolt upright. New agony shot through head and ankle. She bit her lip, not wanting to cry out.

Oh God, don't let him find me here.

She lay still, and in stages, reason asserted itself. The moon hadn't yet risen when she'd walked earlier. The blood on her head was tacky, some of it dried. Hours may have passed. Her tormentor was gone. She shuddered, buried her face in her hands, and wept.

When she lifted her face from her hands, a knife had been taken to the moon. Flat along one side, a jagged sliver of the orb was missing. What remained illuminated her surroundings.

She lay at the bottom of a sandy tunnel. Behind her head, hard-packed earth formed a slanting wall. This wall partially obscured the moon. Across from her, an opposite wall lifted from the sand. Together the walls defined and limited the portion of the night sky she could see.

The arroyo. Stumbling backward from the truck, she'd tumbled into the sandy trench, hit bottom, and knocked herself out. Why hadn't her pursuer simply followed her down and finished the job he'd started?

"Hey, I'm not complaining, God. I'll take whatever

you give me."

But now what?

Theoretically, she could sit right here until someone found her. Her ankle and head seconded that option. Surely someone would notice Alice sitting in the ditch and come looking. But would they think to look on the other side of the mesh fence, or would they stick to the road? How many times had she seen an abandoned car and kept on driving?

Unfortunately, even when she was parked at school, Alice looked like an abandoned car. Most folks would think the owner just wised up and walked away.

Bonnie sighed. She could be here for days.

And it was getting darker. Already the moon had shifted—a mere sixty percent of its area shined down. She didn't fancy the idea of spending a long moonless night at the bottom of a pit.

A six foot length of weather-beaten two-by-four lay just out of reach. Gritting her teeth, she dragged her protesting ankle to the board. As her fingers wrapped around it, she felt like laughing, and the compulsion scared her.

Don't go hysterical, lady.

Ignoring splinters, she hoisted herself to her feet. The pain in her ankle threatened to send her back into oblivion. Breathing like she'd just run a marathon—not that she'd ever do something so stupid—she clung to the precious two-by-four, a drowning woman in a dry river of sand.

Her head almost reached the lip of the arroyo, but

the top may as well have been a hundred feet above her. No way could she climb out. And stretching out before her, the dry stream bed seemed endless.

Leaning heavily on her prop, she took a step. A bolt of pain lanced up her leg and brought tears to her eyes. Her ears rang.

"That wasn't so bad." She fought down the urge to argue with herself.

A handful of steps left her sweating and gasping for air. She felt dizzy and leaned on her board until the feeling passed.

One benefit of standing was that she purchased additional hours of moonlight. Her panorama broadened and now the friendly face of the man-in-the-moon smiled down on her.

"I can do this," she shouted to the moon. "Damn straight, I can do this."

She counted steps, forcing herself to take two more than the first time before she stopped. On the next trial she added five. Each time she halted, the ringing in her ears grew more insistent.

The face of Marcie Englehart, the school nurse, replaced the man-in-the-moon. "You've got a concussion, babe."

"Screw you, Marcie. I'm doing fine." She pressed on, adding still more steps to her halting procession.

Her splintered hands became raw, and she wrapped them in dried grass and kept going.

After an eternity, the arroyo grew shallow. Up ahead, it flattened and disappeared into the desert.

Flashes of light, like fireflies, sparked about her face as she left the dry stream bed. She hobbled to a stop.

Her left leg felt cold. She couldn't remember when it last felt otherwise. Her ringing ears screamed a symphony. The fireflies faded, except one. To the north the mother of all fireflies glowed on the horizon. Bonnie blinked, but the apparition remained.

A fire?

She cupped a hand over her eyes and looked again. Either she was experiencing a very selective hallucination, or someone had built a bonfire atop a hill.

She tried to yell, but only managed a croak. Another attempt proved no better. Setting her jaw, she started up the hill.

She hadn't gone a dozen steps when a raspy woman's voice floated down from above.

"Be joined," the solemn voice sang. "Be joined, Mother. Be joined, Father. Now is the time. In your fruitfulness, let all be fruitful."

A male voice responded, "May all nature be fruitful."

This should be interesting.

Bonnie gritted her teeth and forced one foot before the other. Already, she could feel heat from the massive bonfire.

"In your happiness, let all be happy."

"May all nature rejoice."

The two voices rose, holding a single protracted note.

Bonnie crested the hill. She took a final step, and fell, rolling onto her back in exhaustion. The singing stopped.

She stared at the night sky and thought, *I must be hallucinating.* Standing above her loomed the wild-eyed, raven-haired personage of Rhiannon Griffith, Ali Griffith's mother.

"Missus Pinkwater?" The big woman frowned. "What are you doing here? You look hurt."

Bonnie gave in to a hysterical laugh. "Rhiannon, you look naked."

CHAPTER 5

RHIANNON GRIFFITH ADJUSTED A TILTED costume tiara on her raven mane and delivered a withering glare. Her breasts shook in indignation, threatening to send the Phoenix tattooed across them into flight. "I am the Earth Mother," she rasped, her voice a testament to years of smoking unfiltered cigarettes.

I've fallen down the rabbit hole.

Bonnie sat up and glared back. "And I am the Eggman, coo-coo-ka-choo. Listen, Rhiannon, I'm sorry to burst in on your witchy festival, but I've had a rough evening."

The hammering in her ears threatened to detonate her head. "I need your help."

Just when Bonnie felt her day couldn't turn any more bizarre, a pale naked man sporting a crown of white flowers on his bald head scampered to Rhiannon's side.

"What's the problem, Rhee? I'm freezing." Tall and emaciated, a silver crescent moon adorned his right cheek—the one on his face. He hopped from one bare foot to the other, obviously unaccustomed to subjecting naked tootsies to desert rocks and flora.

This just gets better and better.

"Earth Father?" Bonnie caught Rhiannon's eye and could swear the woman winced before she nodded.

While covering himself with one hand, Earth Father stooped and took Bonnie's hand in his other. "Winston Bellows."

He blanched and pulled his hand away. "You're bleeding."

Terrific. Winston, the bare-assed warlock, has a problem with blood.

Bonnie bit her lip to keep from screaming. "I don't want to be pushy, guys, but my hands are the least of my problems. Someone tried to kill me tonight."

Winston's free hand went to where a suit-coat breast pocket would have been. He patted his chest looking for all the world like a man searching for a cell phone. "That's dreadful."

Bonnie wasn't sure if he meant her ordeal in the desert or his failure to find his phone. She opted for the former. "I, for one, could have gone a long time without the experience. You're a lawyer, right?"

"How did you know?" Winston asked.

"Just a hunch." She held an arm up to Rhiannon.

"I think I can walk if you give me a hand."

Rhiannon considered the proffered arm. "I don't think so." She sat down in the sand then turned back to Winston.

"Be a lamb and bring a phone. Tell everyone, especially Ali, about our guest. Have her bring an ice pack."

Bonnie watched him tip-toe off, wondering what the qualifications were for becoming an Earth Father. She had a feeling he was probably an ace with crossword puzzles, more than likely knew a lot about wine. "I really am sorry for disturbing . . . whatever it was that was going on here tonight."

Rhiannon shifted her naked derriere uncomfortably on the sand and leaned forward. Her face just inches from Bonnie's, she stared first into one eye then the other. "Apology accepted. By the way, did you know one of your pupils is dilated?"

Well, Marcie, you may be right about that concussion. "I took a fall and hit my head." She turned her head and showed Rhiannon the blood.

Earth Mother threw back her head and laughed. "Was this before or after someone tried to kill you?"

I don't need this shit from a pagan lunatic. "I tell you what. How about you let me use that phone, and I'll get the hell out of here?"

Rhiannon laid a henna-decorated hand on Bonnie's knee. "It's Beltane."

Bonnie squinted at the woman. "What?"

"You asked what was going on here tonight. The witchy festival is called Beltane, the celebration of

Spring's fertility."

Bonnie wasn't ready to let go of her anger. "I didn't ask. I said I was sorry for disturbing your festival, that's all. I don't give a furry rat's behind what you call it."

"You're angry."

Bonnie tried to stand. Her ankle shrieked in protest. She gave up the effort, panting in frustration. "Damn right, I'm angry. I come to you for help, and you sit there in your tattooed birthday suit and laugh at me."

"I was sad because I had no shoes until I met a man who had no feet."

"Are you, by any chance, on drugs?"

Rhiannon laughed again. "Thank you, Goddess. One lesson after another. No, Missus Pinkwater, I am not on drugs. Not since nineteen eighty-nine. And I wasn't laughing at you."

Bonnie lost her grip on her indignation. It was just too damn difficult to be angry with someone who might be mentally unbalanced. "Then what?"

Rhiannon removed the tiara from her hair and set it on the ground between them. "We had a break-in earlier this evening. My spirit wasn't right for honoring the Goddess. To tell the truth, I was pissed off. We've also had a number of rednecks coming around to gawk at the witches. I guess I was feeling sorry for myself until you told me about your evening."

"So, it sucks so much being me that I made you feel better about being you?" Bonnie picked up the tiara and placed it on her own head. "Glad to be of service."

Rhiannon scooted forward. She eyed the tiara and

straightened it with a nudge. "Not bad. I wish I had a mirror."

Bonnie looked up at a sound from beyond the dying fire. "We have company."

Wearing a white terrycloth robe and Birkenstock sandals, Winston strode into the firelight. He carried another white robe in one hand and a silver cell phone in the other. A half-dozen people, including Ali Griffith, followed in his wake.

Thank God none of them are nude.

A purple robe covered Ali from her neck to the tops of her bare feet. White baby's-breath was woven into her hair. Henna, in patterns that matched Rhiannon's, decorated her hands and feet. Ali hoisted her robe and knelt in the sand.

"Missus Pinkwater, are you all right?" She offered Bonnie a blue-gel ice-pack.

Bonnie took the pack and catalogued the elements of her evening that separated her from being all right then set them aside. "I'm getting better, sweetie." She laid the ice-pack against her aching head.

Winston tossed the robe to Rhiannon and handed the cell phone to Bonnie.

She flipped open the phone, ready to make a call, then cupped the receiver as if the connection was live. "Can anyone tell me the time?"

A white-haired woman, who looked like she should be playing mah jong rather than attending a witch's celebration, came into the firelight. "Look on the phone, dear."

Ten-thirty. Bonnie reddened. She knew damn well time was displayed on cell phones. She owned one, for pity's sake. *I'm more screwed up than I first thought.* Normally, she never would have forgotten it.

Bonnie nodded to the older woman. "Thank you." She'd have to call Franklin at home.

He picked up on the second ring. "Yo, it's your dime." He sounded sleepy.

Bonnie pushed aside her guilt for waking Franklin. "It's your favorite math teacher."

He groaned. "What time is it?"

"I have it on the best of authority it's past ten. A young man like you shouldn't be sitting at home at ten o'clock on a Friday night, anyway."

"Then how could I be here to take your fascinating late night calls? You know my only wish is to wait upon your pleasure." He sighed. "What can I do for you, Missus P?"

She drew a deep breath. *All right, try not to sound like a crybaby.* "Jesse Poole tried to kill me."

He hesitated, then said, "You got my attention. Tell me everything."

She told him everything.

"This is screwy," Franklin said. "What is Jesse Poole doing off road in the middle of the night? And why would he want to kill you?"

Bonnie felt her anger grow through the telling, and now Franklin questioned her integrity. "I know what I saw, God damn it. How am I supposed to know why that little shit does what he does?"

"Settle down, Missus P."

Her throat contracted. Hot tears welled in her eyes. "Settle down yourself, youngster. He toyed with me, like a cat with a mouse. I don't appreciate being made into a victim." What she couldn't bring herself to say was that Jesse Poole made her feel like a foolish old woman. And *that* she couldn't forgive.

Ali touched her arm. "Can I talk to the policeman?"

Damn, I cursed in front of a student and her mother. Bonnie stared at the girl. "Ali, I need—"

"Jesse was here earlier this evening."

She handed Ali the phone.

Carefully, the girl pulled flower-woven hair away from her ear. "Officer, this is Ali Griffith. Jesse Poole broke into our house this evening."

Rhiannon Griffith had donned the white terrycloth robe. She stood several feet away smoking a cigarette and huddling with the members of her coven.

"Jesse Poole was here?" Bonnie asked, trying not to shout.

Six faces, including Rhiannon's, turned her way. All nodded in agreement.

"It's not the first time the little miscreant's come around here." Winston's deep-set eyes glowed red in the reflected firelight. "Rhiannon's had to chase him off more than once."

Rhiannon took a long pull on her cigarette. "But this is the first time he's been criminal about it. Up until now I've chalked up his trespassing to curiosity. But breaking in . . ." She blew out the smoke, looking disgusted.

"What happened?"

The older woman waved away the smoke. "Ali was the one who actually saw the truck. We were all stacking wood for the balefire when she heard a noise. She ran. She said someone slammed the back door of the house then jumped into a red pickup. It sped away down the frontage road." Her hand shook as she pointed off into the gloom.

"Did you call the police?"

Rhiannon shook her head. "We went through the house but couldn't find anything missing, or even disturbed. We had already started to decorate the five-petal altar. He could easily have vandalized that, but he didn't."

"Missus Pinkwater." Ali held out the phone. "The policeman wants to talk with you again."

Bonnie put the phone to her ear. "What do we do now?"

"I'll phone in the assault, send someone around to pick up Jesse Poole. You get to a hospital. Have your head examined."

She chuckled. "You've been waiting a long time to tell me that."

"Almost makes being woken up worth it. Good-night, Missus P."

"Goodnight yourself, youngster." She closed the phone and looked up to see a dozen-plus eyes staring down at her. She held up her index finger. "Just one more call?"

"I'll stay with her," said Ali.

"We'll all stay," Rhiannon said. "Make your call, Missus Pinkwater."

Bonnie pulled a crumpled wad of paper from her pocket. She unfolded the paper and punched in the number written there. She'd copied the number, it seemed a lifetime ago, when she was having second thoughts on the advisability of sharing coffee with a certain gentleman.

Armen Callahan answered on the third ring. "Hallo."

"Armen, it's me, Bonnie."

"Do you mean the Bonnie Pinkwater who left me sitting at Capulets for over an hour?"

She swallowed, not really sure what do with the anger in his voice. "The very one. I'm sorry, Armen, but I have a good excuse."

"A poor substitute for a coffee date, but try me."

She told him the highlights of her evening.

He whistled. "I'd say that's a pretty good excuse. So, if I understand you right, you're currently injured, sitting on the ground next to a dying fire in the company of witches."

"Why, yes, I am."

"I'll be right there."

She sat up straight as if by doing so she could demonstrate her surprise, or possibly her disapproval. "What?"

"You need to go to the hospital. I'll take you, but it's going to cost you."

She considered declining his offer, but realized she

would have to inconvenience someone if she wanted to get to the hospital that night—and here was Armen volunteering.

"What's the price?"

"You buy me coffee at the hospital."

"Black?"

"You betcha. See you in about half an hour." He hung up.

Bonnie closed the phone and handed it to Winston. She squirmed uncomfortably. "I think my rear end is permanently numb from this hard ground. And I need to visit the little girl's room. Is there really a house out there somewhere in the night, or did you witches make it disappear?"

BONNIE HOBBLED OUT OF THE BATHROOM. HANGING onto the doorjamb, she scanned the rough-hewn log living room for a place to sit.

Good luck.

All furniture of a sitting variety had been removed from the living room. An immense white altar spanned the entirety of the far living room wall. Two-tiered, the altar's upper tier sported more than a dozen white candles burning in brass holders. Aside from this light, the first floor of the ranch-house—which stretched to a family room and den to the right and a kitchen and mud room to the left—lay in darkness.

White flower garlands adorned the altar's lower tier,

spilling onto a satin apron. An honest to God cauldron sat centered on a pentagram rug in front of the apron, much of the cauldron's occult mystique mitigated by its use as a planter. White lobelia festooned over the rim.

Although her head felt like it might remain attached to her neck, her ankle throbbed like the dickens. She needed to get off her feet. She looked wistfully back into the bathroom at what might be the only seat left in the house.

Where the hell was everyone?

In answer to her unspoken question, she heard laughter coming from the family room she'd passed through earlier. Wearing an upside-down winged-back wicker chair like a gigantic hat, Winston Bellows staggered into the room, narrowly avoiding tripping over the cauldron.

He plopped the chair down in front of her. Red-faced, he smiled and patted the seat. "For you, my lady. Rhee sent everyone else home. It's now just her, Ali, and myself." He offered his hand.

"Thank you, sir." She took his hand and hobbled into the chair.

Ali entered next carrying a plush ottoman. "You need to elevate that ankle."

Even though Ali lifted the leg gently, Bonnie had to bite her lip to keep from crying out. Ali set the leg gingerly onto the ottoman.

"Don't get too comfortable." A cigarette dangling from her mouth, Rhiannon brought in a fresh ice-pack. Without a by-your-leave, she lifted the ankle and wrapped the ice-pack around it.

"Jesus, Mary, and Joseph, Rhiannon, that hurts." Bonnie glared at Rhiannon. "If you drop that foot, I'll have to kill you in front of your daughter."

"Stop whining, I'm not going to drop your foot. I'm the Earth Mother. Nurturing is in my blood." She set foot and ice-pack on the ottoman then stepped back, drew heavily on her cigarette, and admired her handiwork. "Leave the ice on there for twenty minutes."

"I know about injuries, you harpy." Bonnie leaned forward and adjusted the pack. "Ali, your mother's a sadist."

Ali put her arm around Rhiannon. "You're telling me? I have to live with her."

The cold made the ankle throb even worse, but Bonnie forced herself to lean back in the chair and relax. The light from the multitude of candles helped. "Thank you, Rhiannon."

Rhiannon winked and took another pull on her cigarette. "Sure thing, couldn't let Ali's favorite teacher suffer. Not on Beltane."

Bonnie nodded to the altar. "This Beltane's a big deal, isn't it?"

Ali spread her purple robe and sat at Bonnie's feet. "One of the major Sabbats. And my favorite. Next year, I'll be Earth Mother."

"Does that include the naked bit?"

"Of course."

Keep your mouth shut, Bonnie. "That's nice, dear."

Winston had left and now returned slurping a lollipop.

Although he existed at the opposite end of the morphology spectrum from the school counselor, Winston's lollipop brought that morning's meeting to mind. "I met with Mister Davenport this morning. I have some good news for you, Ali."

"Mister Davenport called here." Ali leaned an elbow on the ottoman. "Isn't it great about the scholarship?"

Before Bonnie could answer just how great she thought Ali's good fortune actually was, Rhiannon said, "She'll win that scholarship."

She spoke with such conviction, Bonnie felt compelled to speak. "I hope so."

"I know she will. I did a Tarot spread this afternoon, and the cards confirmed Ali's ascension." Rhiannon squared her shoulders and squinted at Bonnie as if daring her to voice disbelief.

Bonnie had seen that true believer look before, although from the other side of the religious continuum. She knew she had very little wiggle room. Rhiannon fully expected her to react with skepticism. Bonnie's Imp of the Perverse prodded her to do just that.

What the hell, silence is just as bad. "The Tarot, you say?" Regardless of her intention, it came out sounding flip.

"That's right. You have a problem with the Tarot?"

"I didn't say that."

"You didn't have to. It's all over your face as plain as your nose."

Bonnie sat up to confront Rhiannon. She'd always been sensitive about her nose. "My nose is not all over my face."

"But your skepticism is." Rhiannon jammed her fists into her hips as if to say—Hah, come back from that.

"I'll have you know I've had lots of Tarot readings."

Rhiannon eyed her suspiciously. "Is that so?"

"You bet. I'm a regular." She could feel the loose earth tumbling beneath her feet with every foolish lie.

"Would you like one more? We have time to kill while waiting for Mister Callahan."

In for a penny.

"Sure, why not?"

"Ali, bring me my Rider's deck."

The girl returned with an oversized pack of cards and a folding card table. She handed the deck to her mother and set up the table.

"Ladies, I'm going to bed." Winston didn't wait for a response, just disappeared into kitchen.

"Good night, Uncle Winston," Ali called.

Uncle Winston?

Bonnie heard his footfalls grow faint. She wondered what the sleeping arrangements were in this strange household.

Rhiannon handed Bonnie the cards. "Shuffle then cut the deck three times. We need the warmth of your hands and your own personal energy to enter the cards."

Bonnie awkwardly shuffled the oversized cards.

Rhiannon nodded toward the deck. "Tarot suits are different from spades, hearts, clubs, and diamonds, but an old hand like you already knew that. You do remember the Tarot suits?"

"Don't be such a wicked witch, mother. Missus P is our guest." Ali offered Bonnie a warm smile. "The suits are wands, cups, pentacles, and swords."

"I knew that." Bonnie refused to meet Rhiannon's stare.

The elder witch cracked her knuckles. "Of course you did. I never doubted it."

Bonnie set the deck onto the card table and cut it three times as instructed. "Now what?" She regretted the question, thinking it showed her for the novice she was.

Rhiannon cupped the deck in her hands looking as if she were readying a card trick. "Now we decide what to ask the cards."

The answer came to Bonnie's mind as if it had been playing solitaire in some dark corner. "What's become of Peyton Newlin?"

Rhiannon riffled through the cards. "Interesting choice, both a person and an inquiry. We need a very specific Significator to represent this dual inquiry. Here we go."

She chose a card showing a young man holding a staff. He seemed to be battling six other animate staffs. "Seven of Wands, a young man under attack."

Rhiannon set down the remainder of the deck and tapped the top card. "This next card shall be what covers him."

Bonnie leaned forward. Despite the low wail of her bullshit alarm, she found herself growing interested.

"What's that mean?"

"The main influence touching the person or inquiry, in your case both." She flipped over a card showing a red heart pierced by three intersecting swords. She laid it directly atop the first card. "Three of Swords." She leaned on the table and studied the card.

A heart pierced by swords didn't seem like it could be any kind of good thing, and Rhiannon's silence made Bonnie even edgier. "Well?"

Rhiannon waved her quiet. "Hold your water. The card indicates dispersion, absence, or in extreme cases forcible removal. That makes sense in light of what happened at Knowledge Bowl."

The meaning seemed too much of a coincidence. "The card actually means that?"

Rhiannon frowned at her. "You think I'm making this stuff up?"

A shiver shot up Bonnie's spine. *Get a grip, girl.* She told herself the shiver was probably an aftershock of her concussion. "Just go on."

Rhiannon turned over the next card and laid it perpendicularly across the pierced heart. "What crosses him. The Knight of Cups reversed." The card showed a knight on a white steed holding a golden chalice.

"This represents obstacles facing the individual. Reversed, the Knight of Cups isn't the noble figure he appears to be. He represents fraud, trickery, and deceit."

"Peyton is being deceived?"

Rhiannon shook her head. "Possibly, but not necessarily. There might be deception inherent in his disappearance. In which case, he would be the deceiver."

Before Bonnie could frame another question, Rhiannon snapped another card onto the table in the space above the three-card pile. "This crowns him. It represents the aim of the individual." The card featured a crowned man in flowing red robes seated on a throne. In one hand he held a sword, in the other a balance. The word Justice was written across the bottom of the card.

"In extreme cases 'what crowns him' represents the last resort of the individual, the best he can hope for under present circumstances."

"I don't understand." She felt dense and resented Rhiannon for making her feel that way.

Rhiannon traded glances with her daughter.

Ali sat up and stretched. In that pose, she looked like a younger version of her mother. "Think of it this way, Missus P. Seeking justice may have been the reason Peyton took off, or the driving force of his desires at this very moment. Does that make sense?"

"I suppose."

Rhiannon flipped the next card. It went below the central three cards. "The Fool is beneath him." The card showed a vacuous young fop and his dog. Both were so absorbed in staring at the clouds and the sky they failed to notice they were about to step off a precipice. "This represents the basis of the matter."

"Basically, Peyton is gone because Peyton is a fool," Bonnie said.

Rhiannon shrugged. "That seems the most logical explanation."

She turned the next card and placed it to the right. "The King of Swords." A stern man sat on a throne situated in a field. He held a sword in his hand as if he intended to use it.

"That which influenced the subject in the most recent past. It either refers to why Peyton may have run away, or what influenced the boy directly in other areas of his life."

This needed no explanation. The man seated on the throne even looked like Colonel Ralph Newlin, right down to the cruel turn of his lip.

The next card, which Rhiannon placed left, showed a woman sitting up in bed, her face buried in her hands in despair. Nine swords hung on a black wall behind her. "Nine of Swords is before him. This is what will influence him in the near future. With this card, what you see is what you get—failure, despair, and hopelessness."

"Is it significant the figure is a woman?"

Rhiannon nodded. "The cards reflect and are influenced by one another. Considering the mother was there the night the boy disappeared, I'd say gender is very significant."

She tapped the next card she intended to upturn. "This card will speak to the individual's actual attitude in the present circumstances." She placed the card face-up to the far right. "Two of Pentacles reversed."

A young man danced on a beach while he held a sidewise eight, the symbol for infinity, in his outstretched arms. In the background two ships sailed on a rolling sea. "Normally this card represents gaiety, but reversed it speaks of agitation, as if the youth is being forced to dance."

Being forced to dance with infinity. What the hell is that supposed to mean?

Bonnie fell back into the wingback chair. Her head throbbed. A part of her wanted this whole Tarot thing done with. "How many more cards?"

Rhiannon stroked the top card of the deck with a diamond encrusted nail. "Three. Do you want to quit?"

Might as well see it to the end. "Go on."

"This is his house." The card showed a blindfolded woman holding two crossed swords. She sat on a stool. Behind her a sea full of rocks and shoals crashed onto the shore. "The two of Swords represents his environment, the influence of the important people in his life."

When Rhiannon hesitated, Bonnie asked, "So what does the card say about Peyton's house?"

Rhiannon shook her head and smiled mischievously. "Impatient little bugger, aren't you? I thought you were tired of this game."

Bonnie stuck out her tongue. "Mainly, I'm tired of you. Would it help it I said please?"

"I wouldn't have you denigrate yourself so on Beltane. The card is a hoodwinked woman, conforming even when conforming is painful. Once again gender is important. Someone in Peyton's house is living a lie." She tapped the card. "An alternative interpretation is friendship. Someone in Peyton's house is reaching out in friendship even though it's against their nature."

Bonnie thought how she left things with Wendy

Newlin. "Come back and see me. I think I'm going to need a friend over the next couple of months."

Two cards to go.

Rhiannon flipped the next and placed it with the last two. "The Wheel of Fortune represents his hopes and fears." A sphinx sat on an amber circle which contained runic symbols.

Bonnie stifled a giggle. Every fiber of her being wanted to shout, "Pat, I'd like to buy a vowel."

Her struggle must have shown on her face. Rhiannon shot her a frown. "The card indicates Peyton worries about his destiny."

Or at least if he should give that big old wheel another spin. "Last Card?"

"Yes, and not a moment too soon." She sighed. "This card represents Peyton's destiny, or at least the end result of his disappearance. You and I need to concentrate and bring to bear all our intuition." She shut her eyes.

Bonnie felt awkward sitting there like she had as a child in church when the praying congregation bowed their heads. She looked at Ali, but the girl had her eyes closed as well.

When Rhiannon opened hers, she said, "Ready?"

"Ready."

The card showed a skeleton in armor riding a red-eyed, white war horse. A bishop in full liturgical garb, including miter, stood before the horse. The bishop clasped his hands in abject supplication. On the ground around the horse's hooves people either swooned or lay prostrate. At the bottom of the card, a single word was printed.

Death.

CHAPTER 6

ALL THOUGHTS OF PEYTON NEWLIN AND the Tarot flew out of Bonnie's mind. The room felt heavy with the dead presence of Stephanie Templeton.

A knock sounded on the front door, and Bonnie just about jumped out of her skin. "Jeeze, Louise." Her heart pounded.

At Rhiannon's nod, Ali got up to answer. She disappeared into the dark family room.

Rhiannon slid the card bearing the skeleton on horseback closer to Bonnie. "The 'Death' card isn't to be taken necessarily at face value. Certainly, death can mean just that, death, but the card can also indicate a major life change."

Having someone take a baseball bat to the back of your head certainly constitutes a major life change.

Had Rhiannon, or even more significantly, Ali heard the news about the murdered girl?

While Bonnie was deciding whether to test the waters on this tragic subject, Ali returned followed by Armen Callahan. Unlike at school, where he wore only sweater vests and ties, tonight he wore blue jeans and a tight navy blue muscle shirt. The shirt bore the message, "I toss peanuts at old ladies."

The ludicrous message deflated Bonnie's tension. She felt tired and light-headed. Of course, that could be the concussion.

In that moment, Bonnie decided she would not be the one to tell Ali of her friend's death.

The strain must have showed on her face because Ali asked, "Are you feeling all right, Missus P?"

Bonnie cast about for something to distract the girl from further questions. "Just admiring this good looking gentleman."

The Science teacher grinned. "Why, thank you, ma'am."

She had to admit Armen did look good. His belly was flat, his arms and shoulders well muscled. From the corner of her eye she caught a smiling Rhiannon Griffith staring at her. She turned her head to stare back. "What?"

Rhiannon shrugged and adopted a wide-eyed innocent look. "Nothing."

"Have I missed something?" Armen asked.

Bonnie reddened. "We should get going."

Armen helped her stand.

She wrapped an arm about his shoulder, and he scooped her into his arms. The move was so sudden and unexpected, she whooped then laughed. "Can you handle this?"

"No problem." Even though the veins in his neck stood out, he put on the patented male expression that asked, "You want to feel my biceps?"

In the sixteen months since Ben's death she'd forgotten the inanity of the male ego. Even when their goatees were gray, little boy hearts beat in their inflated chests. She had to admit, however, it did feel nice to have him hold her so close.

Get a grip, girl.

As Rhiannon and Ali gathered around to make their farewells, the older woman laid a hand on Bonnie. "Wait."

She ran back to the kitchen. When she returned a moment later she was carrying a small purple-velvet bag by its golden drawstring. She took Bonnie's hand and closed it around the bag. "Open it before you go to bed."

Bonnie eyed her suspiciously. She could feel something hard and cylindrical within the bag. "What is it?"

"Open it before you go to bed," Rhiannon repeated. She folded her arms across her chest.

The motion reminded Bonnie of the fiery Phoenix the woman had stenciled across that same bosom. *Time to leave Never-Never Land, boys and girls.* "Thank you both for everything."

When they got out to Armen's car he set her on the

hood. His face red and arms trembling, he dug car keys from his jeans.

So much for Superman. More like Clark Kent in a gray goatee. Still, he'd carried her to the car, and was taking her to the hospital. That counted for something. "This is very nice of you, Armen."

"You just remember your promise. I think I'm going to need that coffee." He opened the passenger door and lifted her off the hood.

She intended to tell him to put her down, let her hobble the few steps into the car, but she couldn't deny him this act of chivalry—even if it killed him. On impulse, she planted a kiss on the side of his cheek.

He cocked his head and grinned then set her on the car seat. "How bold you are, Missus Pinkwater."

"Call me Bonnie."

⟑

Bonnie and Armen had Highway Eighty-Four to themselves, as far as the eye could see, east and west, not a headlight in sight. Now that the moon had dipped below the horizon, the high plains lay in a blackness which was almost complete, except for the sky. Ten thousand stars peeked out of that dark.

Bonnie had driven this road countless times and knew beyond the shoulder, beyond a wide skirt of sand and scrub grass, rose a spine of low hills that followed Highway Eighty-Four almost into Colorado Springs. However, the dark robbed all depth and definition from the landscape. She may as well have been riding on an unchanging blanket of ebony satin.

They'd fallen into a companionable silence. She couldn't remember any time in the last year and a half she'd felt so comfortable with another human being, male or female. She broke the silence with a question. "You know much about the Tarot?"

He shot her a sidelong glance and returned his attention to the dark road. "You mean the deck of seventy-eight cards consisting of twenty-two major and fifty-six minor Arcana popularized in nineteen-ten by A. J. Waite into the well-known Rider deck?"

At the end of this lengthy reciprocal question he drew an exaggerated breath. "Never heard of it."

She slapped his arm. "Showoff."

He shrugged, looking pleased with himself. "My mother told fortunes, first in the old country then on the boardwalk in Wildwood, New Jersey. That's where she met my father."

She studied Armen in the pale glow of the dash lights, trying to discern exactly where this Old Country might be. His face did carry a tan, but nothing too pronounced. His voice gave nothing away. For all Bonnie could tell from his accent he might be from anywhere east of the Mississippi. He certainly didn't sound foreign.

He caught her staring and gave her a wink. "I have this effect on women all the time. First, they're drawn to my striking good looks, but what actually hooks them are my mysterious origins. It's a curse really."

She swiveled in her seat to face him and was pleasantly surprised her ankle didn't protest, at least not too much. "You're a regular tragic figure."

He nodded solemnly. "It takes a woman of rare insight to recognize the inner workings of a man. For that, I'll give you a hint."

"Why not just tell me?"

"Because we both know you'd rather figure me out on your own. Besides, once I tell you, we have to move on and talk of something else besides me."

She chuckled. "Is this going to be worth the trouble?"

It was his turn to laugh. "Definitely not! If I were you I'd refuse to play."

They crested the last remaining hill separating East Plains from Colorado Springs. The lights of the city spread out before them like stars fallen from the heavens. It wouldn't be long before they reached Memorial Hospital. Urgency grabbed Bonnie. She wanted to dope out Armen's ancestry before she crossed the hospital's threshold.

"Let's have your hint." She tried to sound disinterested, but from the look on Armen's face she knew she hadn't fooled him.

"Two hints, actually. First, my mother loved the country of her birth." He stopped as if he needed to give her time to assimilate this all-important piece of information.

When he didn't speak again for almost a minute she wanted to reach across the seat and strangle him. Highway Eighty-Four had turned into Platte Avenue. They were in Colorado Springs already. "Stop stalling."

They came to a red light. When they stopped, he turned to her. "Okay, here it is. My mother gave me something which would remind me every day who I was and where my ancestors lived."

He beat out "Shave and a Haircut" on the steering wheel then extended an open palm to her. "Take it away."

She tried to think of the thousand things a mother could give her child that would remind him every day of his mother's nationality. A flag came to mind, but if he left the flag at home, which he would eventually do, then his reminder would be gone. The same was true for a national anthem or a photograph. "This is hard, since I don't know what your mother gave you."

He grinned mischievously. "But you do."

In the distance she could see the lights of the Olympic Training Center and knew Memorial Hospital was bathed in those same lights. "I know what she gave you?"

"Yep."

She studied him again. This time she looked for anything on his person which might be a mother's gift. In a low-neck, sleeveless muscle shirt, he couldn't hide a chain around his neck. He wore no rings or jewelry of any kind. None of that mattered anyway. Even if he wore a ring, she wouldn't know it came from his mother. And yet, Armen said she knew what the gift was.

What did she know about Armen? Apparently, not much beyond his unusual name.

Oh, my God.

She smacked her hand on the seat cushion. "Your

name! Your mother gave you your name."

He nodded. "For that matter, so did my father. He gave me the name of Callahan."

"And your mother gave you the name of Armen, to remind you every day of Armenia."

Almost in slow motion, he slid his hand across the seat and squeezed hers. "Armenian mother, second generation Irish father, both Carny people. Nice going, lady. You're as clever as they say." He favored her with a smile.

Embarrassed, Bonnie shifted in her seat. A sharp pain shot through her ankle. "Ow, ow, ow, Goddamn that smarts." She tried to settle her leg into a position where it wouldn't hurt. As they slowed for the driveway into Memorial Hospital's emergency lane she found a position where the leg merely ached. Then the rise and fall of a speed bump gifted her with new agony.

Breathing through the pain, she asked, "Who are these people who say I'm clever?"

EXCEPT FOR THE X-RAYS, ARMEN HELD HER HAND through the examination. She wasn't certain when he first took hold, but it felt all right, more than all right. As they poked at her foot, she squeezed his hand. He never complained. They shined light into each of her eyes, and the feel of him made her relax. Her hand settled into his like it belonged there.

The prognoses proved Marcie-in-the-moon correct—

Bonnie had a not too serious concussion. On top of that, the second, third, and fourth metatarsals of her right foot were fractured. They fitted her with a black plastic boot—a walking cast they called it—that looked like a cheap ski boot made by a child. Once again, she squeezed Armen's hand through the pain as an intern closed the snaps to secure the boot in place. The same intern presented her with a shiny new pair of crutches.

"I hate crutches," she complained. She didn't need to be Armen's fortune-telling mother to know that before she'd tottered a dozen steps in these torture devices her hands and armpits would ache. *As if I don't have enough aches and pains already.*

"You're supposed to hate them," Armen deadpanned. "It's your God-given right as an American."

She stepped down off the examination table and onto her aluminum props. For a fleeting moment she considered bopping Armen in the shins, but the moment passed. "I didn't know that."

He nodded, keeping his face solemn. "It's in the Constitution. As Knowledge Bowl coach, I'm surprised at your ignorance."

"I only know useful facts, like the average rainfall of the Amazon Basin." She maneuvered a few steps in the crutches, already feeling the ache. She peeked back over her shoulder and caught him watching her with concern. "You coming?"

He quickly wiped the worried look from his face and adopted an expression of studied nonchalance. "I can see you're going to need my help with the sheer tonnage of minutia that makes life worth living. And yes, Missus Smarty Pants, I'm coming. And another thing, I never did get my coffee." He ran to catch up.

Her heart sank. She didn't want to spend another minute at the hospital. It had to be two in the morning, at least. Her entire ambition lay in getting home and putting head to pillow. "Could I give you a rain check?"

He rubbed a tender spot between her shoulder blades. "Don't sweat it. Coffee would just keep me up the rest of the night anyway."

At the car he took her crutches and helped her into the passenger seat. When she was settled, he shut the door. He came around and threw the crutches into the back. "Let's get you home."

The talk through Colorado Springs and out onto Highway Eighty-Four was just what Bonnie needed, light-hearted and not too demanding. The easy repartee allowed her to drift closer and closer to that dreamy state, not quite asleep but hardly awake. Again she marveled how comfortable she felt with this man she was just getting to know. It wasn't until they'd passed through the Eastern town of Falcon and had turned onto Meridian, the long country artery which took Bonnie to her Black Forest home, that Armen posed a question that brought her completely awake.

"What are you going to do about your car?"

"Oh, my God, Alice." She pictured her poor Subaru crumpled at the scene of some hit and run. What if someone smacked into it and was injured? Or worse?

Armen shifted his weight so he could offer one eye

to the highway and peer at her with the other. "Your car's name is Alice?"

Her mind had gone too far into panic mode to enjoy his gentle jibe. "That's right, Armen, the car's named Alice, and she's sitting half on and half off Coyote Road, right where it makes the hard turn east. Anyone coming too fast going either west or north might plow into her."

He reached across the seat and patted her leg. "Take it easy. That which you cannot change, you must endure."

At that moment all the comfortable feelings Bonnie had been having in Armen's company evaporated. She wanted to tweak his smug nose. *That which you cannot change, you must endure? Sounds like the kind of pop philosophy you could glean out of one of Ben's old Travis McGee mysteries.*

"Do you have a cell phone?"

He gave her a half-smile and shook his head. "Haven't seen the need for one yet. Besides, who would you call?"

She stared at him wishing he would stop asking questions. Her mind and mouth fluttered around words like "emergency" and "after hours," not really sure if she wanted to say them aloud. In her fanny pack she was fairly certain she had an insurance card which would provide a number for the magic "emergency-after hours" people, but then again her fanny pack sat on her desk at school. She also had a duplicate of said insurance card in Alice's glove box. Unfortunately,

Alice sat farther away than the school and was getting farther with every passing moment.

Bonnie folded her arms across her chest and decided the best course of action and the best answer she could give to Armen's question was a pout. She was still fuming when he turned onto her long dirt driveway.

Armen had long since removed his hand from her knee and returned it to the steering wheel. Now he placed it tentatively in the no-man's-land of the seat between them. "I have someone I can call."

She looked at him as if he had said, "God wants you to know that he'll take care of everything. Oh, by the way, he thinks you're the best gosh-darned math teacher he's ever met."

"Really?"

He pulled up in front her house and turned off the car. The syncopated roar of three dogs barking disturbed the silence, but Armen didn't seem to notice. "Sure, it'll only take a moment. I'll have them tow your car right into your driveway." He reached behind the seat and grabbed the crutches.

When he opened the car door he asked, "How many dogs do you have? They sound like the devil's own wolf pack."

She took the crutches, fitted them to her shoulders and was halfway to her door before she said, "Three, and one cat. Bet they're starving."

Euclid, the black Burmese and the only male member of Bonnie's household, met them as soon as they entered the house. He stood on the end table just inside the door looking like a statue from an Egyptian exhibit.

"That's his furious pose. He thinks we'll be devastated by it." Bonnie hobbled past the cat. "Get over yourself, Euclid. You don't even want to know the evening I've had."

The cat jumped down. Meowing, he followed them past the half-wall that separated the combination family room and kitchen from the front section of the house.

Armen passed her in the family room and went right for the kitchen phone hanging next to the microwave. "Euclid would have fit right in at Griffith's. You know, a witch's familiar?"

He smiled, and Bonnie found herself smiling back. She felt guilty for how churlishly she acted. After all, it wasn't Armen's fault she'd left Alice tilted in a ditch way out on Coyote Road.

"Armen?"

He waved away the obvious apology. "Forget it. Like you said, you've had a bad night." He picked up the receiver. "You got a couple of messages."

Bonnie hobbled closer, down the narrow hall which separated the back of the family room couch from the kitchen breakfast island. "Looks like three. Make your call first. I'll let the dogs in. The messages will keep."

She spun on one crutch and left him to make his call. She dreaded the explosion of dogs which would erupt past the steel-reinforced laundry room door once she opened it. Even though the dogs had a massive dog run beyond the laundry room, they'd still been outside far longer than they were used to. They could hardly be expected to understand the significance of crutches or why knocking their mistress off her pinions wouldn't be a good thing. Even now they scratched at the door and whined to be let in.

"Pay attention, ladies. I'm wounded out here. I'm not in any condition to play, so calm down." She twisted the door knob preparing to jump, as best she could, out of the way of the thundering herd. She pushed open the door.

Three dogs—one Golden Retriever, one Black Labrador, and one Border Collie—stood quietly in the doorway. They eyed their mistress for a moment then sauntered past her down the hall, the Border Collie in the lead. Only the Golden Retriever looked back, and that just to give her a glare.

"I'm sorry, Hypatia. I got here as quick as I could."

The dog snorted and followed her mates around the corner toward the kitchen. The message was obvious. "Save your apologies, lady. Do your talking with food."

By the time Bonnie reached the kitchen again Armen had already made his call. The dogs surrounded him, and he looked uneasy. "Henry, my tow guy, should drop Alice off in the next hour and a half."

Bonnie wasn't sure what she expected, but an hour and a half seemed an eternity. *That which you cannot change, you must endure.*

Armen looked exhausted. "Why don't you go on to bed? I've already told Henry I'd be here when he delivered Alice."

Bonnie's heart momentarily leapt at the opportunity before her mother's voice whispered in her ear that leaving this man to wait up half the night alone would be rude. "I'm fine. I'll make us some coffee."

Armen shook his head. "I'll make the coffee. You feed these dogs before they decide Science teacher is on the menu."

"They haven't eaten teacher in ages." She gave him an appraising stare as she opened a can of dog food. "Although, you do look tender."

"You look pretty good yourself. Now, where's this coffee?"

She showed him, and they handled their respective chores in silence. Once the dogs and cat were fed and watered, and the coffee was on the drip, they sat side by side on stools that bordered the island.

Armen nodded to the phone. "You still have those messages."

Bonnie sighed. The phone seemed a half a mile away.

Armen yawned. "I'll get it." He stood for a moment reading the buttons on the phone/answering machine and finally pushed the large central blue one. The machine whirred as it rewound then beeped three times. The first message was from Missus Newlin.

Bonnie winced. "I promised her I'd call tonight."

". . . know the time got away from you with your date and all. Just give me a call tomorrow."

Armen raised an eyebrow a la Mister Spock of Star Trek. "You told her you had a date with me?"

Bonnie reddened. "I told her I was meeting someone for coffee."

The machine beeped again to start the next message. "Missus P, this is Franklin. We took Jesse Poole in for questioning. That's all we could do since he had witnesses who say he never left the hospice during the times of the Griffith break-in or your assault. I don't think we're going to hold him. Catch you later."

The final beep came at the same time as the buzz of the coffee maker. Armen carried the two mugs he'd gotten earlier to the machine while the message played.

"Missus Pinkwater, this is Donna Poole, Jesse's mom."

Bonnie had been watching Armen, but she now turned to face the machine.

"The police came and took my son away tonight, said he tried to run you down with his truck." A long liquid cough emanated from the machine followed by several pronounced inhalations. "Excuse me. I just need to catch my breath. Damn, I can't say all I want to say on this short tape. Please come see me at the hospice tomorrow?"

Another deep cough ended the message.

Armen set a mug of black coffee in front of Bonnie and retook his stool. "Are you going to go?"

Bonnie brought the steaming coffee to her face. She breathed deep, feeling the damp and warmth of it in her nostrils. "I think so."

"Then I'm going with you." He looked away and took a sip of his coffee as if the matter was settled.

Bonnie bristled at what she considered a boorish display of male insolence. "You are?"

He swung his stool around to face her. "Be reasonable. How are you even going to get to the hospice? Think you'll be driving by tomorrow?"

Having so often used logic to back others into corners, Bonnie discovered she didn't much like it when the tables were turned. She dug in her heels. "I could take a cab." *God, a cab would cost a fortune.*

Armen peered at her for a long moment and nodded. "All right. Let's start over. Bonnie Pinkwater, I would like to offer my services as a driver and companion." He shot her a wide toothy grin.

She nodded back. "In the spirit of starting over, I accept."

She held out her hand, and Armen shook it.

" 'Frenchie, this could be the beginning of a beautiful friendship'." Armen's voice came out low with just a hint of a slur.

Bonnie giggled. "Was that an impression?"

Armen looked crestfallen. "Bogart, woman. *Casablanca*, the final scene. Bogart and Claude Raines, the French Chief of Police, walk from the airport in heavy fog. Bogart and Frenchie are off to join the resistance. Bogart turns to Frenchie and says—"

"I got it. 'This could be the beginning of a beautiful friendship'."

Wide eyed, Armen stared at her. "You've never seen *Casablanca*?"

She shook her head. "I've never seen any Bogart movies."

"What! None of them? No *Maltese Falcon*? No *To Have and Have Not*? Never even *The Treasure of*

Sierra Madre? 'We don't need no stinking badges'."
This time he sounded like a man imitating a Mexican weasel.

"What was that?"

Armen buried his face in his hands. When he lifted it again, he sighed. He took both Bonnie's hands in his. "Missus Pinkwater, would you do me the honor of watching the finest movie ever made with me a week from tomorrow?"

"*Casablanca*?"

"*Casablanca*."

She shrugged. "Sure. Why not."

They sat sipping coffee and talking until they heard gravel churning in the drive. Armen leapt up and was gone for over ten minutes before he returned. Bonnie considered joining him. After all, it was her car being delivered to her door, but once again she couldn't deny the charming man another act of chivalry—and this time she was fairly sure it wouldn't kill him.

When he returned Bonnie showed him the guest bedroom and the hall closet containing sheets and blankets. She bid him goodnight and closed the sliding door between the kitchen and the master bedroom.

Bonnie hobbled to her bed and sat down, laying her crutches on the floor. Almost as if it had a will of its own, her hand found its way into her pocket. She pulled out a purple velvet bag by its gold drawstring.

"Open it before you go to bed," Rhiannon had said.

She worked the string and dumped a small amber

vial and a slip of paper onto the coverlet. On the paper were three words—Love Potion: Enjoy.

CHAPTER 7

ESPITE A STIFF NECK AND A DEFINITE ache in her ankle, Bonnie woke feeling almost whole. The amber cylinder containing Rhiannon's Love Potion sat on the end table, glowing in the morning sunlight. Next to it stood the Big Ben alarm Bonnie had owned since she left home for college more than thirty years ago. Eight-twenty. She'd slept a little over four hours, yet strangely she wasn't tired.

Light streamed in from the kitchen. Someone, Armen obviously, had slid back her bedroom door. Had he stood in the doorway watching her sleep? She knew she should be uncomfortable with this image, but she wasn't. Intuition told her Armen had better things to do than play the Peeping Tom.

The sounds and smells of coffee dripping and something frying in butter wafted past her nose. French toast? God, she would kill for some French toast sprinkled with powdered sugar, smothered with maple syrup. She hadn't had decent French toast since Ben died. You'd think a grown woman would learn how to make her favorite breakfast.

She swung her feet over the padded edge of her water bed. They came to rest on the warm flank of a dog. From the size and the way her toes wriggled into soft fur she guessed Hypatia, the Golden Retriever. The dog must have crept in when Armen opened the door. From the snuffles around the bedroom the other two dogs—Hopper, the Border Collie, and Lovelace, the Labrador—had made their way in as well. Euclid lay curled at the end of the bed.

Hypatia stood, compacting Bonnie's leg, and more importantly her injured foot. The shift sent a wakeup call of agony through the leg. Bonnie cried out. The dog slid away, allowing gravity to pull the leg back down. New pain, kind of an inside-out version of the first visited the leg. Again, she cried out.

Armen's face appeared in the doorway. "Are you all right?"

She blinked at him through pain-induced tears. Her upper body, particularly her arms, trembled. Hypatia sat with her furry chin on the padded edge of the bed and regarded Bonnie with sad eyes, apologetic eyes.

Bonnie stroked the dog's face. "I'm fine. I just forgot the foot, that's all."

In the space of a moment, she wondered, then panicked about her sleeping attire, or lack thereof. Her hand closed around the collar of her flannel sleeping gown. For an awkward moment, she felt exposed.

Armen flushed and stepped out of the doorway back into the kitchen.

Bonnie regarded her flannel gown and gave herself hell. *You're wearing more now than you did all last night. Don't go bananas just because a man's in the house for the first time in a year and a half.*

She squeezed Hypatia's loose muzzle in her right hand. Bending down, she gave the dog a kiss on her snout. "And you, madam, don't look so sad. You didn't mean to hurt me. I forgive you." By the time Bonnie straightened up again the other two dogs and the cat had gathered around for some affection as well.

"Later, fur faces. Give me space so I can dress. Shoo. Get out of here, all of you." Bonnie waved her hands, and the dogs and cat reluctantly vacated the bedroom.

She scooped up the crutches and hobbled to the sliding door and closed it.

What to wear?

Last night was easy. She hadn't had to think about what she was wearing. She'd worn her school clothes because she had no choice. Now she was going to spend the day in the company of a man, and she had everything in her closet to choose from—the curse of too many options.

What to wear?

She had to look as if getting dressed hadn't been any big deal. Yet, she wanted to offset the fact that she would be a semi-invalid hopping around with one foot encased in a plastic boot. Good God, how was she going to shower? She felt like crawling back into bed.

"Don't be an idiot, Bonnie," she whispered. "You're not trying to seduce the man. He's just driving you around for some errands. Get a grip, girl."

Her gaze traveled back to the love potion sitting on the clock table. *Hell, if I wanted to seduce him I could just slip a drop or two of Rhiannon's magic elixir into his coffee.*

Standing alone in her bedroom, she blushed. Where did that thought come from? She had no intention of complicating her life by entering into a romance with Armen Callahan. He was a colleague, for Pete's sake. She'd have to see him every day at school.

Bonnie groaned. She already told him she would watch a movie with him next weekend.

"Bonnie," Armen called through the closed door, "how much longer do you think you'll be? Breakfast is almost ready."

She inhaled and let the breath out slowly. What was she going to do? "Give me five minutes."

"I made French toast."

Oh damn, the man makes French toast. "I'll be there in three."

Bonnie wiped her mouth, savoring the last bite of her breakfast. She set her elbows on the breakfast island and sipped at her coffee. She'd chosen to wear an old pair of jeans and a ratty Michigan State Spartans sweatshirt. She wasn't sure what sort of statement she was trying to make, but at least she felt comfortable.

Armen, of course, still wore his "I throw peanuts at old ladies" muscle shirt. Somehow it looked as if he wore it for the first time that morning. He even smelled fresh. Bonnie had earlier snuck a whiff when she reached across him for syrup.

"I throw peanuts at old ladies?" She stared at his shirt across her coffee cup.

He slapped the words on his chest. "You like it? My homeroom got together and bought the shirt for my birthday."

He may as well have said, "I'm donating a kidney to an orphaned child." As far as Bonnie was concerned, there were few things more sacred than the gifts of students. She knew teachers who didn't feel as she did who relegated student gifts to deep drawers, or even tossed them away outright. No doubt, these people are soulless. Yet here sat a man who treasured a student gift so much he wore it away from school.

"Do they consider you someone who bedevils elderly women?" She tried to keep admiration out of her voice. "Am I going to have to watch out for you whenever you have a peanut in your hand?"

Armen stroked his mustache like a villain from some cheesy melodrama. "First of all, the shirt says old ladies. You hardly qualify. Secondly, my homeroom is seventh-graders. Who knows what goes on in their minds? There are days when I'm not sure they and I are members of the same species."

He rubbed the shirt message with the palm of his hand. "Still, they did good. It's a great shirt. I hoped you would like it."

"I love it." In that moment, she realized Armen had worn the shirt as a bit of a test. What would have happened if she hadn't liked it?

"What's on the agenda?" He picked up his coffee cup and walked it to the sink. He swished some water in it and set it to dry in the drainer.

The set of motions was so natural Bonnie had no doubt Armen kept his house meticulous. *And he makes French toast as well. Be still, my beating heart.*

"I need a shower, and I need to get Alice to a garage somewhere. Otherwise I have no way to get to work on Monday." She expected him to volunteer to take her.

He merely nodded. "Tell me exactly what happened when Alice stalled out." He stared at her, chewing the beard surrounding his lower lip.

She told him.

He listened without interruption, grunting at key points in her narrative. When she finished, he asked, "The gas pedal went spongy all at once, or has it been getting that way over time?"

She had to think. Alice had been having problems since the invention of rope, so Bonnie needed to isolate this particular malady. "The pedal's gone weird before."

"Had you tried fluttering it?"

The man was a mind reader. "How did you know?

Yes, and it even worked, but not this time."

Armen nodded, looking pensive. "Do you mind if I take a look while you take your shower?"

She shot him a mischievous smile. "Mister Callahan?"

He went red from his neck to his hairline. "I meant at the car." A smile crept onto his face. "Although—"

"Never you mind." She returned his smile. "You sure you want to get into Alice's engine? She's pretty dirty." Bonnie couldn't imagine anything she'd rather avoid than poking around the greasy innards of an old car.

"You just take your shower."

In the master bathroom, Bonnie stripped down and regarded her reflection in the vanity mirror. "You hardly qualify," Armen had said when she referred to herself as an old lady.

He couldn't mean her steel-gray hair. That dropped her solidly into the old lady camp. She'd stopped dying it since Ben's death, and in the last year and a half, gray had chased off all other colors except white.

Her face, except for laugh lines around her eyes and mouth, remained as it had for the last twenty years. She was proud of those lines. Ben had liked her face, used to kiss her laugh lines, saying they were evidences of every joke he'd ever told her. She pushed that bittersweet memory aside and let her gaze travel to her breasts and stomach.

I guess one of the benefits of starting off flat-chested is that you don't give gravity a whole lot to work with. She laid the palm of her hand on her smooth stomach. Years of hiking the mountain trails around Colorado

Springs had kept her fit. Her muscled thighs and calves were proof of that.

Leaning heavily on one crutch, she flexed her bicep and mugged in the mirror. Not bad. At least, she didn't have that jiggling business hanging beneath her arm. Maybe she wasn't such an old lady after all.

She decided not to inspect her backside, thinking she should quit while she was ahead. *Leave well enough alone, Bonnie.*

It took forever and more than a little self-pity to remove the plastic boot.

After a labored effort involving sponges, wet and slippery crutches, and a lot of cursing, she emerged from the shower bedraggled but clean. She promised herself when she no longer needed the accursed crutches she'd have a ceremony to burn them. Maybe she'd give the damn things to Rhiannon for next year's balefire.

Dressed in the same sweatshirt and jeans she'd worn for breakfast, she slid open the bedroom door. Armen stood at the kitchen sink washing his hands. Patches of grease streaked both arms and a long smear extended from his cheek, through his beard, and down his neck. A tiny speck even adorned one earlobe.

He squirted some dishwashing liquid onto a paper towel and scrubbed his elbows. He offered her a big you-should-be-proud-of-me smile. "Your fuel filter was full of gook from a filthy gas tank. I pulled the filter off—little plastic and screen doohickey—rinsed it out with gasoline from your lawnmower gas can, and hooked the filter back up again. You should have seen the crud that came out."

He tapped his ear. "Listen."

At first Bonnie didn't hear anything, and then the drone of an engine rose above the other outside noises. "Is that—?"

"Alice, the little engine that could?" He nodded, and his grin widened. "You bet your sweet bippy. I think you should get that ancient gas tank of yours flushed, or you're going have this problem again. Also, you might have a problem with your fuel pump, but we can put one of those on later."

The use of the word "we" wasn't lost on Bonnie. It felt comfortable, a good fit, at least for the moment. "You're amazing, Mister Callahan."

Armen spread wide his hands in a gesture that was supposed to indicate, "Shucks, 'twern't nothing, Ma'am."

That, coupled with the grease on his face, made him look like a five-year-old in a fake beard playing at being an adult. A part of Bonnie wanted to hobble over and throw her arms around him. She resisted the temptation. Instead, she took the paper towel from his hand. She squirted on more Dawn and worked the towel into lather.

"Hold still. You have a monster smudge on your face, and I don't want to get soap in your eye." She set her crutches against the breakfast island and took a stool. "Come here."

"Yes, ma'am." He dropped his hands to his side and closed his eyes—once again the child, this time trusting the capable hands of an adult.

The closeness of him made her uneasy, lent a slight tremble to her hand. More than once while she tended him she had to swallow. He must have felt her hand shake, but never did he open his eyes or change his expression. She saved the earlobe for last and gave a token to the voice that wanted her to take him in her arms.

She kissed the clean earlobe and whispered, "Thank you."

He stepped back and opened his eyes. "You're welcome, Bonnie."

The way he said her name made her shiver. The saying held the promise of intimacy, of shared confidences and laughter. For a long moment they stood there, captive in one another's gaze. Then the moment passed. The look she offered him was a mixture of apology and embarrassment. The look he returned said he understood.

He handed her the crutches. "Come on. Let's get you reacquainted with Alice."

$$\bigwedge$$

BONNIE AND ARMEN PULLED ALICE INTO THE SCHOOL parking lot around ten-thirty. The plan was to first swing by the school and pick up the fanny pack. Even if Armen didn't see the point of cell phones, Bonnie couldn't go another day without hers. Once she had her phone, she'd sit down and call Wendy Newlin, make sure the woman was okay, maybe even drop in if Wendy needed company. Later, they'd go see Donna Poole at the hospice.

When they reached Bonnie's classroom the phone was ringing. Bonnie surprised herself with how fast she could motor on her new crutches, beating Armen across the room to her desk. She latched onto the phone a split second before Armen could apprehend it. She stuck out her tongue at him and raised the phone to her ear. "City Dump."

"Nice." Franklin Valsecci chuckled. "You're developing a sense of humor."

"I've always had a sense of humor, youngster. You've just never appreciated it." She leaned the crutches against the desk and sat atop it. The effort left her breathless. "What can I do you for?"

"Just being a responsible civil servant and following up on last night's incident."

"Tell me you're not at Jade Hill. Franklin, don't you have any kind of social life?"

"Thank you so much for that cruel and unnecessary intrusion into my business. Especially since I'm taking time out of my demanding schedule to keep you in the loop." He sighed, a long drawn out affair that spoke of long hours and little sleep. "Yes, I'm here at the precinct. Missus P, I've got what might be a double homicide on my hands—if you consider a worse case scenario with Peyton Newlin. Now, if you're not interested in what I've got to say . . ."

She shifted the phone to her other ear. "Hold on. Of course I'm interested. Would it help if I said I'm sorry?"

"I'm not certain. You haven't said it yet."

It was her turn to sigh. "I'm sorry. Sheesh. You're a fine one to talk about a sense of humor."

A long silence hung in the air. "I guess that's as good as I'm going to get. Okay, here it is. You got my message last night?"

"Uh huh."

"Like I said on the message, we only took Jesse Poole in for questioning since he had a slew of witnesses who swear he never left the hospital. We had to let him go."

Bonnie shifted uneasily on the desktop, unable to get comfortable. She didn't want to hear where this conversation was going. "But I saw him. I'd know that truck anywhere."

"I believe you, but I've got a problem. The truck was in the parking lot when we came for Jesse. So here's the million dollar question. Did you actually see the driver of the vehicle?"

She felt heat rise to her cheeks. Armen gave her an inquiring look, but she held back any questions with a wave of her hand. "The cab was dark and a bright light was shining in my eyes. I didn't see the driver."

Franklin must have heard the despair in her voice because he came back quickly. "Don't open a vein just yet. How about the license plate?"

Images came floating back from the previous night. One-by-one, Bonnie pinned them on the bulletin board of her memory like snapshots from a field trip. A green and white rectangle bearing the characters BCKDRFT stood out in one of the photographs. "I saw it! God damn, I saw it! BCKDRFT."

"I don't mean to malign the much vaunted Pink-water memory, but are you sure?"

"I'm sure."

He exhaled, again long and with feeling. "All right. We'll bring in the truck, check it out. For now I'll use your verbal testimony, but it would help if you came down and did some paperwork. You up to it?"

"Absolutely." Suddenly, the world felt like it was turning on greased grooves. "I have to be in town later this morning to see Donna Poole."

"Jesse's mother?"

She bit her lip to keep from mouthing off and saying, No, some other Donna Poole. "Why yes, the very same, dear boy."

"I'm not sure that's a good idea." He sounded genuinely concerned, like she intended to take up lion taming.

"Truth be told, I'm not so sure either, but I'm still going. I guess it has something to do with a dying woman's request."

"I'll go one step further and declare it a really bad idea. From what I understand, the last time you saw Jesse Poole at school he wanted to knock your block off. He's not going to feel any more kindly toward you after I confiscate his truck."

She stretched to work out a kink in her back, and Armen rubbed between her shoulder-blades.

"Would you feel better if I told you I wasn't going alone?"

"Only marginally. Who's going with you?"

Suddenly, she didn't want to tell him—as if admitting to Armen's assistance was tantamount to admitting something was going on between them. "Just someone."

"I don't have time for this. You're going to do what you want no matter what I say, aren't you?"

"Like ninth-graders love to say, 'You're not the boss of me'."

"Uh huh, be careful, Missus P."

"Get a girlfriend, youngster."

Franklin hung up.

Still stroking the tender spot between her shoulder-blades, Armen sat down beside her. "Now what?"

Bonnie wanted to forget all the promises she made and just enjoy the feel of Armen's soothing hand. *But I've got miles to go before I sleep.* "Another call and we're out of here."

She punched in Wendy Newlin's number. She let it ring six then seven then eight times and was just about to give up when a sleepy voice answered.

"Newlins."

Bonnie checked her class clock—close to eleven. It wasn't unreasonable for the woman to just be getting up considering the condition she'd been in the previous night. "Wendy. It's Bonnie Pinkwater."

"Bonnie?" Wendy spoke the word as if trying to make sense of it. "Forgive me. I'm wearing a swollen head this morning. It feels like it belongs to somebody else."

"Well, I'm not a hundred percent myself." Bonnie recounted her evening, ending with collapsing in front of Rhiannon Griffith.

"Jesus Christ! What are you doing running around? You should be in bed."

Bonnie was just about to protest and explain she felt almost human when she heard a crash come across the phone line.

A startled male voice exclaimed, "Shit."

A long silence followed before either Bonnie or Wendy spoke. Finally, Bonnie broke in with a whisper. "Has Ralph come home?"

Again, an awkward silence.

"Yes," Wendy stammered. "He cruised in early this morning, but so far everything is okay. We've put our differences behind us. We've both agreed the important thing right now is to get Peyton back."

Wendy spoke as if she desperately needed Bonnie to believe something for which her voice carried no conviction.

Bonnie lowered her voice below her previous whisper. "Is he right next to you?"

"Absolutely." Wendy answered brightly, as if the question might have been, "Are you fond of pound cake?"

"Do you want me to come over?"

Wendy sighed. "He's left the room. Please don't come here. It will only set things off again. I can take care of myself."

Like hell you can.

But the idea of storming out to the Newlin place after Wendy told her to stay away felt ludicrous. In no imagined permutation of events did things come out anything but disastrous. "I'm going to call back in a couple of hours. If I don't hear from you, consider me the cavalry, and I'll be on my white horse. Also, let me give you my cell phone number."

She rattled it off. "Things get crazy, you get out of there and tell me where to find you. Deal?"

"Deal. I was right about you. I'm lucky to call you a friend."

Bonnie let loose with one of those dry two-syllable chuckles which live on the opposite side of the solar system from honest laughter. "Damn right, and don't you forget it."

"I've got to go."

"Remember what I said." She felt like she was talking to a child.

"I will." Wendy hung up.

Bonnie sat for a time staring at the phone in her hand before she looked up and met Armen's eyes. "Let's get out of here. I need to move so I can think." She clipped on her fanny pack, fitted the crutches to her hands and was halfway across the room before she realized Armen wasn't with her. She pivoted and caught him shaking his head.

"What?" she asked impatiently.

"From what I heard, Missus Newlin told you her husband showed up at their ranch this morning." As he did when he was trying to dope out the problem with Alice, Armen chewed on his lower lip and the beard surrounding it.

Why doesn't he just say what's on his mind? Bonnie inhaled to keep her impatience from showing. "Yep, that's what she said. What of it?"

Armen crossed the room weaving his way between student desks. He strode ahead and held the classroom door. "Let's walk while we talk."

Once she cleared into the hallway, he was beside her, keeping pace.

"Okay, here's the problem. After starting Alice I turned on the radio and a news flash interrupted B. B. King. I didn't catch it all, but some colorful alert connected with Homeland Security called for all essential personnel, especially flight line folks, to return to Peterson Air Base early this morning. They had to report before seven-thirty."

Bonnie's brain felt as if a goldfish had taken up residence behind her eyes and was now swimming like there was no tomorrow. "That means—"

"Among other things, it means Wendy Newlin lied."

CHAPTER 8

BONNIE'S FOOT ACHED LIKE IT HATED HER. She squirmed in Alice's passenger seat, unable to get comfortable and totally unable to get Wendy Newlin off her mind. What in the name of all that's holy was going on? "I heard the crash and a male voice. Of that I'm certain."

Armen gave her a quick glance before returning his attention to the road. "Then we'll start there. What are the possibilities?"

She wanted to swivel in her seat to face him, but knew better than to try. The way her leg was acting up she'd be better off banging the damn thing against the glove compartment than to move it right now. "Okay, there are two cases. Wendy is either telling the truth or she isn't."

Armen blew a sharp breath through his mustache.

"I thought I explained—"

"Hear me out." She laid a conciliatory hand on his shoulder. "Just follow the logic. Case one—assume Wendy Newlin is telling the truth. What is the next reasonable consequence?"

He gave her a look that said he wasn't fully buying into all of this but would play the game. "Colonel Ralph Newlin actually was at his house."

Bonnie nodded. "Right, which means he wouldn't be at Peterson, at least for the time while I was calling. Did the news report say how long the base lockdown was going to last?"

"I think they said until this evening, certainly for the better part of today."

She dug her cell phone from her fanny pack.

Armen pointed with his chin toward the phone. "What are you up to?"

The gesture reminded her so much of the way Ben would point, it momentarily distracted her. Her thoughts went fuzzy and only with an effort did she bring them back into focus. *Funny how the brain works.*

"From what Wendy said, Ralph showed up at home around the time he should've been reporting for duty. He doesn't report, big trouble follows. By now a lot of people must be wondering where he is."

Armen shook his head. "They're not going to tell you, a civilian, whether or not one of their celebrity pilots is AWOL."

She punched in the first three numbers of Jade Hill. "You're probably right, which is why I'm going to ask

Franklin to do it for us." She finished the number.

Franklin came on the line after only two rings. "Valsecci."

Must be a slow day. "Hello again, youngster."

A sound midway between a whine and a growl came out of the receiver. "What now?"

"We could pretend it's my birthday, and you could be a lot nicer to me."

"Your birthday is in September, and I'm always nice to you." He breathed heavily into the phone. "What the hell, happy birthday, Missus P. What can I do for you?"

She always liked this boy. "Happy birthday to you too, youngster. I've got a favor to ask." She told him about the call to Wendy and the lockdown of Peterson Air Force Base.

When she finished he said, "Have you thought about the possibility it could have been some other male voice you heard at Newlin's?"

"I haven't gotten around to that yet. And there'll be no point if Ralph Newlin never reported in."

"And if we find he has?"

Bonnie tugged at her ear. She had no doubt what was going through Franklin's overworked mind. The same thirteen-year-old genius named Peyton kept dancing through hers. "We can talk about that when I see you this afternoon."

"Count on it. Are you still determined to see Donna Poole?"

She was touched he worried so much about her, but

also more than a little annoyed. The man was like a dog with the last soup bone left in the kitchen. "Let it go, Officer Valsecci. I'm a big girl. Plus, I'm in the company of my protector even as we squeak." She gave Armen a wink.

He silently mouthed, "Call me Mighty Mouse."

"You going to bring this protector with you when you come by?" Franklin asked.

"See you later. Don't forget that call."

When she turned off the phone, she tried to scoot across Alice's bench seat and sit closer to Armen. Unfortunately, her foot gave her several agonized reasons why that was a bad idea. Frustrated and panting for breath, she came to rest back where she started. "Mister Mouse, would you think less of me if I took this opportunity to complain?"

Armen drummed his fingers on the steering wheel. "What kind of super-hero would I be if I lacked compassion? Feel free to vent your spleen."

"Pain sucks." She formed her mouth into an exaggerated pout. "Pain won't listen to reason even when you say please. Pain shouts like a petulant three-year old. And it won't leave me alone. I'm damn tired of this foot, and all told it's been less than a day."

He mirrored her expression then whispered, "Pain sucks. Pithy yet profound. With your permission I believe I'll have this gem of homespun wisdom tattooed on my thigh."

She gave him a two finger salute. "You have our leave. Just remember where you heard it when the T-shirt people come calling."

"Thank you, thank you very much."

Bonnie struggled with this opportunity to tease Armen. *Oscar Wilde, you hit it square on the nose. I can resist anything but temptation.* "That's Elvis, right?"

His lips formed a line so thin they disappeared into his beard. He squinted hard at her. "You know darn well it is. I'd like to see you do better."

She tried to keep a straight face but couldn't. He looked so damn cute with his flashing brown eyes. If she didn't watch herself, this man could be habit forming. "Not a chance. That may possibly have been one of the finest renditions of 'Thank you, thank you very much,' I've ever been subjected to."

He gave her one last piercing stare and said, "Not to change the subject, but shall we consider the more likely Case Two? You know the one where Wendy Newlin is a bald-faced liar?"

Bonnie lay back in her seat and closed her eyes. "I'm too tired, Mister Mouse. Besides, I think I promised Franklin Valsecci we'd do that with him. Wake me when we reach the hospice."

She fell asleep to Armen singing, "Here I come to save the day."

$$\triangle$$

TO SAY THAT DONNA POOLE LOOKED LIKE DEATH would have been kind. Sunken eyes stared from deep inside a face so gaunt the woman's head appeared little more than sallow skin stretched across a skull surmounted by wispy black hair. A disturbing mound extended from her neck to her waist, rising high beneath her blanket—evidence of an enormous tumor giddily devouring everything in its path. One of Donna's feet protruded from her blanket, a swollen mass of musky blue flesh. Bonnie knew that Donna couldn't be more than forty, but the hand punctured by the clear IV tube looked ancient and emaciated. Each breath Donna drew was a labored agony Bonnie could feel in the pit of her stomach.

At the foot of the hospital bed, Jesse Poole slumped on one of two orange plastic chairs. He'd glared when Bonnie entered, but now simply stared at his feet. The boy looked drained.

"Thank you for coming," Donna rasped. She drew a long breath as though the four word sentence had exhausted her. "Jesse, mind your manners. Let Missus Pinkwater and her friend sit down."

"Yes, Mama." Jesse shuffled past Bonnie to stand at his mother's side. He took her fragile hand in his.

Bonnie's ankle didn't really want her to sit, but after Donna's gesture Bonnie felt she should at least stand near the chairs. She limped over and leaned a hand on the back of one. Armen followed her.

Now what?

Bonnie gazed silently at the ravaged woman knowing it was the Donna Poole Show, and Donna would direct every moment of the proceedings.

"Baby?" Donna squeezed Jesse's hand. The tip of her blistered white tongue licked equally white lips.

"Get your mama a Doctor Pepper."

"Sure thing, Mama." Jesse bent down and kissed his mother's pallid cheek. With that same listless gait, he shuffled from the room and into the hall.

Donna watched her son depart then locked her pale blue eyes onto Bonnie's. They were strong, intelligent eyes. They seemed unaffected by the illness that was so obviously killing the rest of her.

Bonnie had to force herself not to look away.

"He's a lot like his daddy. That man felt everything so deeply, but was never a big one for words." Donna covered her mouth and coughed. For a moment color rose into her cheeks, but quickly faded. In short, ragged gasps, she pulled air into her lungs, shuddering with every effort.

Bonnie exchanged an anxious glance with Armen, afraid the woman would die right before their eyes. Then as quickly as the spasm had started, Donna's breathing settled into an even rhythm.

A thin smile crept onto Donna's lips. "Don't worry. The Good Lord ain't ready to send His chariot for this old bag of bones yet." Her eyes were the only thing that retained any color. They were faintly bloodshot.

"I sleep a lot these days, so I better get down to business. Bring your chairs around here so I can see your faces." She patted the side of the bed where Jesse had stood.

Once Bonnie and Armen were settled, Donna nodded her head in weary acknowledgement. "Jesse told me how he knocked you down at school. He felt real bad about that."

I felt pretty bad myself. Bonnie immediately regretted the thought, as if Donna's cancer had given the woman telepathy. "He was angry."

Donna drew a deep breath. "No excuse. He's been told to apologize to you, and if he knows what's good for him, he will."

Bonnie couldn't imagine how this dry husk of a woman might enforce this demand, but at the same time had no doubt she'd have her way with him.

"That brings us to last night's business with the truck."

Bonnie had seen the red pickup in the parking lot and had hoped she could get in and out of the hospice before the police came and hauled it away. At the very least, she prayed Jesse wouldn't discover it gone. "I know it was Jesse's pickup, Missus Poole. I saw the license plate, BCKDRFT."

Donna inclined her head in what had to be an approximation of a nod. "I don't doubt it. Jesse told me himself someone had been driving the pickup. He could smell them in the cab. Jesse has a real good sense of smell."

The woman seemed very proud of her son's olfactory prowess. She fixed Bonnie with those sharp eyes, daring Bonnie to refute her.

You must have been hell on wheels before you were sick. "Someone stole the truck right out of the parking lot and then returned it?" She couldn't bring herself to complete the thought, which was, *Why bring the truck back after you've stolen it?*

Again, Donna inclined her head. "That's right. Did those things—chased you, broke into that house of—" A coughing fit interrupted the sentence. Donna's white tongue protruded from her mouth as she struggled for air.

Jesse Poole chose that moment to return. In the same loping gait he used to shamble from the school Thursday morning, he ran across the room, pushing between Bonnie and Armen. He dropped the Doctor Pepper—Armen apprehended the can before it could roll off the bed to the floor—and squeezed a buff colored button taped to the bed railing. Unselfconsciously, he began to sing. The words were unclear but Bonnie recognized "Oh Sinner Man" by the refrain ". . . all on that day."

By the time a male nurse named Winslow arrived, Donna had regained her breath. Bonnie and Armen slid back their chairs to allow the nurse access to the sick woman, but there was nothing that needed doing.

Nevertheless, Winslow checked the drip on Donna's IV and fluffed her pillow. He had to work around Jesse, who continued to sing and refused to give ground. It was evident Jesse made Winslow uncomfortable.

Way to go, Jesse, Bonnie thought, not really sure why she admired this starkly primitive protectiveness. *Good God, Peyton Newlin must have been insane to insult this boy's mother to his face.* She could just imagine the torrent of grief and anger unleashed on the foolish genius. She could also imagine that this boy would stay by his mother's side come hell or high water. He probably slept at the foot of her bed like a faithful dog.

"Looks like you're in good hands, Missus Poole," Winslow said, backing out of the room.

"Doing just dandy, Johnny. My boy's here to take care of me."

Winslow mumbled something incoherent and was gone.

A hint of a smile played at the edges of Jesse's mouth—a smile that didn't escape Donna's notice.

"Nurse Johnny is a good man, Jesse. Don't you go making sport of him."

The smile disappeared from Jesse's face. "Sorry, Mama."

"Speaking of sorry, don't you have something you need to say to Missus Pinkwater?"

The boy's shoulders slumped, his chin dropped to his chest, he scuffed one tennis shoe against the floor. "Do I have to, Mama?"

Yeah, Mama, does he really have to? I think I'd rather forego it.

"Of course you have to. A gentleman never takes a rough hand to a lady. Now, go on."

Donna used her expressive eyes to direct her son's next action the way some mothers would use a swat on the butt.

Jesse turned toward Bonnie as if physically handled. "I'm sorry I pushed you. I didn't know it was you behind me Thursday morning."

A long silence followed, so long in fact Bonnie was

preparing herself to respond when Jesse continued. "When I got outside the school that day, I knew I was in big trouble."

He banged a fist against the side of his bald head. "Stupid, stupid—I shoved a teacher then cursed at her."

Donna Poole's thin lips formed into a smile. Maybe head-banging was normal in the Poole household. Different strokes for different folks.

Rolling back a year's worth of memories, Bonnie couldn't recall ever having heard Jesse string together this many words. The effect was startling. She had to admit, to her shame, she hadn't thought the boy capable of true human articulation.

Great lemon-drop tears welled in Jesse's eyes. His jaw tightened. "But you should have heard the things he said about my mama." He bared his teeth.

For a moment Bonnie was sure he intended to growl. "He said more than just 'Your mother would be real proud of you picking on a thirteen-year old'?"

Jesse's eyes went wide, and in that moment Bonnie saw the same intelligence she'd seen in his mother's eyes.

He blew out a derisive breath. "He said that, but first he said a lot more." Jesse turned back to his mother. "Don't make me tell what he said, Mama."

Donna Poole inclined her head by way of agreement.

Bonnie felt like her brain was full of jigsaw pieces that simply didn't fit together. "Help me out here. Friday I talked to Mister Davenport. He said you came to see him Thursday morning because you were already angry with Peyton."

At the mention of Freddy Davenport's name, Jesse's fists unclenched, his breathing slowed. "That's right. Me and Counselor Davenport, we got a deal. Whenever I think I'm gonna blow, I come see him. He keeps me out of trouble."

Not that morning.

"From seeing Mister Davenport you ran into Peyton Newlin at the water fountain, and there begins the fight."

Jesse now studied Bonnie warily as if she were trying to trick him. "I suppose."

Bonnie had seen that look a thousand times and knew if she weren't careful Jesse would clam up completely. She had leaned forward when she began questioning him. Now she eased herself back into the orange chair to give the boy space. "I'm not saying you're lying, and Lord knows you had ample reason to clean Peyton Newlin's clock."

She took a deep breath to steady her voice. "What's troubling me is that I can't see when you and Peyton could have crossed paths before you went to see Counselor Davenport."

At first Jesse didn't seem to understand the question, then color rose out of his collar into his cheeks. "Me and Peyton didn't actually talk before I went to the counselor."

"Then how . . . ?" She squeezed Armen's hand as the answer came to her. *How could you have been so dense, Bonnie?* "Someone else told you."

Jesse nodded.

Donna hissed like steam escaping an ancient loco-motive. "Boy, how many times have I said that temper of yours would get you in trouble? Did you stop and think this person may have been lying?"

The outburst cost Donna. When she attempted to inhale, she gurgled as though she drew breath through a sopping wet dishrag. Great hacking coughs ripped from her throat. Blood sprayed from her nose and lips, speckling the bedspread.

"Mama!" Jesse shouted and pushed the call button again and again.

Armen raced to the door. "We need help in here," he shouted down the hall.

"She died?" Franklin came around his battered gray desk and leaned his rear end against his desk blotter. He hooked his thumbs into his pants' pockets. "Remind me not to invite you to visit if I ever go in the hospital."

"Not funny, youngster." Bonnie felt guilty enough without Franklin making light of the situation. Maybe if she hadn't gotten Donna so worked up about Thursday morning, the woman would still be alive. "First of all, it's a hospice. People go there to die. The one doctor and Nurse Winslow didn't try very hard to save Donna Poole. For that matter, I don't think Donna herself tried very hard."

You were wrong, Donna. Today was your day for

a chariot ride.

Bonnie sat on one of three chairs arrayed in front of Franklin's desk. Armen took up another. The third was unoccupied, but from the way Franklin kept eyeing it, he expected someone soon.

"How did Jesse take his mama's death?" Franklin asked.

"Better than I thought he would. Once they proclaimed her dead, he went quiet. Her cancer had been hard on him, so maybe her death was a relief." *Sure, Bonnie, just keep telling yourself that.* "I don't know how long he'll keep his cool once he notices his truck is gone. I felt like slitting my wrists when we got to the parking lot, and no red truck."

Franklin shrugged. "By now, he already knows. We had to inform him the truck was being taken in for evidence, had to give him a receipt. I'm surprised you weren't there when it happened."

She whistled. "Thank God I wasn't."

Armen squeezed her hand. "We left not long after they declared her dead. We probably passed the officers on their way in."

Unsmiling, Franklin let his gaze linger overlong on Armen. He'd done the same thing when Bonnie introduced them. Armen, for his part, unblinkingly returned the gaze.

What is it with men and their proprietary issues? She felt like clapping her hands between their faces before a pissing contest ensued. "What did you find out about old Ralphy boy?"

Franklin reluctantly turned toward Bonnie. "At first they weren't going to tell me. Some business about base security, blah, blah, blah. I played the murder and kidnapping card, and they caved."

He shot her a thumbs-up. "You were right."

"What?" Armen said, then reddened, obviously embarrassed at his own outburst. "Colonel Newlin never reported?"

Franklin shook his head, a hint of smile playing on his lips. "Nope. He's listed as AWOL."

"Did they call his home?" Bonnie tried to imagine the dynamic of a phone call where one or more of the Newlins had to lie to the United States Air Force. She didn't think Ralph had it in him.

"I didn't ask, and they didn't tell." Franklin looked up as a heavyset man with tired eyes and an even more tired looking suit approached the desk.

He flopped down in the third seat without invitation.

"Bonnie Pinkwater," Franklin said, "this is Sergeant Keene, the statehouse coordinator for Peyton Newlin's Amber Alert."

The big man swallowed Bonnie's hand into his surprisingly soft and damp one. When it became evident Franklin had no intention of introducing Armen, Armen introduced himself.

"What do we know?" Keene sounded like a card-carrying member of the Cosa Nostra—clipped monosyllables, heavy East Coast accent. He tilted his chair precariously back, hands laced behind his head.

Regardless of his authenticity, the word "asshole"

applied for citizenship in Bonnie's frontal lobe.

While Franklin related his conversation with Peterson Air Base, Keene closed his eyes and nodded ever so slightly, just enough to show he hadn't fallen asleep. He held up a meaty hand when Franklin waxed philosophical about Ralph Newlin's reasons for going AWOL. He opened his eyes and brought the legs of his chair down to the floor. "We don't know anything like that for sure. Stick with what we know, bubby."

Franklin took the mild rebuke without comment. He turned toward Bonnie. "I invited Sergeant Keene here because he expressed interest when I told him about your phone call to the Newlins."

"Before we get into that . . ." Keene removed a small tape recorder from his pocket. "Bonnie, is it?"

You damn well know what my name is, bubby. She nodded.

Keene impatiently waved the small recorder toward where Franklin sat. When Franklin had removed himself back to the other side of the desk, Keene set the recorder on the edge close to Bonnie. Finger poised over the button, he asked, "Do you mind if I tape our interview?"

What would you do if I said yes? "Go ahead."

He depressed the record button and tiny wheels began to revolve. "I understand you went to see Jesse Newlin and his mother today. How did that go?"

"She died."

Keene never batted an eye. "That's unfortunate. Did she or Jesse say anything of interest before she passed on?"

You sir, are the Mother Theresa of law enforce-
ment. "She told me someone else had been driving
Jesse's truck the night I was attacked."

Keene and Franklin exchanged brief, unreadable
glances. "Do you believe her?"

Armen, who had been sandwiched between Keene
and Bonnie got up. "I'm going to get some coffee."

He laid a hand on Bonnie's arm. "Can I get you
anything?"

"No, thank you."

Franklin waggled a large mug toward Armen.
"There's a squad room just before you get to the elevators. I'd love a cup."

Armen stared hard at the mug and chuckled. "Sure
thing, officer. I'll bring you a scone if they have them."
He snatched the mug from Franklin's hand. Waving
backward over his shoulder, he made for the elevators.

"What's his problem?" Franklin frowned at Armen's
retreating back.

I could ask you the same thing. "I can't imagine."

Keene moved into Armen's seat. The man smelled
of garlic and cigarettes.

Bonnie found herself fascinated by a green something or other poking out between two front teeth.

"If we could get back to business, Missus Pinkwater, do you believe Donna Poole?"

The question brought home a thought that had been
percolating across Bonnie's brain. How much did she
trust the now deceased Donna Poole? And if she did,

how much of that trust was based on the fact Donna had been dying of cancer? "I think I do."

"Why?"

You odious man, you would ask the one question I've got no real answer for.

She leaned back from him as far as she could. "Before we go round and round, could you tell me why my visit to Donna Poole is of interest?" *And why, in God's name, would they put you in charge of anything to do with children?*

Frowning, Keene shot Franklin another glance. Unlike its predecessor, this look was far from unreadable. *What was this civilian doing questioning police procedure?* "Could we just stick to my questions?"

Bonnie tendered Keene the smile she reserved for children she wanted to throttle. "I know your thoughts are far above the thoughts of a non-combatant like myself, but let me offer a guess."

She paused, enjoying the throb of a tiny blood vessel in Keene's forehead. "If I'm incorrect, feel free to stop me at any time. We math teachers so hate to be incorrect."

Keene's face had become stone, all planes and angles. He grunted.

"If Jesse Poole can be eliminated as a possible suspect in Peyton Newlin's disappearance, then the necessity for an Amber Alert becomes questionable. Maybe even a mistake in the first place." She wanted to hurry on before Keene lost his temper in earnest, but she couldn't resist prodding the man just a little.

"I mean, an important man like yourself shouldn't be saddled with a simple runaway case."

"Missus P," Franklin cautioned.

"Let her rave on." Keene once again tilted back his chair, but that pesky blood vessel just kept throbbing.

Bingo, you're stuck on the flypaper, Sergeant Keene. How do you like it? "Except, it's not that simple. Colonel Ralph Newlin and his family are important people. You can't risk something happening to Peyton Newlin, even though every cop instinct in your body is telling you the boy was never snatched."

"What do you know?" Keene annunciated each word through clenched teeth.

Bonnie raised both hands palms forward. "These are guesses, remember? But, to add one more guess to the string of sevens I seem to be rolling, if Jesse didn't snatch Peyton—and I, like you, believe he didn't—then Peyton Newlin walked away from the Interfaith Christian Academy of his own volition."

Keene let his chair slam back down onto the tile floor, signaling it was his turn to talk.

Bonnie's Imp of the Perverse urged her to cut him off before he could speak. She leaned forward until her mouth was just a few inches from the tape recorder. "I believed Donna Poole because not only did she convince me she was sincere, but also because Jesse wouldn't have left his mother's side unless someone led him away at gunpoint, maybe not even then. Certainly, not for the time it would have taken him to kidnap Peyton Newlin. It's as simple as that."

Keene drew in a great breath and released it in a sigh. "You're right, Valsecci. She's a mountain-sized pain in the poop chute, but she's got *chutzpah*."

Bonnie shot Franklin a major glare and returned her gaze to Keene. "I'll take that as a compliment. So, where does this leave you guys?"

Even though Bonnie addressed the question to Keene, Franklin picked it up. "With a few unanswered questions, the main one being—What has Peyton Newlin been up to since Thursday night?"

With certainty Bonnie could see where Franklin, and from the look on his face, Keene were heading with this train of thought. "This isn't about Thursday. You're talking Friday morning and in particular early Friday morning up on Fulton Hill. Don't tell me you members of the Jade Hill Brain Trust think Peyton killed Stephanie Templeton?"

CHAPTER 9

At the risk of repeatin' myself, do you know something we don't?" Keene fixed Bonnie with a malevolent stare.

Don't pull this cowboy stuff on me, Keene. You don't know glaring until you've been given the devil-eye by a fourteen-year old girl with a pierced eyebrow. "Yeah, I think I do. I know Peyton Newlin, and I knew Stephanie Templeton. Peyton worshiped her."

Franklin spread wide his hands and adopted his best be-reasonable-Missus P smile. "You said yourself Stephanie peeled back Newlin's paint. Here's the girl of his thirteen-year-old dreams toasting his muffins in public, in front of his mother, no less. It's a short trip from adoration to angry humiliation."

Armen chose that moment to return. He set Franklin's mug in front him. "Nice turn of phrase, Valsecci.

Another bit of wisdom for the T-shirt consortium?"

Armen took the vacant seat. "Sorry, no scones."

Even with a Styrofoam cup covering his mouth, Bonnie could see the amusement on Armen's face. *For an old fart Science teacher, you drive pretty close to the edge, Callahan. I like that.*

From the look on his face, Franklin didn't share her admiration.

Keene gave Armen a disinterested glance and dismissed him with a curl of his lip. "If everybody has their hot cocoa, let's get back to business."

He reached over and shut off the recorder then shook his head like a bison getting ready to charge. "Templeton dies within hours of Peyton Newlin making like Houdini. A coincidence? I don't buy it."

"I didn't think you bought it either, Missus P," Franklin said.

Bonnie tugged at her ear. "I'm not saying there's no connection. I just can't picture Peyton beating Stephanie Templeton to death with a baseball bat. Adding to my incredulity is the nagging question of how Peyton got to Fulton Hill to do the deed."

She stared from one face to the next, challenging anyone present to answer the "nagging question." "Remember, at thirteen, Peyton doesn't yet drive."

"Then someone drove him," Keene said, obviously not used to civilians questioning his theories. "What's the big deal?"

Bonnie gave Keene her best bless-your-heart-but-you're-not-the-sharpest-crayon-in-the-box sigh. "Now you have two people in on this murder. Three, if you include the fact Stephanie must have voluntarily gone with this ever burgeoning group. By the way, who was this mystery driver?"

Franklin cleared his throat. "Back up, Missus P. Why should we assume Stephanie went with her murderers voluntarily?

"Murderers? All right, let's keep the multiple killers option open. Answer me this. When you questioned the Templetons, did they hear anyone come into their house and drag away their daughter?"

Franklin reddened from his neck to his hairline. "Doesn't mean it didn't happen. Maybe the girl met with Peyton and—"

"Whomever." Bonnie waved him on.

"And whomever. Then they kept her quiet with the threat of violence."

"With a weapon?" Bonnie cringed at the sarcastic tone in her voice. She knew the effect it had on children and had been trying to wean herself off it for years, with limited success. *Put it together, Franklin. You're too intelligent to let me lead you down the dumbass path.*

To Bonnie's relief, Keene picked up the inquiry. No matter if he plowed through a pile of stupid. He was probably used to it anyway.

"Yeah, with a weapon, a knife or a gun."

Bonnie put an innocent expression on her face. She'd used this technique over the years to soften the blow of sarcasm. "Let me get this straight. Peyton Newlin first wakes up Stephanie, by say, tossing pebbles at her bedroom window, like that Nazi boy in *The Sound of Music?*"

"I loved that movie," Armen whispered from the other side of Keene.

"So did I," Bonnie said.

Keene's nostrils flared. "I don't know about no pebbles, but Peyton got her up somehow."

Bonnie thought better of continuing any more movie talk. She held up her index finger. "Hold that thought."

Her foot was complaining something awful, so she used the opportunity to get more comfortable and to also turn to Franklin. "I'll bet Stephanie wasn't in a nightgown when you found her on Fulton Hill. I'll wager she even had shoes on."

Her statement was rewarded with a raised eyebrow from Franklin. "No bet. She was fully dressed. I'm not even going to ask where that wild guess came from."

Wild guess, my sagging derriere.

"So now, instead of just opening her window and speaking with Peyton, Stephanie gets fully dressed, and without informing her parents, goes outside. We on the same page here?"

Keene looked as if he still wanted to pursue the crumbling line of logic, but to Bonnie's gratification Franklin nodded.

"Okay, I see what you're saying. Why get fully dressed just to talk?" He nodded agreement. "Templeton knew she wasn't coming back for a while. Maybe even knew she was leaving home."

"Makes sense to me, youngster. Especially if she was wearing shoes. You don't need shoes to maintain your modesty."

Keene shook his head, again the lumbering bison. "You do if you don't want to scrape your tender toes on rocks and dirt."

Bonnie traded glances with Franklin and saw he already knew the answer to Keene's proposition. "I've got the advantage over you," she said. "I knew Stephanie. Like most of these country girls, she'd go barefoot at the drop of a hat. Feet tough as leather."

Keene squinted at her. "Okay, I'll have to take your word for that one, but I still don't understand how you knew she was fully clothed in the first place."

Bonnie hated lazy thinking in children. She really found the trait unattractive in people who supposedly used deduction for a living. "Because I knew there wasn't a knife or a gun. She wasn't forced to go with anyone."

From the corner of her eye, Bonnie saw Franklin's expression change as he picked up the answer. *Tell him, my beamish boy.*

"Because she was killed with a baseball bat. If the killers had a knife or gun, why not use the weapon at hand?"

Keene still appeared unconvinced. "All right, Templeton goes with Peyton of her own free will. Then he and his driver kill her."

"I don't think so."

Keene's nostrils flared even wider than before. The man looked as if he might exhale flames. "Damn it, why not?"

The fact that even Armen peered at her doubtfully gave her pause. *You better have your ducks in a row, Pinkwater, or this bozo Keene will discount everything you say after this.* She eyed Franklin uneasily. *And so will the youngster.*

"Because I don't believe Stephanie Templeton was awakened by her killer. She was waiting for him."

She hastily added, "Or her."

Keene's eyes became slits. "There's no way to know that."

Bonnie hated the idea of taking these men by the hands and showing them every thought in her head. If this were a classroom math problem, she'd have her students work their way from what they knew to where they had to go. Fortunately, very few math problems involved murder.

Oh, what the hell.

"Let's go back to what we know. Franklin, you went out and talked to the Templetons after Stephanie's death?"

Franklin eyed her cautiously. "Yes."

She recognized the please-don't-call-on-me-look from when he used it in Algebra One. "Did you meet Zeebo?"

"What kinda name is Zeebo?" Keene's voice, which had been running almost in neutral, slipped back into heavy East Coast.

Any second Bonnie expected him to exclaim, "F'gedd about it."

As she hoped, the answer came to Franklin. "The dog! The little yipping fur ball."

She nodded, feeling a disjointed sense of pride this former student could still use his brain with a little prodding. "Zeebo is a cockapoo, a noble, albeit miniscule creation of crossbreeding. From your description, I have to assume Zeebo gave you a sampling of his voice."

"If you mean he's a yipper, you'd be right as rain."

To his credit, Keene kept his mouth shut although Bonnie could tell he was growing impatient with all this talk of dogs and their barks. From the expression on Armen's kisser he already saw where she was headed. *You got a good head on your shoulders, Mister Callahan.*

She leaned closer to Franklin, as much to exclude Keene as anything else. "Would it be probable, how'd you put it, 'the little yipping fur ball' never barked Thursday night? Remember now, the entire household is supposedly asleep, and Peyton with his mystery driver comes to the Templeton house in the middle of the night."

Franklin sighed. "Possible, but not probable."

She addressed her next question to Keene. "What is more likely?" *Even lummoxes need an opportunity to be smart.*

"Templeton pretends to go to bed and waits, all her clothes on, for whoever was coming. She keeps the pooch quiet. Parents don't get disturbed." Like a teenager with a right answer, Keene looked proud of himself.

Saints be praised. Ladies and gentlemen, proof positive it's never too late for an education.

Keene waggled a finger at her. "That still doesn't

mean it couldn't have been Peyton Newlin with a driver."

Oh damn, I had such high hopes for you.

"Do you believe Stephanie's death had something to do with Peyton's disappearance?"

"You bet." He reaffirmed this assertion with a decisive nod of the head.

"So do I. Then would you agree the probability is high that whoever Stephanie was waiting on must have set up to meet in the minutes or hours after our absent genius's evaporation?"

Keene chewed his lip, and already Bonnie knew she might be moving too fast for him.

Bonnie laid a hand on his arm. "Give me this one, and you can dope it out later." She shot Armen a surreptitious wink.

Keene grunted.

Time for the throat shot. "Stephanie spoke to a number of people, myself included, after Peyton's disappearance, but she couldn't have spoken with Peyton. He was already gone."

"What about a cell phone?" Keene spit out the words like he'd caught Bonnie in a lie. "The Templeton girl could have called Peyton because she was worried about him."

Bonnie extended a palm toward Franklin.

Her former student took the cue. "No cell phone. Ralph Newlin told me himself Peyton was too young to own one."

Bonnie picked up her crutches and stood. "As much

fun as this has been, I'm getting hungry and grumpy. Would anyone here like to buy me a late lunch?"

Armen raised his hand. "Pick me, teacher."

"Sold to the man with the sexy goatee."

Keene stood and barred her way. "Hold on. I've got a few more questions."

She considered *accidentally* jamming the tip of her crutch down on Keene's instep. "Make it quick, constable. You have no idea how hungry I am."

"We'll need a list of all the people Stephanie Templeton talked to that night after Peyton walked away."

Bonnie played back Thursday evening frame-by-frame. She knew whenever she did this, her lips moved and made her appear loopy, but it couldn't be helped. That was just the way the machinery worked. "Ali Griffith, Edmund Sheridan, and Missus Templeton. Those are all I know for sure. To whom she spoke at Knowledge Bowl is anybody's guess, but the principal at the Evangelical Academy can give you a list of the other schools. I have no way of knowing who Stephanie might have contacted once she arrived home, but you guys could get that information from the phone company."

Franklin wrote on a yellow legal pad. He nodded to Keene. "This gives us plenty to do, and I still have to talk with the Griffiths. We can call Missus P on her cell if we need her. She appears to be wasting away."

Keene gave her just enough room to get by.

Bonnie fit the crutches to her hands. "Am I to assume that you two will be working together?"

A half-smile lifted one corner of Keene's mouth.

"For the time being. Is that a problem?"

Bonnie squeezed past him to stand next to Armen. "Not at all, sergeant."

She pulled a tissue from a box on Franklin's desk and handed it to Keene. "We don't know one another very well so this is a little awkward."

"Just spit it out, Pinkwater."

She leaned to Keene, bringing her lips within an inch of his ear. "Funny you should put it that way. You have something stuck between your teeth."

SITTING AT A BACK BOOTH AT GERALDINE'S DINER, Armen paused between bites of his BLT, his elbows propped on the polished oak table, a sandwich in both hands. He eyed Bonnie in the crescent of a recent bite. "Very impressive. I never knew the police consulted you on cases."

Bonnie thought she heard the subtle hint of disapproval, and hoped she was wrong. It was so hard to tell with a man and his ego, which poked into everything like a spare Adam's apple.

"This is only the second time. The first time, in fact, had a lot to do with your coming to East Plains." She tried to act casual by swiping a glop of hummus from the edge of her sandwich and depositing it in her mouth.

"I heard about Luther Devereaux. I have to admit the story made me think twice about taking the job."

She patted his hand. "Relax. Very few of our Science teachers get their throats cut these days. Now Social Studies, that's another thing altogether."

The joke worked. Armen noticeably relaxed. "I'm not kidding. I was impressed, but I have a few problems with your logic."

Her mind shifted into competition mode. Warily, she asked, "How so?"

"How can you be certain Peyton didn't talk to Stephanie before he disappeared?" Armen put down his sandwich and leaned back in his chair—a reasonable man asking a reasonable question.

She had to admit the question merited thought. "About meeting with her in the middle of the night?"

"Yes, that, and his imminent plan to run away."

I love the way your mind works, Mister Callahan. "You're assuming Stephanie and the debacle at Knowledge Bowl wasn't the reason he ran away."

He frowned at her, showing disappointment. "Don't play Devil's Advocate with me. You no more believe that was the reason than I do."

His admonition was like a splash of cold water to the face. At first she recoiled, then after a moment's consideration realized she liked this meeting of equal minds. "All right, no Devil's Advocate. Since nothing is really certain, we'll deal in probabilities. I think it highly probable Wendy Newlin was correct when she said Peyton ran away rather than face the Colonel." *Much the same as Wendy herself did.*

Armen nodded, and she could see him using her last

statement as a building block in his argument.

"Okay, Peyton means to run away and tells Stephanie early on. They make plans to get together to talk about Peyton's problems." Armen's voice softened on the final two words. His face went cloudy.

It was Bonnie's turn to nod. "You see the difficulty, don't you? Who drove him to Stephanie's in the middle of the night?"

She splayed the fingers of her left hand and stared down at them. "It's a finite list."

Armen tapped her pinky. "All right, how about that Korean boy Edmund? He drives. You said you took him to his car Thursday evening. Could he also have known about Peyton's plan, picked him up from wherever he was hiding, and driven him to Stephanie's?"

Bonnie tugged at her ear, considering the scenario. "Forget for a moment what I know about Stephanie and Peyton. The timing is certainly right. Of course, you know that means Edmund was in on Stephanie's murder?"

"How well do you know Edmund?"

She was about to say she had Edmund in class and on the Knowledge Bowl team and knew him damn well. But it wouldn't be true. She didn't really know Edmund at all. Certainly there might be a set of circumstances whereby this seemingly quiet Asian boy could become a murderer. An image of Peyton and Edmund shouting triumphantly as they slaughtered electronic adversaries floated into her mind. "I'm not sure."

Armen tapped his lips with his index finger, wearing

a well-that's-interesting frown. "There's always been one aspect of the aftermath of the Knowledge Bowl that troubled me."

"Just one?"

He chuckled and leaned forward, smoothing down his beard, his face just inches from hers. "Now that you mention it, there's two. Remember telling me how Ali Griffith and Stephanie left the Academy with Stephanie's mother?"

She replayed the scenes from that evening until Edmund stepped on stage with his late-night announcement. "Edmund couldn't reach his parents, so he stayed behind."

"Why would he do that?"

To annoy me, was the first thing that popped into Bonnie's mind, then she saw Armen's conundrum. She took both of his hands in her own and squeezed. "Why indeed would he do that? His parents wouldn't be picking him up at the Academy or back in East Plains. He drove himself. What did it matter if he couldn't contact them at home except to inform them he'd be late, and for that he could leave a message?"

Their breaths fell into synchronous rhythm, Armen inhabiting the world of his thoughts and she in hers. She let her gaze drift over his intelligent features. A pleasant warmth filled her. Even with Ben she hadn't felt this kind of kinship. A sudden pang of guilt swept over her, and she let go of Armen's hands as if she were scalded.

Thankfully, he chose that moment to respond and

didn't seem to notice her anxiety.

"Even more perplexing, wouldn't Missus Templeton have to pass by the school and Edmund's car to get to the Griffith place?"

Bonnie tried to focus her thoughts and swim out of her current soup of emotions. *Get a grip, girl.* She nodded, perhaps a little too energetically. "Straight past the school, not even a little out of her way."

Armen jabbed a finger down on the Formica tabletop. "So why does a teenage boy choose to give up several hours of his precious evening rather than take the obvious ride back to school?"

She was no longer enjoying this intellectual give and take. The dead presence of Ben Pinkwater filled the empty seat beside her. Armen blithely pressed his hypotheses, and it was all she could do not to tell him to shut up and leave her alone. She had to get away.

"I need to visit the little girl's room." She blurted out the statement knowing how awkward and artificial it sounded.

Armen squinted at her. "Sure." His mouth tightened into a strained smile. "You're on your own, though. They don't let me near the Women's room anymore. Not since that incident involving sheep and plastic grocery bags."

She stared at him wanting to scream, "Stop being so damn clever." She collected her crutches and left without another word, or even a look back.

She reached the bathroom and thanked her lucky stars it was empty. With a steadiness that belied her turmoil, she laid her crutches against the tiled wall, leaned heavily onto a sink, staring at herself in the mirror. "What's your problem, Pinkwater?"

The answer came as if someone scrawled it with lipstick across the glass. *I'm a married woman.*

A sonorous voice from the back of her mind answered, *Since when?* Ben's voice. The voice he used when teasing her, trying to get her to smile.

"Since forever, you reprobate Indian." she said aloud. "Twenty-five years, remember?"

You could have fooled me. I thought I was singing in the heavenly choir these last sixteen months.

"You know what I mean." This time she almost shouted but caught herself, not really sure how thick the bathroom walls were. "Besides, you never believed in heaven. You were a damn redskin pagan."

Still am, babe, but that's beside the point.

A pair of black women entered the bathroom, looked at her like they thought she might be dangerous and disappeared into adjacent stalls.

"What is the point?" she whispered.

The point is you like what's his name. And in spite of the fact that he's a scrawny little son of a bitch, I like him, too. The question is, what are you going to do about it?

"I don't know. I probably already freaked him out with my abrupt exit." Her mind framed Armen tip-toeing out of the restaurant, sneaking backward glances as the door shut behind him.

You know better than that. Give yourself and this

pale-face time to figure it out. Remember what I always used to say?

Both women emerged from their respective stalls like they'd invented a new Olympic event—synchronized urination.

Screw it.

Bonnie locked eyes with one of the women. "Ben used to say, 'Take it easy, but don't forget to take it.' Good advice, wouldn't you say?"

The two black women exchanged looks and the one Bonnie had spoken to nodded. "Good advice."

"Damn right. And that's just what I'm going to do." Bonnie gathered her crutches and left.

Armen stood when she approached. His eyes searched hers. "You okay?"

Depends on whether you consider a ladies' room conversation with a dead husband anywhere in the vicinity of okay. "I'll let you know after I figure it out."

He leaned in and kissed her square on the lips. It wasn't the most passionate or expert kiss in the history of kisses, but it wasn't bad.

She pulled back just enough to see his face. "How bold you are, Mister Callahan."

"You better believe it, sweetheart." Armen slurred the last word.

"Humphrey Bogart?"

He kissed her again, this time on the tip of the nose. "There's hope for you yet."

Bonnie hunkered into Alice's passenger seat staring at Highway Eighty-Four and the hogback ridge that ran parallel a quarter mile away. A herd of antelope grazed on the ridge's slope. A red-tailed hawk soared above them. Its shadow swam like a winged gray fish across the prairie grass. "You said you had two problems with Edmund Sheridan. I'm not saying we're done with the first, but tell me about the second."

Armen had been humming to himself, tapping his fingers on the steering wheel. He stopped and regarded her. His eyes looked tired. "Actually, Keene put me onto the thought when he asked if you believed Missus Poole."

She had to think a moment to place the memory in context. "About whether someone else drove Jesse's truck?"

He alternately waggled his fingers, his hands a pair of pistols. "Yes and no. This time I'm thinking about the night of Peyton's disappearance. The whole business of Peyton's supposed kidnapping is rooted in one boy's sighting of that same truck."

God damn, you're good. "Edmund."

Armen nodded, now looking more excited than tired. "Give the lady a cigar. Except we already know that Jesse was at the hospice and not at the Academy. So, either this was the first instance of someone borrowing Jesse's truck, or—"

Bonnie laughed and slapped the seat. "Or Jesse's truck was never at the Interfaith Academy!"

"Or Jesse's truck was never there," Armen agreed. "Edmund was the only one who actually said he saw it."

The unspoken thought that Edmund was lying stalled in Bonnie's mind. "You know the boy could have been mistaken about the truck."

"Oh, really?"

The remark stopped just short of sarcastic.

You're a lot more polite than I am, Armen Callahan. If I heard you make that ridiculous assertion I would have laughed in your face. She sighed. "Yes, the probability is high that if Edmund saw Jesse's truck he also saw the front license plate. And yes, Edmund, like most of East Plains High School, is familiar with Jesse's BCKDRFT vanity plate."

Armen tapped his chin, adopting a what-can-we-deduce-from-this smirk.

If he wasn't driving, Bonnie would have dug her fingers into his ribs and tickled away that expression. "Remember what happened when you thought Wendy Newlin was lying."

Armen waved his hand in protest. "What's the alternative? That some wacko stole the truck, drove out to East Plains so he could follow the school van to within a few blocks of the Interfaith Academy, then high-tail it back to the hospice? Why?"

"So he could be seen following the van."

Armen pursed his lips as if he meant to object, but she cut him off. "Don't get your Joe Boxers in a knot. It sounds screwy to me, too."

He glanced down at his lap and smiled. "How did

you know?"

She reddened. "Men. I'm just psychic, you dirty old fart." She dug her phone from her fanny pack, but stopped short of turning it on. "This won't do."

"You thinking of calling Edmund?"

You got a pipeline into my brain, Callahan? "I was, but I need to read his face when I ask him about the truck." She tugged at her ear. "You live close to Edmund, don't you?"

Armen nodded. "My trailer park is about three miles from the Sheridan place." He smiled conspiratorially. "And I do need to change my clothes. Been wearing these stinkeroos for the past two days."

Bonnie pinched her nose. "You're telling me."

"You going to give Edmund any warning you're coming?"

She yawned, thinking of the long drive to the Sheridan place. She certainly didn't want Edmund to take it into his blond spiked head to split once he knew they were coming. "Let's surprise the little bugger. What's the worst that could happen?"

CHAPTER
10

T HE HUM OF TIRES ON BLACKTOP HAD almost lulled Bonnie to sleep when her cell phone rang. She dragged herself back to wakefulness the way a spelunker might hoist herself out of a limestone pit. She yawned.

The phone lay heavy in her hand. "Speak to me."

Bonnie arranged herself for minimum pain and maximum attentiveness on Alice's passenger seat. Hopefully, the act would fool whoever was calling into thinking they'd reached someone who wasn't as torpid as a beached whale. With any luck she'd even fool herself.

"Missus Pinkwater?" Ali Griffith's voice trembled. The girl sounded afraid, but there was something else, a hint of steel.

Bonnie sat up straight, ignoring the dull ache in her foot. "You got me, honey. What's going on?"

"Mother and I just got off the phone with that policeman I talked to last night. He told us about Stephanie's murder."

How the hell do I respond to that? Console the girl about the death of her friend or apologize for not telling her? This having to be sharp while in sleep mode is the pits. Posture doesn't help a tinker's dam.

The problem was taken out of Bonnie's incapable hands by Rhiannon breaking onto the line. "What's the big idea, Pinkwater? Why didn't you tell us about Stephanie's murder when you were here? This is a hell of a way for Ali to find out about her friend's death."

Bonnie's instinct to fight grabbed hold. "Hello to you too, Rhiannon. Happy Beltane."

"Mother, get off the line." Ali spoke the five words with the authority of someone who would brook no argument. If there were recriminations to make, she would make them.

A long silence ensued. Bonnie pictured a war raging between Rhiannon's desire to comply with her daughter and the overwhelming urge to harangue Bonnie Pinkwater, deceiver and abuser of witch hospitality. The former won out with a final grumble followed by an even more final click.

"I'm sorry, Ali. I should have told you." Bonnie felt roughly three inches tall. Whereas she would have grappled with Rhiannon, she had no wish to bandy words with this woman-child. Whatever the girl wanted to dish out she'd grin and take it.

"Damn right, you should have." Ali's voice broke,

and time passed while she wept at her end.

Armen laid a sympathetic hand on Bonnie's knee. She offered him a sad, pained smile. "Thanks."

Ali sniffled and drew ragged breath, signaling a respite in tears. "I was so mad at you, my hand shook when I tried to punch in your number. I wasn't sure if I was allowed to be mad at you, not like this."

In the strange world of teacher-student relationships, the revelation made sense. The give and take of distance versus friendship defined a peculiar type of synergy—one, which at this moment, needed to be neutralized. "You're allowed. I screwed up, sweetie. You should have heard about Stephanie from me. The best defense I can muster is to say the time never seemed right."

Ali drew a long breath and released it. "I feel so awful, Missus P. I don't know how to be angry with you and so sad about Steph at the same time."

Bonnie wanted to reach through the phone and wrap this injured child in her arms. Bonnie's world went hazy as liquid collected in her eyes. She blinked it away.

You don't get to be weepy, Pinkwater. Right now, your job is to be strong. "How about you save your anger and share it with your mother? Let her blast me a good one the next time we meet. I'm thinking she's probably better at it."

Ali laughed, sounding more like a little girl than an eighteen-year old woman. "Count on it. Mother's working on a curse."

Bonnie joined in the laughter, more than a little

alarmed that a long time witch was mixing potions to do her hurt. "Tell your mother she's too nice a person to do any such thing. Also tell her quickly how sorry I am. What about you? Do you want to talk?"

Again a long silence. When Ali finally spoke she whispered, "Mother's in the next room. I needed to make sure she wasn't listening. I'm kind of mixed up right now."

Join the club.

Something was going on here that went beyond grief for a murdered friend. What did Ali have to say that couldn't be said in front of Rhiannon? "Take your time, honey. I'm not going anywhere."

"I lied to the policeman."

Well, that's certainly unexpected.

Bonnie tugged at her ear trying to draft her next sentence and the right tone of voice to go with it. "Run that by me again with a tad more detail."

"Missus P, I know he had nothing to do with Stephanie's murder. He may be screwy and immature, but he's no murderer."

In a back-assward sort of way, Ali's blurted assertions eased Bonnie's growing concern. "Relax, Ali. I don't think Peyton had anything to do with Stephanie's murder."

"I'm not talking about Peyton. He loved Stephanie."

"Then who . . . ?" No sooner had the words cleared her lips than she knew the answer. "Edmund?"

"I didn't exactly lie. I just kept something from Officer Valsecci. I didn't want to get Edmund in trouble."

Holy shit.

"What exactly did you hold back?" She struggled to keep the anxiety out of her voice. No point in telling this already upset girl that Edmund fit, in unknown ways, into the Peyton Newlin puzzle. Was he also a corner-piece in Stephanie's death?

"Do you remember how angry Stephanie was with Peyton the night of the competition?" Ali asked.

"Uh huh. She felt Peyton was the reason we played poorly, but she changed her mind. By the time I came outside she was blaming herself."

"There's a reason for her change of heart."

Bonnie was losing patience with this piecemeal form of revelation. Why wouldn't Ali just say what she wanted to say? "Edmund told her something?"

"All the way to the parking lot, Stephanie went on about how Peyton had let us down. By the time we reached the van she wanted to strangle him. I'd never seen her so mad. Edmund took her aside, and in a heartbeat she came back crying."

Connections formed in Bonnie's mind so fast she could barely speak. She shunted them aside and asked, "Do you know what Edmund told Stephanie?"

"Not really. Just before you showed up, Edmund reminded Stephanie about some promise. He made a special point that Stephanie say nothing to you."

"To me?" Bonnie wasn't exactly sure why that bothered her so much.

Let it go, you big baby. You're a grown-up, remember? "Looking back, what do you guess Edmund told her?"

"Once Peyton turned up missing, I figured it had to do with him running away and the reasons he did it."

I'm figuring the same thing. "But you didn't tell any of this to Officer Valsecci?"

"I didn't think the two things were related. You know, Peyton's disappearance and Stephanie's murder. I didn't want to get Edmund in trouble. Now I'm not so sure."

Well, I'm damn well sure. The boy's standing hip deep in bad Kim Chi. "Ali, Sergeant Valsecci needs to know this stuff."

Armen turned onto East Plains Road. They'd be at Edmund's in a matter of minutes.

"Is there anything else you haven't told me?"

"I don't think so." Ali let some time pass before she spoke again. "Missus P?"

Uh oh. I don't like the sound of that Missus P. "Ali G?"

"About that business of not telling me about Stephanie. Do you figure you owe me . . . just a little?"

There was something sleazy and manipulative in the way Ali was using the death of her friend to finagle a favor. *You said you would take whatever the girl dished out.* "You want me to smooth the waters with Sergeant Valsecci?"

"Would you?"

Again she sounded more like a little girl than a woman, but this time the effect was studied. While Bonnie considered her reply, the blue and red fortress that was East Plains Junior/Senior High School passed by on the left. The next left turn would be Belleview, the road to Edmund's.

What the hell, why not? "Look, I'm heading out to the Sheridan place. I'll get a hold of Valsecci when I'm done there."

"You're going to Edmund's?"

Something in the way Ali asked the question made Bonnie wary. *You shouldn't have told her, Pinkwater. What a blabbermouth you are.* A mental picture of Ali phoning Edmund to warn him sprang full-blown into her mind.

"It has nothing to do with you, or what you've told me. I just need to ask Edmund some questions about the time after Stephanie's mom took the two of you home."

Armen turned onto Belleview. In the distance, the TV antenna rising above the Sheridan's chimney looked like a stick man dancing against the slate of the afternoon sky.

"Thank you, Missus Pinkwater. I knew I could count on you."

My full name? My, my, she's laying it on thick. "I've got to go, honey."

"I'll try to slow mother up on that curse."

"You do that. I've got no desire to lose my hair or grow another limb. See you later."

As Bonnie turned off her phone, Armen brought Alice to a stop. "You want to tell me what's going on? You look like you just swallowed a lemon."

"Two lemons, Callahan—one Asian, the other

pagan. Okay, let me lay it out for you." She ran down what Ali had told her and her final impression of the girl. "What do you think?"

All through the telling Armen had grown increasingly animated. His ears were pink and looked like they were getting ready to twitch. "You want the conservative opinion, or the gonzo gut reaction?"

"Both."

"Conservative first. Let's put aside your feelings about Ali Griffith and concentrate on this business with Edmund. Also, let's not allow our other suspicions about the boy to color our judgment."

"Wow. I've always been a sucker for an articulate man." She fanned the front of her face as if she might faint. "Speak on, MacDuff."

"Then you hush, Lady Macbeth. Here's the bottom line. We don't know what Edmund said to Stephanie, but it might have been something as innocent as telling her about the abusive situation in Peyton's home. To a young girl with a strong sense of justice this alone could have brought on tears and made her forgive the boy."

Bonnie had to admit she loved the sound of this Science teacher's voice. "Now give me your gonzo take."

He laced his fingers together and cracked his knuckles. "Edmund Sheridan knew all and told all. He knew before he entered that school Peyton meant to run away. He probably helped the boy genius escape. He came back later and picked him up."

"Then Edmund deceived me from the beginning. It also explains why he hung around the Academy."

Armen nodded, his face grave. "He wanted to keep an eye on you and make darn sure Peyton wasn't found. Now we come to the business of Stephanie Templeton."

Bonnie's heart sank with the direction the logic was taking them. "Edmund had second thoughts about Stephanie's trustworthiness. He killed her to shut her up."

She shook her head as if by doing so she could negate this line of reasoning. "It seems far too severe a solution. We're talking about a teenager running away, not Mafia secrets. And where was Peyton in the middle of all of this? Surely he wouldn't stand by and let harm come to Stephanie."

Armen waved an impatient hand. "Slow down. It didn't have to be planned. Try this scenario. Edmund and Stephanie agree to meet later that evening to further discuss Peyton's situation. They have a disagreement. Things get out of hand. Edmund kills Stephanie."

"With a baseball bat? And where is Peyton during all of this?"

Armen stroked his beard. "Fulton Hill. Stephanie rode there with Edmund to see Peyton."

She shook her head so violently her foot protested. "That still makes Peyton Newlin an accomplice to Stephanie's murderer. I don't believe it."

Armen spread wide his hands, once again the reasonable man, this time giving the problem back to her. "You have a more likely scenario?"

Bonnie wanted to scream. She could feel the elements of this conundrum circulating about her brain, but somehow she was still missing something key to finding a solution.

"No, damn it." She nodded toward Edmund's house. "But I think some of our answers are in there."

He took hold of her upper arm. "If I'm right, we're talking about confronting a murderer on his own turf."

"Turf?" She formed her mouth around the ludicrous sounding word and laughed. "Armen, this isn't *West Side Story*, and you're not Officer Krapski."

"That's Krupke and don't change the subject." Armen grabbed the top of his head like it might explode. "You know, you might be one of the most exasperating women I've ever grown fond of. Have you considered this boy may have already tried to kill you?"

The smile froze on her face. She couldn't laugh this question away. "Yes, it's occurred to me Edmund might be the driver that tried to run me down."

Armen had laid his hand in the space between them, and she covered it with her own. "I have to do this, Armen. If it was Edmund, I'll know it when I speak to him."

He nodded. "No chance of calling Valsecci? You did tell Ali you would."

"I didn't say when."

$$\bigwedge$$

"I'M REMINDED OF WHAT BROWNING HAD TO SAY about one unfortunate Scottish mousey." Armen ground to a halt in the Sheridan's driveway and turned off the ignition. He offered Bonnie a sympathetic half-smile.

"The best laid plans of mice and math teachers." She stared down a long empty driveway of pink pea-gravel extending to an equally empty graveled rear courtyard. Past the courtyard, framed in the green embrace of a stand of massive cottonwoods, stood a traditionally painted red and white barn. Not a hint of a vehicle was in evidence, not even a bicycle. No light came from the white-paneled two-story farm house.

Try as she might, Bonnie heard no sound coming from within. "Maybe the Sheridans are just sleeping?"

"It's possible." Armen found a way to say the short sentence and have it mean just the opposite. "There's only one way to find out."

"Right." This might even be better. No telling what they might find even with a quick look around. "Would you give the front door a knock?"

By the time she'd exited and snatched up her crutches, Armen was already at the white screen door rapping away. There seemed no point in joining him if no one was home. She left him to his task and hobbled up the driveway toward the rear of the house.

The centerpiece of the courtyard was a white wishing well surrounded by an apron of yellow petunias. Small hillocks of pansies, snapdragons, and petunias defined the two borders of the yard not already defined by the house and barn. Someone had put in a lot of work planting and weeding these small berms. Bonnie was reminded of the fact that the Sheridans were a retired couple.

When I retire, I'll have gardens like these. She'd

told herself this lie before when confronted by other enviable gardens. It was a lie that felt better every time she told it.

A triple switchback of wooden ramps led from the rear screen door to the ground. At the base of the ramp, grooves had been worn into the hard-packed earth and gravel where a pair of thin wheelchair tires had attacked the ramp over the years—a wheelchair belonging to Molly, Edmund Sheridan's sister.

Bonnie headed for the barn. If Peyton had stayed with Edmund, that would be the perfect place to hide. With effort and prerequisite cursing, she slid open the heavy wooden door. Although the barn hosted six horse stalls—three to each side of a wide dirt aisle—the absence of the musky smell of horse told a tale of long disuse as a paddock. No tack hung on the walls.

The Sheridans probably got rid of their horses after Molly's accident.

Before she'd taken half a dozen steps, Armen joined her. "No one home, which is just as well for a pair of amateur burglars."

"I have no intention of burgling. I just want to look around."

"Uh huh. If I'd had known you were into breaking and entering, I'd have asked you out for coffee long ago." He pointed with his chin to the far stall on the right. "Something's in that one."

He strode past her to stand tall on the first rail of the galvanized steel gate. "Hello. A sleeping bag."

By the time Bonnie hobbled to the gate, Armen was

rooting around in the stall. He rejoined her holding a white strip of cloth or paper. "I think it's athletic tape."

She took the strip and laid it in one palm. "Not athletic, medical. See the diagonal folds? This was once a butterfly suture. Peyton had one on his face."

Armen chewed his beard and lower lip. "Not any more."

"The boy probably came here Thursday night." She pocketed the tape. "I've been such a blockhead. Everybody—Franklin, you, Keene—you all tried to tell me Peyton had a hand in Stephanie's murder. I wouldn't hear of it. Damn, I thought I knew that boy."

Jesse Poole was right. I don't know shit.

A standard sized door equipped with a brass dead bolt broke the symmetry of the barn's rear wall. The bolt had been thrown open. "This is most likely the way Edmund let Peyton in. The pair could come and go at will. Anyone in the house would stay clueless."

Bonnie swung wide the door. A weedy path of sand and gravel led away from the barn and into a stand of cottonwoods. From somewhere lost in the trees came the skittering sounds and clean smell of rushing water—a small creek probably. Insects and birds chirped. The last dying gasps of afternoon sunlight fell dappled through tree branches.

A slurry of shallow footprints gathered at the barn door and disappeared into the trees. Through the middle of the footprints a wide swath of smooth dirt ran in the same direction.

"Someone tried to erase their footprints," Armen

said.

Bonnie stooped to get a closer look, inching herself down on one crutch. "They sure did a poor job of it. Most of the footprints are still here."

Armen took her by the arm and helped her up. "We may have stopped them in the act," he whispered. "They could be watching us from those trees right now."

Bonnie felt exposed standing in the doorway. She stepped back, shut the door, and threw the bolt. Gloom reintroduced itself into the rear of the barn. "We probably ought not to disturb the footprints. Keene and Franklin will want to see them."

"I couldn't agree more." Armen shivered, though the heat in the barn seemed more than adequate.

Bonnie pivoted on her crutches.

Molly Sheridan, Edmund's sister, sat in her wheelchair, blocking the entrance to the barn. She had a shotgun leveled in their direction, and from the way she held it she knew what she was doing. "Come out of there, both of you. Put your hands where I can see them."

"So ends the criminal career of the Pinkwater and Callahan gang," Armen whispered. He raised his hands and walked slowly toward Molly.

Bonnie raised hers as well then found she couldn't walk. *Well, this just sucks. I'm going to be shot because I'm a cripple.* "Molly, it's Missus Pinkwater, Edmund's math teacher. I'm on crutches. I need to put my hands down to walk."

The girl lowered the rifle maybe ten degrees. "Missus P? What are you doing in our barn?"

Armen, having already reached the girl, looked back at Bonnie as if to say, "You have to admit, it's a reasonable question. I can't wait to hear your answer."

Bonnie hobbled to Molly, still considering viable responses. *I've always wanted to see the inside of a barn. I can come back if this is a bad time.*

Of course, there was always the truth. *I was looking for Edmund because he and a classmate, who by the way has been missing for two days, may have murdered a young girl. You haven't by any chance seen them?*

Molly laid the shotgun across her lap. "It's Edmund, isn't it? He's in trouble."

Bonnie studied Molly's guileless face wondering just how much she could trust the girl. Supposedly, Edmund and this invalid sister were close. How would this same sister react to the news that her beloved brother might be a murderer? "I'd feel more comfortable if you let my friend hold your shotgun before I answered your question."

Molly peered up at Armen. Her soft almond eyes regarded him and she nodded. She extended the shotgun, barrel first. At the last moment, she appeared as if she'd changed her mind and refused Armen's attempt to take the weapon. From the look of her well-muscled arms, she could easily have given him a fight.

Then she relented and let Armen have the rifle. "He's in that bad of trouble?"

You have no idea, sweetie. "Are your parents here?"

Molly shook her head, her straight, black hair

tossing first right then left. "They left for the Springs early this morning. Sometimes I have trouble sleeping at night, so I took a pill and went back to bed."

That explains no answer at the door. "How about Edmund?"

Molly shrugged. The expression carried the weight of miserable resignation. "He's gone, but who knows where? He doesn't tell me anything, not any more." Her face contorted.

Bonnie prepared herself for the young woman's tears, but Molly recovered, fighting her way back to control. Her face grew tight. "He's gone all the time. Sometimes sneaks out in the middle of the night. I'm worried sick about him."

"Can we go inside and talk?" *I don't think I'm about to make you feel any better.*

BONNIE HUDDLED OVER HER GLASS OF ICE TEA. THE three of them sat at a long maple dining table, in a semi-lit dining room, not drinking drinks and taking turns clearing their throats. Molly couldn't seem to take her eyes off Armen's "I throw peanuts at old ladies" shirt, her lips moving as she read. Bonnie had been assigned the head of the table with Armen on her left and Molly's wheelchair pulled up to the table on the right. The seating arrangement seemed to dictate Bonnie assume the task of leading the conversation.

How do I tell this girl I intend to phone the police

and rat out her brother? "Did you know Peyton New-lin had run away, that he'd been hiding in your barn?" The question sounded smoother in her mind, but what the hell, she was winging it.

Molly's face went to stone. She glanced first at Armen, who by his own hard expression gave noth-ing away. When she came back to Bonnie, she blew out a long breath. "I knew Edmund was out there, but not Peyton. Like always, I was having trouble sleep-ing Thursday night. I was staring out the back window when I saw the barn door slide open. Edmund carefully slid it shut then snuck into the house."

Bonnie rubbed her sweating palms on her jeans. "Did he see you?"

She shook her head. "My bedroom door was closed. My lights were out. I heard him pass my door in the hall heading for his own room."

"In the days since, you never confronted him?"

Molly opened her mouth then closed it. "There's more to this than Peyton sleeping in our barn, isn't there?" Her lips flattened into a tight line.

Armen folded his arms across his chest, as if to remove himself from the possibility of answering this difficult question.

Thanks a lot, Callahan. "Yeah, honey. There's quite a bit more. We think Edmund may be involved in a murder."

Bonnie had been prepared for denial, anger, or even a physical response. But the young woman surprised her.

With a jarring shove, Molly pushed her wheelchair

away from the table. "That bitch. It's all her fault. I know it. Edmund is no murderer."

Stephanie?

Bonnie inhaled slowly to get her voice and emotions under control. "Exactly what bitch might we talking about?"

Molly cocked her head and tendered a look dripping with disdain. "His girlfriend, of course." Molly had her hands raised since pushing off the table, now she lowered them into her lap—two fists pressed one against the other like butting rams.

The air felt close and hot about Bonnie's face. She turned to Armen, and he mouthed the name Bonnie had been thinking just a moment ago.

She shook her head. "I don't think so," she mouthed back. "Molly?"

Edmund's big sister raised her eyes from her fists to Bonnie's face. Her compact little Korean face looked lopsided with rage and sorrow.

"What?" She sniffled wetly.

"Do you know this girlfriend's name?"

Like a child, Molly unselfconsciously wiped her sleeve across her nose. "She never signed her name on her e-mails, but I think I know who she is."

Oh, my God. "She wrote e-mails to Edmund?" *And you read them. Clever girl.*

Molly nodded. "About a dozen. You should see the crap she says to him."

"I'd like to, very much."

CHAPTER 11

DMUND SHERIDAN'S BEDROOM LOOKED like a local branch of the Library of Congress. Bookshelves lined every wall including around the window and the spaces beside and above his twin bed. Black binders filled every shelf. A niche had been grudgingly carved out of the ubiquitous shelves for a small computer desk. A poster hung in the space above the computer. Casper the Friendly Ghost had his marshmallow arm around a young witch clad in a red cape and conical hat.

Molly Sheridan sat in front of a flat-screen monitor firing up a Gateway computer.

A gigantic throw rug covered the floor from wall to wall. It featured an obese boy wearing Harry Potter glasses and brandishing a lollipop like a weapon. The caption next to the boy's head read, "You want I should bop you with this here lollipop?"

"Herbie Popnecker," Armen whispered as if he had just entered the sacristy of the Sistine Chapel.

"Who?" Bonnie asked, although the name sounded vaguely familiar. She'd been preoccupied with a full-sized fiberglass statue of Wonder Woman. As always, the female superhero looked as if her pointed bosoms just might explode out of her costume.

"Herbie Popnecker," Armen repeated. "A fat little boy who fought crime and saved the world using a collection of supernatural lollipops."

Molly punched "enter" to finish logging on and pivoted in her wheelchair. "Do you remember Herbie's favorite flavor of lollipop?"

A wide grin that spoke of not quite forgotten childhood memories split Armen's face. "Hard-To-Get-Cinnamon."

He turned his smile and enthusiasm on Bonnie. "Herbie once went back in time and saved the American Revolution using Hard-To-Get-Cinnamon."

Bonnie stared at this fifty-year old Science teacher, amazed he could still speak of comic books with such reverence. Once again, her belief that men never stopped being little boys was validated. "That's nice, Armen."

If he caught the hint of sarcasm in her voice, Armen didn't acknowledge it. "I once owned every issue of Herbie Popnecker. Read them all a dozen times."

Molly pointed to a binder on a shelf one removed from the top. "Edmund owns the entire Herbie run, including his first appearance in Forbidden Worlds."

Armen reached for the binder then stopped. "May I?"

Molly nodded. "I'm sure Edmund wouldn't mind as long as you're careful. None of the issues are in anything above Very Good condition."

Armen slid the binder free and opened it for Bonnie and himself. Encased in a plastic sleeve lay a comic book featuring the same rotund boy, this time towing George Washington and his troops across the Delaware.

"Comic books are rated according to their condition, the best being Mint condition. Then follows Near Mint, Very Fine, Fine, then Very Good all the way down to Poor." He peered above the volume at Molly. "Even in Very Good condition a complete collection of Herbie Popneckers must be worth a considerable sum."

Molly spread wide her hands. "I'm not an expert like Edmund. I'd have to look up the price in Overstreet." She took the binder gingerly from Armen's hand.

In spite of herself, Bonnie felt her interest being tickled. "Overstreet?"

Molly smiled indulgently. "The bible of comic book collectors—current prices, news-worthy sales, notices from collectors looking for specifics, ads from commercial collectors."

For the first time Bonnie became fully aware that all the binders wore labels. Some of the titles she recognized from the recent spate of comic book movies—*Daredevil*, *Spiderman*, *Hulk*. Some unknown to her—*Punisher, Doctor Strange, Justice League of America*. Four thick binders were titled *Mad Magazine*. "My God, we're talking hundreds, maybe thousands of comic books. Edmund must have a small fortune tied up in these."

Or at least his parents have.

Molly tilted her head and scanned the binders. Her lips moved as she checked off titles. "Not as much as you think. Maybe ten, fifteen thousand dollars tops. But then again, none of these are in better than Very Good condition."

"Fifteen thousand dollars?" Bonnie forced down a giggle she knew would be interpreted as disrespectful. "Edmund must have quite an allowance."

Molly shot her a shows-what-you-know frown. "Edmund doesn't get an allowance. He's a serious collector. Last year, buying and selling, he made a profit of twenty-eight thousand dollars."

"But I thought you said all of these were only worth between ten and fifteen thousand."

"This isn't the good stuff." Molly smiled mischievously, her almond eyes twinkling. "Edmund keeps his prized pieces in a de-humidifying vault in the basement."

"Mint condition?" Armen looked as if he might salivate.

A spark of something indefinable passed between Molly and Armen. "Of course. He's got a mint original *Secret Origins* from DC comics. And a mint collection of the first fifty issues of *Omni Magazine*."

Armen laced his fingers behind his head and exhaled. "I'd love to see them, especially the *Secret* Origins."

"No can do." Molly pursed her lips, looking apologetic. "Edmund has the only key. He loves that collection more than he loves me."

She lowered her eyes. "Especially now."

Oh, sweetie, don't let Edmund's problems become yours.

"What else does he have?" Armen's hands shook with the asking.

Molly took a long breath and released it. "He just picked up *Mad Magazine* number twenty-four in Very Fine condition. I think he paid four thousand for it."

"Four thousand dollars?" Bonnie immediately regretted her outburst. *No Pinkwater, four thousand lira.*

Molly was looking at Bonnie as if she might be mentally challenged. "Edmund could sell it right now for fifty-one hundred. He also has *Daredevil* number one in Very Fine condition—bought for five hundred, worth eight."

"*Daredevil* number one," Armen said as if he intoned the sacred name Jehovah. "He wouldn't really sell it, would he?"

"He once told me that if the price was right he'd sell it all." Molly waved a hand to indicate Edmund's entire collection.

Sensible young man, Bonnie thought, then remembered Edmund might be a murderer. *A sensible young murderer.*

"But Edmund's a liar," Molly said, a little too vehemently. "He's got a small run in the vault he'd never sell. Have you ever heard of Harvey comics?"

Bonnie knew the girl couldn't be talking to her. She'd lost face since the embarrassing "four-thousand dollars" outburst. But even Armen was shaking his head.

"In the last few months, Harvey has become Edmund's obsession and spesh-ee-al-i-ty." Molly elongated the syllables of the word to show she didn't think much of this section of Edmund's collection. "Their most famous title is *Casper the Friendly Ghost*, but Harvey also printed *Hot Stuff*—"

"The little devil in the diaper who roasted apples on his pitchfork!" Armen exclaimed. "I loved him."

Molly grimaced. "The very same. Also *Little Audrey, Wendy, The Good Little Witch, Little Lotta, Little Dot*, and *Baby Huey*." She ticked off the titles on her fingers.

Armen nodded the I-know-those nod with each title.

Bonnie eyed the computer screen thinking she'd had enough comic book talk to last her a lifetime. Unfortunately, she couldn't see any way to steer the conversation back to Edmund's e-mails without being rude. After all, Molly was doing them a favor. "You sure know a lot about Harvey comics."

Molly shrugged an it's-no-big-deal shrug. "Edmund's most recent acquisitions are from Harvey. He won't shut up about it—calls it his *coup*. He picked up the first five issues of *Casper the Friendly Ghost*, Mint condition for six hundred. Issue number one alone, the one that introduces both Casper and Wendy, the Good Little Witch, is worth almost that much."

Molly must have noticed Bonnie's eyes glazing over. "We probably ought to look at those e-mails."

Thank you, Jesus. Thank you, Jesus. "We could

do that."

Molly clicked the icon for AOL. Following a series of dips and dives through America On-Line's roller
coaster ride, Molly arrived at the mail center. She first
checked new mail and found it empty. "Nothing since
yesterday."

She clicked the old mail tab—equally vacant.
"Don't worry. AOL automatically archives its mail.
Two days ago, Edmund's archive had at least a dozen
letters from his honey bunny."

Molly's face had grown pinched, her hands small
hammers pounding the keys with ferocious precision.
*She's pissed at Edmund, and especially hates this girl-
friend, whoever she is. Hell hath no fury . . .*

Bonnie took Armen's hand in hers and gave it a
squeeze.

"Here they are." Molly punched a triumphant fist
into the air. "Brother mine, I told you to clean out your
archives."

Bonnie squinted at the list of e-mails. Her own address appeared in the list from when she'd written the
Knowledge Bowl team concerning a canceled practice.
At least a dozen were titled YWLW. Molly double-
clicked on the last of these, dated April 30th, Thursday,
ten-ten PM—the night of Knowledge Bowl.

A single paragraph filled the screen.

Dear Samurai,
Keep the faith. It won't be long before we
can be together. Mother doesn't suspect

a thing, and neither does that busybody
Pinkwater. I promise you, the risk will be
worth the reward, if you know what I mean.
I can't wait to feel your body next to mine.
Be strong.
Your Wicked Little Witch.

Molly turned from the screen to stare up at Bonnie. Cold triumph shone on her face. "That's how the bitch signs all her e-mails—Your Wicked Little Witch. Get it—YWLW. The Samurai is different, though. She usually calls Edmund Casper."

Bonnie nodded, feeling as if she'd been kicked in the stomach. She tried to gather her wits, not willing to say aloud what each of them was thinking. "Did you check this address against Edmund's address book?"

The elated look on Molly's face faded to a glimmer. "I couldn't find it in there."

"But you did find Ali's address, and it wasn't the same?"

"That's right. They're not the same. But it's got to be her."

"Fair enough." Bonnie drew a deep breath so her impatience wouldn't show. "I think I know a way through this problem. Go back to the archives."

The girl gave Bonnie a hard stare then did as she was told.

When the list reappeared, Bonnie noticed what she should have seen before. Several of the addresses, while all containing YWLW, differed in suffixes. "Someone's gone to a lot of trouble to make it difficult to trace these. This Wicked Little Witch has at least four different addresses. Molly, would you print out the list?"

"This is a waste of time. Who else could it be besides the Griffith girl?"

Bonnie's hand wrapped around an imaginary lollipop. *You want I should bop you with this here hard-to-get-cinnamon? Just do it.*

She forced a smile onto her face. "Honey, we can give the e-mail addresses to the police, and let them try to ferret out the writer. That's what we all want, isn't it?"

"I suppose." She clicked on Print. The printer sprang to life.

"Thank you." A pain was building between Bonnie's eyes. Right then, her dearest wish was, with list in hand, to see this house grow small in Alice's rearview mirror.

Molly gathered up both pages of the list and handed them to Bonnie. She wanted to say something encouraging to the girl, but came up empty. No matter that right now Molly was angry with her brother. It wouldn't be long before anger mutated into guilt and guilt into sadness. Edmund had made some bad choices, but this crippled girl would reap at least some of the consequences.

Shit. Bonnie turned to Armen. "Mister Mouse. How 'bout we get out of here?"

"You got it, lady."

Molly ushered them to the back door and out onto

the ramp landing. She sat in the doorway, her hands on her lap. "I did the right thing . . .didn't I?"

This was no time for equivocation. "You did."

Bonnie held up the printed lists. "The police will find these extremely helpful."

Molly looked dubious. "But the lists won't help Edmund."

How can I lie to this young woman? "No, sweetie. I don't think they'll help Edmund."

Without another word, Molly rolled her wheelchair back and closed the door, leaving Bonnie and Armen standing together in the fading twilight.

"Your chariot awaits, my lady."

Armen extended an arm, and Bonnie noticed the time on his wristwatch. "Oh, my God."

He looked back at her nonplussed. "What?"

"Missus Newlin. I promised I'd call her hours ago."

$$\triangle$$

THE PLAN WAS TO CALL WENDY NEWLIN ON THE WAY to Armen's, where the man could change clothes and perhaps procure a shower. After that, who knew? If everything was okay with Wendy then there was the vague promise of dinner prepared ala Callahan.

The plan died in infancy. Armen hadn't driven Alice out of shouting distance from the Sheridans when a battered silver El Camino came fishtailing down Belleview.

"That's Franklin's car. Pull over, and make sure he

does the same."

As he stopped, Armen laid into the horn.

The El Camino and its corresponding cloud of dust came alongside, Franklin driving, Keene at shotgun. Franklin rolled down his window. "We're in a hurry, Missus P. Got reason to ask Edmund Sheridan some pointed questions."

Bonnie leaned across Armen. "We just came from there. Edmund's not home." She went so far as to hand the printed lists out the window then pulled them back. *Not so fast, my Beamish Boy.*

"You need to know a few things." She snatched her crutches and hobbled around to Alice's driver side.

Keene was out of the El Camino and leaning on the fender. The big man pulled a toothpick from his mouth. He held it up like he was making a toast. "Just for you, Pinkwater."

She nodded to him. "Let's see."

Keene smiled what in some circles might be considered a shit-eating grin.

Bonnie moved in close to make her inspection. "Clean as a whistle. You, sir, shall set a new standard for oral hygiene."

Keene reinserted the toothpick. "Now that we're past the bullshit, just what in hell are you doing here?"

The man kind of grows on you. She handed him the lists. "A girlfriend has been writing Edmund." She recounted Friday's e-mail verbatim.

"Busybody, huh?" Keene chewed his toothpick and chuckled. He bent down and threw the list onto

Franklin's lap. "We'll take the computer into the station. See what we can find."

He turned back to Bonnie. "Still haven't answered my question."

There's no way to do this except through the front door and down the long hall. Peppered with interruptions from both Franklin and Keene and seasoned with Armen's embellishments, Bonnie walked everyone through the mental gymnastics she and Armen had performed that afternoon. She finished with Ali's phone call and shrugged. "I ask you. After all that, wouldn't you feel the need to talk to Edmund?"

Keene and Franklin exchanged glances.

"She's your friend," Keene said.

"I know." Franklin drew in a couple of quick breaths as if he was gathering resources. "As a matter of fact, Missus P, I probably would have. Of course, the difference between you and me is that I'm a cop, and you're an algebra teacher."

"You got me there, youngster. There's no denying our contrasting vocations but—"

"But what?" Keene asked impatiently.

"How about the fact we found the spot where Peyton Newlin spent Thursday and probably Friday night," Armen shouted. This time most of his face matched his pink ears. "Put that in your pipe."

My white knight to the rescue. "In the barn, we found a sleeping bag and this."

She handed Keene the strip of medical tape. "I saw Peyton wearing this butterfly suture Thursday morning.

You also need to search behind the barn. We found some footprints."

"You done?" Keene took the edge of the tape with the tips of his thumb and forefinger and handed it to Franklin who deposited it in a small plastic baggie.

Bonnie held up a hand to quiet Armen before he could lay into Keene again. "I think that about covers it."

"Good. Now you listen to me. This ain't no game, math lady. We got it on the best of authority this Edmund character already tried to flatten you once."

She locked eyes with Franklin. "The lab report on the truck came back?"

Franklin nodded then got out of the El Camino. He stepped between her and Keene. "That's why we drove out here . . . to get this bad boy. And what do we find? Two school teachers leaving the suspect's house admitting they came there to interrogate him."

"It sounds bad when you say it like that."

Franklin slapped his hands to the sides of his face, giving himself a hangdog look. "You're not listening to me."

She laid a hand on his arm. "I hear you. And to show you how much, I promise to back off, no more risks. Just tell me what they found in Poole's truck."

Franklin whacked Alice's driver door, startling Armen. He pointed at the Science teacher like he was shooting a pistol. "You heard her. I expect you to hold her to it. Okay, Missus P, here goes. On the headrest of Jesse Poole's pickup truck they found a single hair."

"What kind of hair?"

"One blond hair with black roots—Asian."

"I KNOW DAMN WELL I'M FORGETTING SOMETHING." Bonnie braced herself as Armen navigated Alice over the ruts and potholes decorating East Plains Acres trailer park. "It's gnawing at the back of my head like a rabid beaver."

"Nice imagery." Armen slowed and eased the car through a particularly deep rut. "But I thought you didn't forget anything—ever."

Bonnie waved away the notion. "Not true. If I want, I can most times recall a name or an event, but I have to know what I'm after. I can't dredge up things without that first hook to hang onto. And right now, like Never-Never Land after the crocodile ate him, I'm hook-less."

From the corner of her eye, she spied someone smoking a cigarette in the glow of a yellow bug light—a bald-headed someone.

She spun around, but too quickly intervening trailers hid the man from view. "Is that who I think it is?"

"That depends." He shrugged with his mouth. "Do you think it's Geraldo Rivera?"

She cocked her head and stared at him, unable to keep from smiling. "Armen Callahan, you are peculiar in the extreme."

Armen put his hand to his chest and bowed his head. "I do what I can. How about Jesse Poole? Did it look like him?"

A dip followed by a mud speed bump sent Bonnie sailing to the ceiling where she bumped her head. "God damn it!" The pain shot the length of her body and ricocheted back, causing both her foot and head to ache simultaneously. "Slow down, you madman. Of course, I mean Jesse Poole."

Armen steered around the next bump. "Well, then, yes. That was Jesse back there."

"You never told me you lived in the same park as Jesse Poole."

"It never came up." He slowed in front of a faux wood-sided and white double-wide trailer. "Here we are, home sweet home."

He parked Alice beneath a fiberglass awning constructed to look like an aquarium—fish and all. He reached for the door release.

"Hold on. We have to go back and talk to Jesse."

Armen's eyes expressed everything he had to be thinking. "I'm tired and hungry." "We've been on the road since early this morning." "I'm working on about four hours sleep." "I need a shower."

To his credit he said none of these. "You're darn lucky you're so cute."

He kicked Alice into reverse and pulled back onto the trailer park's rutted lane. "I hesitate to mention that not twenty minutes ago you made a promise to Franklin Valsecci."

Bonnie laid a hand to his cheek. "You really think I'm cute?"

"Don't change the subject." He shot her a frown. "And yes, I think you're plenty cute."

As they approached the killer speed bump Bonnie braced herself against the dash. She stared a hole in the side of Armen's head. "I wouldn't mind taking this puppy a little slower this time, please."

At the last moment, Armen slowed and crept over the bump.

"Thank you, Mighty Mouse," she whispered in her best sexy voice.

He didn't respond. Still frowning, he kept his eyes on the rough road.

Men.

"Armen, be reasonable. I promised not to put myself at risk. This shouldn't be anything close to risky."

"Uh huh. Whatever you say. We're here."

Jesse was sitting on the top of three wooden steps rising to a powder blue double-wide. The yellow bug light glowing in a holder next to the side door lent a sickly pallor to his face and white sleeveless T-shirt.

Armen pulled Alice onto an oil-stained concrete slab. If Jesse was surprised or anxious about their arrival, he didn't show it. He took once last drag on his cigarette and stubbed it onto the step beside him. He leaned back, his arms folded across his chest.

Now what, Pinkwater? She struggled out of the car and settled into her crutches. Maybe if she took enough time, she'd think of something to say. Surprisingly, Poole came to her and took her elbow.

He guided her to the steps and brushed away the

remains of the cigarette.

Even though a streak of ash painted the top step, Bonnie sat. "Thank you, Jesse."

Without a word, he took her crutches and leaned them against the trailer.

Armen slammed Alice's door. "Jesse."

The young man nodded, tight-lipped and solemn. "Mister Callahan. Can I get you a beer?"

Armen ignored Bonnie's wide-eyed disapproval. "I think I'd like that."

Bonnie waited to be asked and when the offer wasn't forthcoming answered, "Nothing for me, thanks."

Jesse grunted and squeezed past Bonnie into the trailer. The sounds of bottles being opened came from within. When Bonnie next looked, he stood framed in the screen door, holding a pair of bottles. He stood there for a long moment watching her.

I don't think I want to know how a seventeen-year-old comes to have beer in his refrigerator. She slid to one side, and Jesse sat down beside her.

He handed the beer to Armen, keeping a tall bottle of Doctor Pepper for himself. The hint of a smile made a fleeting appearance at the corner of Jesse's mouth.

He saluted her with the bottle. "You expecting something else?"

You little son of a bitch, you were right all along. I don't know shit. She shook her head. "Expectations never fail to get me in trouble. What's more, I think you're a young man full of surprises. How are you holding up?"

Jesse shrugged. "It ain't really hit me yet. I came home to this empty trailer every night for the past month and a half. The only difference is tomorrow I won't be going to the hospice."

He stared up into the night sky and took a long drink of his soda. When he looked back, he said, "One thing I do know, I ain't going to no foster home."

Armen put a foot on the lower step, glancing first at Bonnie then at Jesse. "I don't think you have to. How old are you, son?"

"I'll be eighteen in July." Jesse gave Armen a wary look. "Why you want to know?"

Armen waved away the question. "I'll get to that in a minute. Do you have a plan to keep social services at bay?"

Jesse stood, forcing Armen to step back. "I sure as hell . . ." He shot an embarrassed glance Bonnie's way. "I sure do. I'm going to get my G.E.D. then become a fireman like my pa was."

"A noble goal. Kurt Vonnegut proclaimed firemen the last true heroes in America. I couldn't agree more. I foresee only one problem." Armen raised both hands palms forward, as if he meant to distance himself from the aforementioned problem.

The boy shook his head. "I got money. When Pa was killed fighting that fire, Mama and I saved most of the insurance money. And this here trailer's paid for."

"You got a good start, but money's not the difficulty, Jesse."

Armen's voice had taken on a soft yet commanding

tone. Bonnie was sure if the man adopted this tone with her he could talk her into anything. *I'm not sure I find that thought comforting.*

"I think you have the makings of a splendid fireman. The problem lies with the G.E.D. There was a time when a young man could become a policeman or fireman after taking the Equivalency Test, but those days are long gone. Anymore, the competition is too stiff. These days you need at least a high school diploma . . . a few years of college wouldn't hurt."

Jesse opened his mouth to protest.

Armen silenced him by once again raising a hand. "Not an insurmountable problem. First you need to be emancipated. This is where your age plays in your favor."

"Like the slaves and Abraham Lincoln?" Jesse squinted at Armen in disbelief.

"Very much so. Emancipation declares you a free individual able to make decisions for yourself. And to be emancipated you need a sponsor. One would be nice. Two would be better."

A long silence hung in the air. Jesse's deep chest rose and fell as he regarded first Armen then Bonnie. "I would bet a pair of schoolteachers would make great sponsors."

Bonnie felt as if she'd somehow booked passage on a whitewater raft. Each bend in the river caught her by surprise. But she'd always been a quick study, and she could see now where Armen was steering this raft.

Make a good bargain, Callahan.

"And tutors." Armen took a long pull on his beer,

and offered the bottle to Bonnie. He avoided looking at Jesse.

Oh, what the hell. She took a drink and handed the bottle back. She couldn't remember when beer tasted as sweet. "After all, you do want to be a fireman, don't you?"

Jesse waved his hands like what he really wanted was everyone to keep quiet. "We ain't talking about the G.E.D. test anymore, are we?"

"No, Jess, we're talking about you, an emancipated young man, living here and finishing high school." Armen cocked his head with a what-do-you-say expression plastered on his face.

"I don't know. I'm in big trouble at school. Got in a fight, you know?" Crimson spread from his neck up until it covered most of his bald pate. "Hit a teacher."

"I can tell you right now you're going to have to quit the teacher hitting." Bonnie laid a hand on the boy's shoulder. "But I know that particular teacher pretty well, and I'll bet we can get her to forgive you. Rumor has it, she's pretty cool."

Jesse hadn't shed one tear at the hospice, and Bonnie didn't expect he'd shed any now, but she thought she saw a quiver in his lower lip.

"Why you guys doing this?"

Armen gave Jesse an exaggerated wink. "I don't know about her, but me, I'm trying to impress a lady."

It's working, Callahan.

"What about it, Jesse? Sound like a plan? You'd have to stay out of trouble."

Jesse licked his lips, and Bonnie could see the old synapses firing.

"I don't want to sound ungrateful, but could I get back with you guys?"

Before Bonnie could mount a protest, Armen said, "You do that. When you make up your mind, you know where I live."

Bonnie held out a hand, and Jesse helped her up.

"Let's have those crutches." When she'd reached the car she turned back. "Just one more thing. Thursday morning."

Jesse seemed to stiffen. "What about it?"

"At the hospice you said someone told you that Peyton Newlin said unkind things about your mother."

Jesse laced his fingers behind his bald head, obviously ill at ease. "That's right. But I'm not sure about ratting this person out."

Bonnie threw her crutches into Alice's back seat and slammed the door. She leaned unsteadily against Alice. "Fair enough. I won't ask you to say a thing. I'm going give you a name. You do what you want after that."

Jesse didn't move.

"Edmund Sheridan."

The boy did nothing for so long Bonnie decided to let the issue die. *Nice try, Pinkwater.* She opened Alice's passenger door and plopped onto the seat. When she looked back, Jesse Poole was standing behind his screen door. He nodded once and disappeared from view.

CHAPTER 12

BONNIE SNUCK A QUICK PEEK AT ARMEN'S *derriere* as he slid the casserole dish into the oven. By the time he'd closed the door and turned back around, she'd lowered her eyes to her coffee cup.

"You make a mean cup of coffee, Callahan." *Very smooth, Bonnie.*

"You ain't seen nothing yet." He wiped his hands on his apron. A caricature of ex-president Richard Nixon, arms raised making the V for victory sign filled the bib. A cartoon balloon read, "I am not a cook." "Cheese enchiladas ala Callahan. Ambrosia."

Untying his apron as he walked, he strode past where she sat at a small claw-footed table. He threw Richard Nixon face-down on a gray leather futon. "You like Van Morrison?"

She'd turned round so she could follow him with her eyes. "Yes, I do, which is strange, considering I rarely understand a thing he's singing."

Armen placed a CD in a slim black player. Almost immediately the familiar guitar opening of "Into the Mystic" trickled out of a pair of oak-trimmed speakers. He crossed the room and stood before her, his hands extended. "May I have this dance?"

"Excuse me?" She nodded to where her crutches leaned against the kitchen counter. "I don't think I'd make a very good dance partner right now."

He bent low. "I'll dance for both of us. Trust me."

She hesitated then wrapped her arms about his neck. As he had done at Griffith's, he scooped her from the chair. Unlike that first time, he held her firm, the two of them swaying to Van Morrison's sure voice and soft guitar.

Armen's hair was still damp from his shower.

Bonnie breathed deep his aroma of soap and aftershave. *The essence of clean boy.* She laid her head on his shoulder. "You know how to show a girl a good time, Armen Callahan."

"We aim to please."

She closed her eyes, and Armen became her world— the smell of him, the feel of his arms, the gentle rhythm of his dancing. She didn't want to ask where these feelings would lead. Her life was a lazy river, and she intended to float. When the song went into a long instrumental, Armen whirled her. They both laughed. His beard brushed her face. She liked the soft yet scratchy feel of it on her cheek and nestled in closer.

Bonnie wasn't exactly aware when Van Morrison switched from "Into the Mystic" to "Crazy Love." If anything, the new song was more romantic than the first, and yet it conjured images of Edmund and Ali—both in black, conical hats. Bonnie tried to put them out of her mind, to slide back into that comfortable haven where only she and Armen populated the planet. The pair of teenagers would have none of it. Leering, they whispered together and laughed.

"Where have you gone?" Armen asked into her hair.

Bonnie lifted her head so she could see his face. "Is it so obvious?"

His eyes held a mixture of understanding tinged with the barest hint of sadness. "Your whole body tensed. Edmund?"

She nodded. "And Ali. I'm sorry, Armen. I really loved our dance."

"Don't be sorry. I'm going to accept the four minutes we had as a gift from the universe." He carried her back to the kitchen/dining room and set her at the claw-foot table.

He tapped her nose with an outstretched finger. "The next time we trip the light fantastic we take a longer whirl."

At least he wants a second dance. "Count on it."

Armen went to a matte-black coffee maker and returned with his own cup. "I'm so hungry, I could eat school food." He frowned at her. "No long faces. I won't have you feeling bad."

Easy for you to say. You didn't turn a romantic moment into a bad dream. "I spoiled our dance."

Armen reached across the table and took her hands in his. "Have you ever seen *Old Yeller?*"

She blinked at the unexpected question. "The Disney movie about the dog?"

"Yep." He hummed the opening bars of the theme song finishing with, "Best doggone dog in the west."

She smiled at this man who had succeeded in keeping her off balance for the better part of two days. "I'm not sure why we're talking about a dog movie, but yes, I saw *Old Yeller* when I was a little girl."

"I own it. It's one of my prized possessions." He rubbed his thumbs across the tops of her hands. "Not many people know this, but *Old Yeller* is a repository of Zen wisdom."

"As in Zen Buddhism?"

"Absolutely." He nodded, showing not a hint he wasn't serious. "If you ask anybody what scene they remember, they'll tell you the scene where the boy has to shoot the beloved dog because it has contracted rabies. They think that's what the movie's about."

Where are you going with this, Armen? "Isn't it?"

He shrugged. "Not for me. For me the heart of the movie happens a few scenes later after the father, played by Fess Parker, comes home from a cattle thing-a-ma-jig."

The image of a large man wearing a buckskin vest came into focus. "I remember him—the actor who played Davy Crocket."

"Give the lady a cigar. He also played Daniel Boone, now he runs a winery somewhere. For my whole generation, Boone and Davy Crocket got sort of blended into one person, Fess Parker. However, I digress."

He let go of her hands and sat tall in his chair. "I'll be the father, Fess Parker." He straightened an imaginary cowboy hat.

God, you're cute. Strange, but cute. She caught herself nodding with amusement. "Okay, you're the father."

"And you're the eldest son who is unable to get over Yeller's death." Armen reached across the table and laid a consoling hand on Bonnie's arm. " 'Boy, a lot of life is mighty fine. You can't afford to waste the good part frettin' about the bad. That makes it all bad.' " Armen's voice had gone unexpectedly deep with a trace of a southern accent.

She waited for him to continue, but the look of accomplishment on his face told her he had nothing more to offer. "That's it?" She immediately regretted the accusatory tone. She needn't have worried. Her incomprehension only served to prime Armen's philosophical pump.

He slumped forward, resting his bearded chin on his forearm, staring up at her. "That's everything. The heart and soul of Zen—focus on the moment, restart your life from where you are right now, view the world with a beginner's mind. What Fess, like any great Zen master, was trying to teach his boy is that the present should never be colored by the past, especially if all the past has to offer is bad news."

Bonnie lowered her head so she could be eye-to-eye with Armen. "Soooooooo, you're telling me I shouldn't let this little setback taint future dances. Leave the past in the past, even if it was only five minutes ago."

He winked at her. "The great Fess Parker has connected with yet another convert."

"Not so quick. I still have Edmund Sheridan on the brain. And furthermore, can we sit up straight again? This table-level talk is killing my back." Twisting, she sat erect. She heard a pop in her neck. "That's more like it."

Armen followed suit minus the audible neck-pop. "I'm surprised you could wait this long after Poole's revelation."

"You want to know the truth?"

He shook his head. "Absolutely not. Give me a veiled lie any old time."

She stuck out her tongue at him. "I'm not sure why I said Edmund's name back there with Jesse. My mouth was forming Ali Griffith when I blurted out Edmund. Surprised the hell out of me when Jesse told me I was right."

"Me, too. It makes no sense whatsoever. He rescues Peyton at Knowledge Bowl then goes out of his way to get Jesse Poole to unleash the wrath of God on Peyton's skinny behind. What's up with that?"

She spun her index fingers one around the other. "Reverse those."

"What?"

"First, he gets Peyton's ass kicked then he rescues

him.   And don't forget, somewhere in there he murders Stephanie Templeton." *And tries to run over the world's greatest math teacher.*

"Then there's the e-mail from Ali Griffith, which he takes the time from his busy macabre schedule to read."

"We don't know that for sure."

Armen took a sip of his coffee. "Which don't we know for sure—that he read the e-mail or that it was written by Ali?"

"Either . . . both."   She threw up her hands in frustration. "I don't know, but just because the letter is archived doesn't prove Edmund read it, and Your Wicked Little Witch doesn't have to be Ali."

"I see."   He scowled, and gave her a look of disappointment. "I didn't know your denial ran that deep."

Her first reaction was to lash out at him. *How dare he? I'm Bonnie Pinkwater, God damn it. Doesn't he know most people consider me an institution?*

Maybe it was that very thought that extinguished her anger like a torch thrust in a rain barrel. Institutions didn't take crap from anybody, but they didn't have a lot of friends either. And right now she wanted this cranky Science teacher to be her friend—and maybe a little more.

She gave birth to an honest chuckle. "Don't pull your punches, Callahan. Tell me what you really think."

The remark set just the right tone. Armen matched her smile for smile, and the tension bled from the room. "Whad-a-ya-say we put the letter on the back burner for a moment."

"I'd say good idea."

He scratched at his beard. "I don't know if you're going to find this any easier to hear, but something else about Ali Griffith has been chewing on me."

"You mean beside the fact that like Edmund at the Academy, she was the only one at her home who actually saw the red pickup truck?" She loved the look of surprise on Armen's face. *That's right, Callahan. You'll always get my A-game.*

He blinked like a cat that's been stared at too long. "Well, yes . . . I mean no. Whatever. Don't you think it's funny both of these teenagers saw Jesse's truck, but no one else did?"

"I saw it." She raised her eyebrows ever so slightly, keeping her expression impassive.

"You know what I mean." He made a steeple of his fingers and regarded her over the tips. "Bon, I've got to tell you. With all that's going on with Ali Griffith, to find out she lied about the truck would cinch it for me."

"Sounds like you're convinced of Ali's guilt already." She went out of her way to emulate Armen's reasonable tone of voice. She didn't want or need to sound strident.

"I don't understand your recalcitrance. The girl did everything but sign her name on that e-mail."

Bonnie slapped the table. "That's just the point. Every word, every punctuation mark in that letter pointed to Ali Griffith. Hells bells, she might as well have signed her damned name. If she wrote that letter, Ali Griffith showed the intelligence of a bar of soap."

"So, the girl made an error in judgment. She's just a kid."

Bonnie wanted to shout out her reply, but first she took a sip of coffee to give herself a chance to settle down. "She's not a member of that club. For that matter none of the teenagers in this affair are mere kids. Peyton Newlin might be a boy genius, but Ali and Edmund aren't anybody's slouches. These are acutely intelligent individuals."

"And your point?"

"I'll bet when the police run down the e-mail addresses on those letters they lead to an untraceable sender. From the beginning the letter writer covered her tracks. If Ali is the author then why write a letter that circumvents all her precautions?" She surprised herself with the vehemence of her objections.

Armen leaned back in his chair, his arms folded across his chest. He studied her, looking like a man who needed to make a proclamation but was choosing each word carefully.

Bonnie let the silence hang uninterrupted. Friends gave one another time to think even if they feared what the other might propose.

He pulled at his goatee. "Bon, I know you'd just as soon not consider this subject, but we need to be able to talk about Ali Griffith being the actual author of that letter. So I'm asking you to entertain that supposition."

Easy for you to say. I've already lost Stephanie, Peyton, and Edmund. Now Ali? Did all four children hold me in contempt? Her head felt heavy as she nodded. "Fair enough. Assume Ali is the author."

"Thank you." He squeezed her hand. "Consider the letter itself—dated Thursday, and if I remember correctly the archives listed the time at ten-ten p.m."

"Ali was home by then." Bonnie drew in a long breath. "She definitely had the opportunity."

"She comes home and the first thing she does is fire off an e-mail to Edmund. The letter refers to you and her mother. Neither of you suspect a thing, the letter says. Suspect what?"

"Their love affair?"

Armen chewed at his lower lip and beard. "There's always that. She also could have been speaking about Stephanie's death."

"Time's all wrong." Bonnie waved her hand to indicate time past. "Stephanie wouldn't be murdered for another four to five hours."

"All right, Stephanie's impending death." Again silence hung in the air.

Bonnie's throat felt dry. The implications of Armen's assumption brought back the earlier leering images of Ali and Edmund. "You're saying the e-mail was Ali pushing Edmund to go out and murder Stephanie?"

"She does encourage him to be strong. I don't think anything in a simple teenage love affair would require that sort of encouragement."

"What about Peyton's disappearance? We know the boy spent time in Sheridan's barn. Suppose Ali knew about Edmund's plans and was just encouraging Edmund to keep Peyton safe from his father?"

Armen cocked his head and frowned at her. "Are we talking about the same letter? The one I remember is mean-spirited and contains hints and promises of sexual rewards, hardly the altruistic urgings of a Pollyanna."

Bonnie closed her eyes and played the letter across her mental teleprompter. She mumbled the words, "busybody Pinkwater," and "the risk will be worth the reward, if you know what I mean." Then there was the bit about holding her body close to his. Nodding, she said in a voice barely above a whisper, "The probability seems high the letter isn't referring to either an innocent love affair or hiding Peyton."

The inexorable downward spiral of the logic had a dizzying effect on Bonnie's mind. She shook off her lethargy. "Let's try another tack. If Edmund was driving that truck Friday night, and Ali and he were lovers, then why break into her house?"

Armen leaned back in his chair and said nothing. His empty expression answered her question.

"You don't believe the break-in happened?" she asked.

"Not for a moment."

The timer on the stove buzzed. Armen rose and slipped on a pair of oven mitts. He returned with a glass casserole dish in which a concoction of red sauce, corn tortillas, and cheese bubbled furiously. After a juggling act involving the transfer of one of the mitts to his mouth, Armen deftly placed the enchiladas in the center of the table. He was heading back toward the oven when the kitchen phone rang.

"Callahan's Pleasure Palace." Almost as soon as the words left his mouth, Armen's expression changed to a grim mask. "Uh huh. My God! I'll tell her. I don't think it'll do any good." He re-cradled the phone.

When he hesitated in speaking, Bonnie felt the hair on the back of her neck bristle. "Who was that?"

He wiped the back of his hand across his mouth. "Franklin. He and Keene investigated the footsteps behind the Sheridan barn. They found the body of Peyton Newlin buried in a shallow grave."

"WELL, HERE'S ANOTHER FIRST FOR ME." ARMEN nodded and patted Bonnie's leg. "I would've never guessed this evening would've ended in a morgue."

Bonnie recognized Armen's attempt to subtly cheer her, but she wanted none of it. The world had become a madhouse—two of her beautiful children dead, the other two suspects in their murder.

She and Armen sat on a pair of hard metal folding chairs outside the office of Kevin, the County Coroner's solitary night attendant. A tall blonde with multiple facial piercings, Kevin looked as though he'd be more at home carrying a surf board or playing hacky-sack than spending his evenings babysitting corpses.

He'd been surprised at their arrival.

No, Bonnie corrected herself. Kevin had been annoyed.

No doubt, most nights he could count on no one

sharing his nocturnal vigil, at least no one capable of conversation. He'd informed Bonnie it might take hours for the crime scene investigators to release Peyton's body, hinting she'd be wise to go on home.

Bonnie declined.

Kevin's tiny Spartan office, big enough for a filing cabinet, desk and chair, felt like the walls were closing in, so Bonnie chose the hall. Here she sat, feeling like God's first fool.

She glanced nervously at Armen. "You think I'm crazy, don't you?"

Armen shook his head. "You're not as good at reading people as you believe you are. I don't think you're crazy. I think you feel guilty. The guilt may have led you to this irrational late-night decision to see Wendy Newlin."

It was her turn to undermine an assumption, even though it was true. "I promised Wendy I'd be there for her then promptly—and conveniently—forgot about her while I . . ."

"While you what? Spent time with me?" He turned away, his face hard.

Well, yes.

"I didn't say that. All I meant was someone needed me, and I forgot about them. That's not like me to forget a promise."

Armen dug the edge of his fist into his eye and yawned. The hard edges of his brow and jaw softened. "That wouldn't have prevented Peyton's death. You could've stood by Wendy's side all day. Peyton would be just as dead."

Damn you and damn your logic, Armen Callahan. "What would you have me do?"

For the first time since they'd sat, he turned his tired face her way. "Just what you're doing, being Juanita-on-the-spot to comfort this Newlin woman. But do it for the right reasons. None of this is your fault."

"Should I chant that as a mantra?"

"If it helps to give you perspective." He offered an I'm-on-your-side shrug. "There's an APB out on Edmund's car. They'll find him, Bonnie."

"I know." She rubbed Armen's shoulder. "I'm glad you're with me."

"I wouldn't miss it for the world." He pointed at their stark surroundings. "You're opening up new vistas to me."

He yawned again.

"And you're looking a little haggard there, Mister Mouse."

The smile he offered drooped a little at the edges. "Does this mean you no longer find me the ridiculously handsome hero of your secret love fantasies?"

She kissed his cheek. "Don't push it." She nestled against his side.

"You know Franklin's not going to be happy to see us here."

She waved away the statement without lifting her head. "The boy just doesn't know his own mind. If he didn't want me to come, then why call? No call, no Pinkwater and Callahan treading water in the depths of the City and County Building."

"Your logic contains more holes than a Robert Trent Jones golf vacation, but I'm too tired to argue."

She reached up and patted his face. "Wise man. Did Franklin say anything about Ali?"

Armen jostled her with the shaking of his head. "I told you everything he said. Not a word about Ali. I didn't get a sense as to whether he'd read the e-mails yet."

Bonnie sat up straight. "But Wendy is definitely coming here?"

Armen regarded her for a long moment. "That's what the man said. They wanted her to identify Peyton away from the scene, and Wendy agreed."

A twinge of uneasiness rippled through Bonnie. She had no idea how Wendy would view this intrusion. That was the funny thing about good intentions. More often than not when they reared their innocent heads the world played whack-a-mole with them. Here she and Armen sat on these bottom-numbing chairs just waiting to offer whatever assistance they could to a grieving Wendy Newlin, but it was just as likely the woman would want to be left alone.

And what about Ralph-the-Creep? "Holy Moley, you don't think Ralph Newlin will show, do you?"

Armen winced. "Will you relax? There's no way to know what happened with the good Colonel in the last twelve hours. Considering the man's status with the powers that be, if he finally made an appearance at Peterson then all may have been forgiven. On the other hand, the Colonel could be incarcerated or a fugitive."

The Fugitive?

For a fleeting moment Bonnie held the image of Ralph Newlin chasing the infamous One-Armed Man up an electrical tower. *If there's any justice in this world, Ralph should be cooling his heels in some smelly stockade.* She smiled at the thought, then just as quickly remembered their reason for being here.

Peyton was dead. First Stephanie, now Peyton. That scholarship was proving more fatal than Ebola. The sound of a buzzer sliced through her reverie.

Kevin emerged from his office. He was past where they sat before Bonnie could ask what was happening. He didn't say not to follow so Armen helped Bonnie to stand. She kept a discreet distance behind the night attendant.

Kevin pressed a button on the hallway wall, and a small garage door rumbled into life. A moment later, Bonnie shielded her eyes against the headlamps of Franklin Valsecci's El Camino.

Kevin met Franklin at his driver's door. After what seemed a heated exchange with Kevin gesturing and pointing up the entrance ramp, Wendy Newlin emerged out of the passenger side of the car.

Bonnie gasped and clutched Armen's forearm. Except for the brilliant shock of red hair, Wendy was unrecognizable. The entire left side of her face was bloated in gruesome asymmetry, with the eye on that side swollen shut. The left side of her mouth looked as if the woman's usually full lips had been replaced with engorged night-crawlers crisscrossed with stitches. Her nose appeared broken.

Wendy hesitated then strode past Kevin until she stood face to face with Bonnie. A single tear crept from beneath the swollen eyelid. "Hell of a day."

CHAPTER 13

As Bonnie waited for Franklin, the ambulance arrived. She kept an eye on Wendy, not sure how the woman would handle the delivery of her dead son. Afraid Wendy might faint, Bonnie captured Armen's attention.

"Stay close," she mouthed. "Be ready with an arm."

He nodded understanding and sidled up next to Wendy.

If she was aware of anything happening, she made no mention of it. Her body was ramrod straight, her good eye fixed on the stretcher rolling through the morgue door. She bobbed her head to some unheard rhythm, lips moving in wordless repetition.

A song, or maybe a litany from the rosary? Bonnie had no doubt she was witnessing someone in emotional and spiritual dissolution. In the face of such heartache,

Bonnie felt impotent.

Keene came around the rear of the ambulance in the company of Franklin. The former had a toothpick in his mouth, his hands jammed in the pockets of his grey trench coat, his eyes downcast as if searching the entrance for evidence. Though the night was calm, he appeared disheveled, windblown.

By contrast, Franklin looked crisp—his thinning hair combed, his tie pulled straight and tight. He picked up his pace, falling in behind the stretcher. Glancing at Bonnie, he offered a cheerless perfunctory nod.

Kevin, the night attendant, led the stretcher and its bearers past where Bonnie stood propped on her crutches. On the rolling platform, a zipped, black bag revealed the outline of the small figure contained within. For the briefest moment she felt anxiety for Peyton.

How could the boy breathe all shut up in that sealed bag?

Her vision blurred before she blinked back tears.

Wendy made no move to follow the litter bearing her son.

"Are you ready?" Franklin's face was a studied mixture of concern and cool reserve.

You've done this before, Mister Valsecci. What a life you've chosen for yourself.

Wendy nodded. She let Franklin take her elbow then turned back to Bonnie. "I need to do this without you."

At first, Bonnie heard the words as separate entities, empty of meaning. When, seconds later, the significance sank in, she was stunned. She nodded and heard herself say, "Whatever you want."

Franklin led Wendy away.

Without you, Bonnie thought. *Not—I've got to do this on my own—but specifically, "without you."* She wasn't sure what to make of the statement, but a part of her—the Catholic schoolgirl part no doubt—accepted it as a form of retribution. After all, she'd abandoned Wendy just when the woman needed her most.

At the end of the wide hall, past Kevin's office and the behind-numbing chairs, Kevin slid open an over-sized, smoke-glass door labeled Examination Rooms.

From what Bonnie could see, the decoration scheme beyond the door was basic—black-on-white tile and acres of stainless steel. Steel cabinets sporting steel handles, gleaming steel tables, steel troughs emptying into steel basins. Even the overhead lights appeared to be cowled in polished metal.

Bonnie stood with Keene and Armen in awkward silence as the sliding-glass door slid shut. Through its smoky translucent surface, the blurred shapes of Wendy and the rest dissipated as if into mist.

The smell of cigarettes, coffee, and garlic caught Bonnie's attention. Keene stood at her elbow.

More to keep from obsessing on "without you" than any real desire for conversation, she asked, "Shouldn't you be in there?"

The big man picked his teeth with a toothpick in the final stages of decomposition. "My job was to find Peyton Newlin. He's been found." Keene's bulldog face was an unreadable stony mask.

He scratched his chest near his shoulder holster, and Bonnie could swear the fingers of that hand appeared to be aching for the pistol in residence there.

Bonnie couldn't blame him. She'd like to shoot something or someone right about now. "How did Peyton die?"

Keene's eyes flashed when he turned his gaze on her.

She braced herself for another lecture—she had no business in these matters of murder.

The big cop's gaze softened. "What the hell?"

He pointed with his lantern jaw toward the examination room. "That's what they'll figure out when the medical examiner gets here, but I'd say his neck was broken sometime early Friday morning."

The same night as Stephanie.

Bonnie tried to swallow her next question, but it demanded voice. "You saw Wendy Newlin's face?"

Keene squinted at her. "Yeah, I saw it." His tone was wary, with an accompanying air of finality.

"Has it occurred to anyone that in the middle of all this violence there's a violent man on the loose?"

Keene's nostrils flared. "You're a real piece of work. You know that?" He brushed past her, heading for the smoky-glass door.

"No, math lady," he called back over his shoulder. "It would never have crossed the minds of us slow-thinkin' flatfoots to consider Colonel Newlin. Thank God we got you to keep us in line."

He slid open the door to the examination room.

Without a look back he shut it between them.

"That went well." Armen patted her hand.

Bonnie felt heat rise from her neck to her face. "I suppose I should work on my tact."

He created a centimeter gap with thumb and forefinger. "Maybe a little."

An uncomfortable pang shot through her lower extremities, particularly her insistent right foot. *Need to get off these damn crutches.* She hobbled to a hard-metal chair and plopped down.

Staring up at Armen, she said, "It just makes me nuts. You'd think Ralph Newlin would try to keep it together so he and his wife could get through this nightmare. Instead, what's he do? He beats her almost unrecognizable."

From the look on his face, it was evident Armen had no answer for the perverseness of the human race, let alone Colonel Ralph Newlin. "I think Sergeant Keene would like to get Colonel Ralph alone in an empty interrogation room for a little one-on-one."

She reached up and took Armen's hand. "You think?"

"Like I told you before, you're not as good at reading people as you believe you are. Keene's no tin man. He may be rough around the edges, but the man's got a heart."

He has no trouble hiding it around me.

With a hiss, the door to the examination slid open. Franklin Valsecci emerged first. Without hesitation, he strode the thirty paces to where Bonnie sat and squared up on Armen. "Do you mind if the lady and I have a private conversation?"

Armen glanced uncertainly at Bonnie. She nodded, and Armen released her hand.

As fast as her crutches allowed, she followed Franklin into Kevin's small office. Her former student shut the door. Ten seconds passed then another ten and still Franklin didn't turn around.

Okay, Mister Valsecci, what's on your mind? She pulled out the desk chair and sat.

With his back still to her, Franklin said, "That woman out there is on the brink of a nervous breakdown."

The statement was so obvious Bonnie held her breath waiting for what Franklin would add.

He turned around and leaned against the door, his hand on the knob. His posture indicated he meant to keep her prisoner in the tiny office until he had his say.

With a motion Bonnie had come to recognize as his I'm-about-to-get-serious-gesture, Franklin used his thumb and forefinger to wipe the corners of his mouth. "She doesn't need someone in her face right now making demands on her."

"By someone, you mean me."

Franklin nodded and held Bonnie's steady gaze. "By someone, I mean you."

The room began to feel claustrophobic, and she found herself liking this conversation less and less. *You're a big boy now, Franklin, and this isn't Algebra One. Spit out what you really have to say.* "You can't think I'm that insensitive. Of course I won't make demands of Wendy."

"Do I have your word on that?"

Bonnie opened her mouth to agree, but something made her hold back the promise. "What's going on, Franklin?"

Another long moment passed before Franklin spoke. "Wendy Newlin refuses to press charges against her husband."

"You're kidding me?"

Bonnie winced. She'd always hated that phrase. People invariably used it at the most inappropriate times. It rang out no less stupid when she was the one giving it voice.

"Did Wendy have a reason?"

Franklin approached her. Hands on both arms of the desk chair, he leaned close. "I didn't ask. I was escorting a woman to identify the dead body of her son."

Bonnie felt as if she were being violently wrenched in opposite directions. A large part of her wanted to see Ralph Newlin drawn and quartered. She wanted Wendy to be his executioner all the while screaming, "Enough is enough."

But Franklin was right. For whatever reason, Wendy had made a decision—a misguided one to be sure—but one of her own choosing. The city morgue, where Peyton lay dead, wasn't the place to try to change her mind.

"I won't say a word." *For now.*

Franklin held her eyes a moment longer then pushed

off the chair. He towered over her. "Thanks, Missus P."

Somehow she didn't feel kindly enough to respond to Franklin's gesture of gratitude. She'd always hated being shamed into doing the right thing.

"At least tell me the police are looking for this maniac."

"He's wanted for questioning by both civil and military police."

She could almost taste his eagerness to throw her this bone. *Thank God for small favors.* Her sense of claustrophobia returned. "What say we get the hell out of here?"

Outside the small office, Wendy stood next to Armen, her arm linked through his. As Bonnie and Franklin approached, Wendy turned her disfigured face in their direction. "Your charming man has volunteered to take me home."

RIDING IN THE BACK OF ALICE, WITH WENDY AND Armen up front, put Bonnie in mind of an interminable New England car vacation she took, as a child, with her father—three, no four states—on one sweltering, eternal July day.

His moon-face aglow with a maniacal mixture of fatigue and hubris, her father had turned back to her and exalted, "We're making good time now, shrimp-boat."

Bonnie hadn't wanted to burst her father's bubble

by telling him she was carsick. Ten minutes later when she threw up all over her little brother, her secret came abruptly, and disgustingly, out of the closet.

Perched dead-center on the edge of the back seat, trying to peer through the front windshield, she felt a little like that nauseous child right now. More than likely the fact that Alice should have had her shocks replaced some time in the administration of the first George Bush was a major contributing factor. Every bump, every swerve in the road went straight to her head or the pit of her stomach, most times both. And just like that long ago vacation, she didn't want her nausea to be the focal point of the trip.

Face it, Pinkwater. You don't want Armen to see you hurl your cookies. And if she didn't want a repetition of that embarrassment, she needed to do something, anything to take her mind off the road. Unfortunately, she'd promised away the subject starring center stage on her mind—Colonel Ralph Newlin being drawn and quartered.

Wendy solved the problem for her. "You're mighty quiet back there."

"I wasn't sure you wanted to talk."

Wendy swiveled in her seat to give Bonnie a one-eyed stare. "Depends on the subject." She sighed as if she held back an ocean of tears.

Bonnie laid a hand on the woman's arm. "I want you to know how sorry I am for not being there today."

"You have nothing to apologize for." She curled her fingers around Bonnie's hand. "No sooner had I hung up the phone than Ralph came storming into the living room, bristling for a fight. I knew what I was in for and should have ducked and covered. Instead, I let him know that when Peyton . . ."

The life went out of her voice. She sat for a time shaking her head and staring into the space between the seats. Like at the morgue, her lips moved, but no words came out.

Bonnie reached to embrace her.

Pulling away, Wendy raised her fists. Her chest heaved, her breathing becoming rapid and shallow. She regarded Bonnie warily.

Not sure what to do, Bonnie leaned back, putting as much distance as she could between herself and the anxious woman. She knew damned well it wasn't a good time to speak inanities.

Little by little the tension eased in the car until Wendy lowered her hands. She tried to smile, but the asymmetry of her face made the expression seem more like a grimace.

Bonnie was once again sure she was in the company of someone destined to fall into a thousand pieces.

"I told him." The three words fell from Wendy's lips in a soft whisper. "When Peyton came home we were leaving."

Silently, she mouthed, "I told him."

"Wendy, this can wait."

The woman cocked her head and leveled her good eye in Bonnie's direction. "Are you sure? It doesn't feel like it can." Her fist came to her face, and she abraded the swollen cheek like she could sand it back into conformity.

A pearl of moisture gathered at the damaged corner of her mouth, and she licked it away. "He went crazy, screaming that he'd never allow me to take his son. Then the hitting started."

Bonnie expected tears, but Wendy's face became hard, all shadow and dark lines. In that face was the promise that Ralph Newlin would never make her cry again.

"When he was finished with the punches and the slaps, he tried to rape me." She cast an anxious glance toward Armen. "The bastard couldn't get it up."

She nodded, color rushing to her face. "He tore out of the house. I laid there, my blouse ripped open, until I heard the rumble of his Stingray fade."

She shrugged an all-in-a-day's-work shrug. "I drove myself to the hospital. I know I said I'd call, but right then I wasn't in the mood for company."

All through the long quiet before and the recitation after, Armen had divided his attention between the road and Wendy's face. In that time, he'd driven past the school, past the turn onto Coyote, and now the double rows of poplars loomed dark, like a small mountain range against the starlit sky. He turned so he could see both Wendy and Bonnie and not drive Alice into a ditch. "Maybe we should stay with you . . . in case he shows up tonight."

Good thinking, Callahan. "I second that."

Shaking her head, Wendy made a small earthquake

of her red curls. "Absolutely not. I won't hear of it.
I'm going to take one of the bastard's softball bats into
my bedroom."

She curled her hand around an imaginary haft. "If
the son of a bitch shows up, I'll make him wish he was
never born."

She shoved Armen hard enough that he had to correct his steering. "I won't be the victim again."

How to put this delicately? "You said yourself it's
been a hell of a day. I'm just wondering if you're making a clear-headed decision here."

"My mind is made up." For the third time that
night she leveled her good eye at Bonnie and glared.
"And don't be so stupid as to park in the shadows
thinking I won't see you."

So much for that plan. "You're sure?"

Wendy sighed a bless-your-heart sigh. "Take my
word for it. He won't bother me tonight."

Although she never could have explained it even to
herself, Bonnie took the woman's word.

$$\bigwedge$$

THE DECISION TO SPEND THE NIGHT AT ARMEN'S TRAILER
seemed to make itself. Neither of them wanted to take
that long trek back to Black Forest. The kicker came
when Armen reminded her the grey futon opened into
a bed. At least she wouldn't be exiling the poor man
from his bed onto an uncomfortable couch.

As she lay under Armen's downy quilt staring up at

his white-on-white four-poster canopy, he entered the bedroom wearing heliotrope silk pajamas with a gold griffin on the breast pocket. She wore a silk royal-blue pajama set Armen had laboriously selected for her from his closet.

"Very continental, Mister Callahan. Hugh Hefner has nothing on you."

He turned and struck a pose straight from *Gentleman's Quarterly*. "Thank you for validating something I've felt for a very long time. You know, of course, what that would make you?"

Bonnie smiled and pulled the covers to her chin. "I'm nobody's bunny, Callahan. And don't you forget it."

The chuckle he let loose carried no shred of repentance or self-consciousness. "Oh, I don't know. You look pretty much the cottontail to me."

Abruptly, he leaned over, and planted a warm, moist, lingering kiss on her lips. Before she could respond or even reciprocate, he made for the door. He waved over his shoulder. "Sleep tight. Don't let the Cimex Lectularius bite."

Sleep tight, my sagging fanny. Bum foot or no bum foot, she wanted to go after the big tease and give back as good as she got.

Then the lights went out, and the door clicked shut.

"Sweet dreams yourself, Mighty Mouse," she whispered.

She lay in the dark, her hands behind her head. *Where's all this going? Wasn't it just this morning I told myself the last thing I wanted was a romantic relation-*

ship with a colleague? "Bonnie Pinkwater, you better sort this out before it goes too far," she said out loud.

Just who do you think you're fooling? Here you lay between Armen's sheets, your head on his oh-so-soft down pillow, the taste of his kiss still on your lips. The truth was—the sign for too far was already dwindling in the rearview mirror.

She woke feeling like she lay in the hand of God, Armen's down pillow curled about her ears. She wriggled the toes of her good foot, luxuriating in the soft warmth of the comforter. Giving in to a feeling that rose like a geyser from her abdomen, she squealed in delight.

"I heard that," Armen called from the next room.

"You shouldn't be listening." She peeled back the covers and stretched like a Cheshire cat. Her eyes blurred, and the room went soft as a yawn overtook her face.

"What time is it?"

"Almost nine."

I'm starving.

She grabbed her crutches and stumbled into the living room. "Is there any of that enchilada casserole left?"

When they'd arrived at the trailer the previous night, they each grabbed a spoon and burrowed into the cold dinner; no one had mentioned microwaves or the use of plates.

Even though he still wore his pajamas, Armen had been awake long enough to scrub the spoons and coffee cups from the night before. He wiped his damp hands on a dish towel and tossed it into the dish drainer.

"On the table."

As if he'd anticipated her request, along with the casserole, knives, forks, plates and napkins were in evidence.

He regarded her admiringly. "I must say you look better in those pajamas than I ever have."

She didn't feel very pretty, standing there with her bedroom hair and a crutch tucked under each arm, but the pajamas did feel exquisite. *Maybe clothes do make the woman.* "You are just shameless, Armen Callahan."

Standing at the coffee maker, his back was to her. He turned around holding a cup in each hand. "I have no idea what you're talking about."

"Then I'll tell you. I'm a semi-invalid. My hair is a mess. God knows how many folds and creases are still in my face from sleeping the sleep of the dead. And you . . ." She swung up one of the crutches and pointed at him. ". . . wise smart about looking good in pajamas." *But please, don't say you were only kidding.*

"That's my story, and I'm sticking to it." He peeled back the plastic wrap and ladled a glop of enchilada onto a plate. "Come eat."

She gathered the crutches into one hand and was preparing to sit when something about the uncluttered space on the tabletop disturbed her. "I don't suppose you have the paper delivered."

Armen wiped at his mouth with a paper napkin. "As a matter of fact, I am a daily student of current events. I'll go get it." He tossed down his napkin and stood.

"Sit yourself back down. I'm already up." Before he could protest, she snagged her crutches and made for the door. As she opened it, white-yellow sunlight stole her vision.

Armen called, "I like a woman who knows what she wants and goes after it."

Once outside, she wasn't as sure. At her home in Black Forest, she could have strode out her front door naked, but here with the nearest neighbor in spitting distance, she felt exposed. *Suck it up, Pinkwater. You're covered from head to toe, and the damned paper can't be more than ten feet away.* Sure enough, off to her left, almost at the end of the faux-aquarium car-port lay a blue plastic bag—the morning and only edition of the Sunday Gazette. It would be the work of fifteen seconds to retrieve.

She had the paper in her hand and had taken a few steps back when a high-pitched voice rang out. "Missus Pinkwater?"

The hair on the back of Bonnie's neck rose straight up.

Shit, shit, shit.

Clutching the paper to her breast, as if it might conceal her, Bonnie turned around.

Lindsay Robinson, a girl in Bonnie's third period Geometry class, looked as if she couldn't decide what she wanted most to stare at. Her gaze shifted from Bonnie to Armen's trailer to her own feet.

Just bluff your way out of this. "How you doing, Lindsay? Soooooo, you live in this trailer park?"

Color rose into the girl's cheeks. "Right here." She pointed to the tan and brown double-wide. "Mister Callahan is our neighbor."

As if on cue, Armen poked his head out of the door. "Did I hear my name being used in vain?"

Now the girl had two pairs of pajamas to try not to stare at.

Shit, shit, and double shit.

The three of them stood as if frozen in time. There was no telling how long the awkward scene might have continued, but Armen's attention was drawn to the rutted dirt lane at the end of the car port. "What's that?"

Then Bonnie saw it, too. Alternately, the path was bathed in first red then blue light. She hadn't heard it before—probably embarrassment had made her deaf—but now she recognized crowd sounds. Grateful to escape before Lindsay asked something truly mortifying, she hobbled toward the end of the trailer.

A young blond boy on a BMX bike came up fast on the right.

"What's going on?" Bonnie shouted.

In a spray of dust the bike spun to a halt. Half-facing her, with at least fifty-percent of his attention on the lights, he bellowed, "Cop cars . . . at the Poole place."

CHAPTER 14

SHAMELESSLY, BONNIE TOOK ADVANTAGE of her new status as a cripple to edge her way to the front of the crowd. Either unable or unwilling to elbow through at her side, Armen waved her on.

In the short time she and Armen spent changing out of their pajamas, the gawking mob had spilled across the rutted lane and onto properties opposite and adjacent Jesse Poole's double-wide—one pair of enterprising youngsters perched atop a trailer, little children astride their parent's shoulders, people cross-legged on the roofs of pickup trucks.

Within a border of caution tape, a section of the powder blue trailer's white lattice skirt had been removed. Down on one knee Franklin Valsecci peered beneath.

Jesse stood at the back end of the concrete parking slab, book-ended by two state patrol officers. Bonnie recognized the blond pair from a multiple murder she had the misfortune of stumbling upon some sixteen months previous. Male and female, the Aryan giants towered over Jesse. From the boy's body language, Bonnie found it impossible to tell if he was in trouble or just standing out of the way.

Maybe both.

The crowd around her seemed to have already made up its mind. Murmuring grew louder. A palpable animosity filled the air. A woman pulled her young daughter close. A tall black man in paint-splattered white coveralls scowled. People who'd been Jesse's neighbors and possibly even friends now stared at him like he'd been transformed into something unholy.

This isn't good.

Pressing close against painter-man, Bonnie craned her neck to see beneath the trailer.

"It's a corpse," Painter-man's deep voice boomed. He nodded toward the trailer without looking at her.

Franklin stood, and revealed the disturbing truth. Unmistakably, a body lay partially hidden in the gloom behind the lattice. Someone had crammed the corpse into the narrow recess. A blue-jeaned leg and corresponding white tennis shoe protruded into the morning light. Across the bottom of the shoe, in red block letters, the word Samurai was printed from toe to heel. The corpse's face was obscured by gloom, but Bonnie didn't need to see a face to identify the corpse. A shaft of sunlight reflected starkly off the blond-on-brunette highlighted hair.

Oh God, Edmund, how the hell did you end up here?

Franklin spotted her. She tried to disappear back into the obscurity of the crowd, fully expecting him to read her the riot act for being at yet another crime scene. Much to her surprise, he signaled her forward.

He lifted the tape to let her within the cordon. "I never thought I'd hear myself saying this, but I'm glad you're here." He steered her to the trailer. "This is a lot to ask, but do you think you could handle a quick look at Edmund?"

She nodded.

Evidently, the plan was for her to squat down. Using her crutch as support, she lowered herself to one knee.

This close she could make out Edmund's face. The boy's eyes were wide open, staring upward. He appeared to be snarling, lips curled away from his upper teeth. *Dear God, he died in pain or in extreme fear.* Even though she knew Edmund was almost surely a murderer, her heart broke for this clever boy who played video games and collected comic books.

And what about his parents? "How did he die?"

"We won't know for sure until the crime scene guys clear the scene, and we can extract the body. There's no violence evident."

The body? Edmund Clark Sheridan had been reduced to this common denominator. "But his face?"

"Don't go there, Missus P. Very few of us go peacefully into that dark night." From inside his jacket, Franklin extracted a penlight and shone it on Edmund's flannel shirt. "Look in the breast pocket."

Maybe twenty percent of a silver circlet was visible sticking out of the boy's wide flannel pocket. It was enough. A cobra's ruby eyes glittered.

"It's a necklace, a choker." She wanted to be any place but here. She certainly didn't want to say what she had to say next. "It belongs to Ali Griffith. She wore it to Knowledge Bowl last Thursday."

Franklin must have seen how much it pained her to finger a student. Tight-lipped, he said, "I'm sorry, Missus P."

She swallowed down the storm of emotions flooding her. She needed to know everything as if in the knowing she could turn confusion into order. "Who found the body . . . Edmund?"

Franklin nodded toward Jesse. "Poole called it in. About six o'clock this morning."

She gave Franklin a questioning glance and looked past him to the blond officers who still had Poole between them.

Jesse's anxious gaze darted from her to the crowd. Gone was the grieving but confident young man from the previous night. Also gone was the angry sophomore from Thursday morning's fight. The new Jesse looked beaten down, defeated.

"And you arrested him?" *How much is one young man supposed to endure?* Even as she regarded Jesse she tried to ignore an inner voice that whispered, *He could easily have murdered Edmund then called it in. Remember, Edmund stole Jesse's pickup and tried to frame him.*

Franklin helped her to stand. "He's not under arrest. We have to ask him some questions."

An angry shout came from the crowd.

"You need to do something, youngster." Bonnie whispered like she was walking through a graveyard. "These folks seem woefully unaware of the subtle difference between apprehension and questioning. This could get ugly."

"Can you blame them? They need to believe their children are safe. That we, and by that I don't include you, have everything under control."

"They damn well need to know Jesse didn't murder Edmund."

"I can't promise them that. Can you?"

There it was out in the open. And she couldn't condemn Franklin for voicing what she herself half suspected. "If you take him away in custody, it won't be safe for him to return." *Assuming he does return.*

"I'm sorry about that, Missus P, but I've got three homicides to solve. I can't concern myself with niceties. Right now, Griffith and Poole are the most likely places to get some answers."

Again, she stared at Jesse. She had sat with him less than ten hours ago. Without any vehicle, how in hell could the boy have snatched Edmund let alone murdered him?

"Would you have any objection to Jesse coming

home with me after you're done with him?" The words spilled out of her mouth a few steps ahead of the half-baked thought that formed them.

"That's a real bad idea, Missus P."

She couldn't disagree. She found herself worrying what Armen would say. "Jesse comes back here—someone's going to get hurt."

Franklin held her gaze, and she had no trouble reading his thoughts. *He goes home with you, you could get hurt.*

"I'll be okay. Armen will be with me."

Franklin snorted. "That makes all the difference in the world."

He shook his head in resignation. "We both know you're going to do what you want to do, and nothing I say will change your mind."

She wanted to offer something that would convince Franklin she was right, but first she'd have to convince herself. Instead, she searched the crowd for Armen. When she couldn't find him she turned back to Franklin.

"What happens now?"

"I've called for sheriff and trooper backup to maintain the integrity of the crime scene until the CSI boys can release the body. We'll get the locals to pick up Ali Griffith and take her to Jade Hill." He hooked a thumb back toward Jesse. "As soon as I can leave, I'm out of here with Poole."

"Do you mind if I talk to him?"

Franklin gave her an up-from-under glare.

I'll take that for a yes. She hobbled over to Jesse. "You're not under arrest, but Sergeant Valsecci is going to take you in for questioning."

Head down, Jesse blinked back angry tears. "I don't know how Edmund got there." He nodded toward the trailer.

She lifted his chin with a forefinger until his eyes met hers. "Be that as it may, you're going to have to go with him in a few minutes."

She patted her pockets. When she couldn't find what she was looking for, she turned to the woman state trooper. "Emily, isn't it? Do you have paper and pencil?"

The woman looked stunned that Bonnie knew her name. She extracted a small pad of paper from her breast pocket, and the male officer offered a pen.

Bonnie accepted both and wrote her cell phone number onto the paper. "Take this." She ripped free the upper sheet. "When you're done at Jade Hill, call me."

"Missus P, I—"

"No arguments. Just do it."

Jesse nodded.

"Good. Don't forget, and don't lose that number."

ON THE WAY BACK TO ARMEN'S TRAILER, BONNIE informed him of her plan to let Jesse Poole stay at her house. She fully expected Armen to pour forth a number of logical and, as always, reasonable objections. He surprised her by agreeing.

"Jesse certainly can't remain in this park. I wouldn't put it past several members of East Plains' esteemed trailer community to let fly with a preemptive strike." Armen hesitated, pursing his lips. "You're not worried Jesse might actually have killed Edmund?"

Even as her mind formed around a lie, she released it like a balloon in the wind. She wasn't sure when it happened, but she didn't want to lie anymore to this man. "A little, but only a little."

He nodded, saying nothing. Neither of them needed to voice aloud the understanding that he'd be at her house as well. His hand found its way to the small of her back, and they walked together back to Armen's trailer.

She stopped at the door and faced him. "I need to go home, feed my animals, change clothes. A good soak in a hot bath wouldn't be unwelcome either. This boot itches like the dickens."

"Sounds like a plan. Valsecci won't be done with Jesse any time soon." He opened the door and held it wide to let her in.

As she squeezed by him, she kissed him. "You really are one darling of a man."

He pulled her close. "And don't you forget it. Uh oh."

She turned to stare the way he was looking. A curtain in the next-door trailer pulled shut.

Armen chuckled. "I'm afraid I may have compromised your reputation."

Bonnie slapped his chest. "It's your reputation, too."

Armen made a poor effort at appearing contrite. "You

know how it works. A man's reputation only improves if a beautiful woman is seen wearing his pajamas."

She groaned, knowing he was right. The conservative tongues of East Plains would wag, and her name was the one they'd be repeating.

Screw it. She planted another kiss on Armen.

"Give 'em something to talk about." As she passed into the trailer and started gathering the last of her possessions, she found herself smiling.

Beautiful, eh? You're not so bad yourself Mister Callahan.

They were out the door and on their way within ten minutes. Having driven the back roads from East Plains to Black Forest for the past thirty years, Bonnie directed Armen away from the main highways. The shortcut would save ten miles and fifteen minutes. Besides, Alice seemed to like dirt roads.

"I've been thinking," Armen said, once they were rumbling down one particularly isolated red dirt lane.

She squeezed his knee. "Don't hurt yourself."

Eyes wide, he regarded her hand. "Now you've got me thinking about something else entirely."

"Sorry about that." She blushed and removed her hand. "As you were saying, Mister Callahan?"

He chuckled. "As I was about to say, regardless of Edmund's culpability in Stephanie's or Peyton's deaths, we have a whole new ball game now that Edmund has been murdered."

An understatement, to say the least. "Any ideas?"

"A few. First, there's Ralph Newlin. He had means,

opportunity, and possibly motive, to kill all three students."

She arranged herself, particularly her cast, so she could give Armen her full attention. "One of those students was his own son."

Armen waved away the comment. "Forget that for a moment. Take Stephanie. Thursday night, the good colonel bolted from his home long before Stephanie died on Fulton Hill. If he discovered Stephanie knew something about Peyton's disappearance—"

"Oh, my God, Ralph Newlin plays softball! He probably has baseball bats in the trunk of that yellow Stingray."

Armen didn't say anything, but she could tell he'd reached the same conclusion.

"And Peyton?" she asked.

Armen drummed "Shave and a Haircut" on the steering wheel. "Suppose, in terror, Stephanie told Ralph where Peyton was hiding before she died. It's now early Friday morning. Ralph drives to the Sheridan's, slips into the barn from the rear, and finds his son."

"His famous temper gets the better of him."

"Precisely."

"Does Edmund stumble upon this violence and get himself killed?"

"Something like that."

Bonnie tugged at her ear. "Much as I'd like to lay all of this on Ralph Newlin, I have a few problems with your theory."

"I welcome your criticism, Holmes."

"More in the nature of questions, my good Watson. Imagine yourself Ralph Newlin in the Sheridan's barn. You've just murdered two teenagers, one of whom is your son. Why do you take the time to bury one then drive the other to Jesse Poole's two nights later?"

Armen stroked his goatee. "Keep in mind Peyton was the one buried—a final goodbye from father to son. The burial could be seen as an act of remorse. As for why Newlin carried Edmund's body around in his car for two days before depositing it beneath Jesse's trailer, I chalk that up to the workings of a desperate mind."

Bonnie nodded. "Fair enough. Any theory as to how Ali's cobra choker got into Edmund's pocket?"

This question caused Armen a moment of hesitation. "We can still assume the love affair between Ali and Edmund. She gave the necklace to Edmund as a token of her affection, and it was still in Edmund's pocket when he stumbled upon Ralph murdering Peyton." Armen drew in a long breath as if the explanation had exhausted him.

"Very neat." She had to admire Armen's cleverness, if not the theory itself. "It also ties up the loose end of the incriminating e-mail. Do you really buy this theory? Keep in mind Stephanie would have to get in a car with Ralph."

This time he didn't hesitate. "Not so much now that I hear that part spoken aloud, although the Ralph-as-Murderer-Hypothesis might explain why Ralph didn't report to Peterson Air Base Friday morning. If a guy has a corpse in his trunk, he doesn't much want to

256 ROBERT SPILLER

go onto a restricted base where that same trunk might be searched."

"Then why not just dump the body? East Plains has no shortage of isolated locales."

If Armen had an answer to her question, he kept it to himself.

"I don't want to browbeat your hypothesis into a coma, but it also fails to explain how one of Edmund's hairs made its way into Jesse Poole's truck—a truck that tried to run me down—not Thursday when Peyton, Edmund, and Stephanie supposedly died, but Friday night."

Armen bit at his lower lip, pulling his beard into his mouth. "It keeps coming back to Edmund even after his death."

"Seems like it."

"Which still begs the twenty-thousand dollar question."

You got that right. "Who killed Edmund Sheridan?"

BONNIE EXPECTED AND RECEIVED NO WELCOME FROM her brood of animals. Euclid scolded her then displayed his pink and puckered rear end by way of raised tail and indignant departure.

"I have a good excuse," she called after him.

The three dogs glowered when she released them from the laundry room/dog run antechamber. Hypatia, always the spokeswoman for the group, shook her shaggy head in disappointment.

"Give me a break, lady," Bonnie entreated. "I spent the night in a morgue."

The beasts would hear none of it. Bonnie had left them, not just through mealtime, but overnight. The period of shunning would be pronounced.

Bonnie poured copious amounts of dry food in their massive bowls and filled a water bowl the size of a truck tire. "Fine! I can do the silent treatment, too." Her strident words made a lie of her proclamation. Besides, she'd never seen her four pets this angry.

She handed Armen a can of cat food and the opener. "I can't face them a moment longer. Would you feed Euclid? I'm going to soak in a bath."

Armen saluted her with the opener. *"Oui, Mon Capitan."*

Stow it, Callahan.

She was in no mood to be cheered up. She passed through the living room to the guest bedroom, which held the house's only bathtub. A major funk sat heavily on her. She was going to need an especially hot bath to wash it off. The hot full on, she barely turned the cold tap.

As she shed her boot and her clothes, her brain continued the conversation she'd had with Armen. *If not Ralph Newlin, then who?*

She slipped gingerly into the steaming water, scarcely aware of the temperature. *Ali Griffith?*

Certainly, the e-mail Molly Sheridan had shared implicated Ali, but why would Ali have wanted Stephanie dead? Two responses presented themselves.

First, there was the heated argument in Math Analysis. Could Ali have been nursing a grudge and only pretended to have forgiven Stephanie at Knowledge Bowl? If asked that question two days ago, Bonnie would have emphatically answered, "No." That was before the e-mail. Now, she wasn't so sure.

Bonnie turned off the water and slid down until only her head and knees remained above water. The heat felt blessedly good on her mangled foot.

What about the scholarship? Of the four students, Ali Griffith was the only one who actually needed college assistance. Each of the other three—the other dead three—came from well-to-do families. Even without the free ride the Sullivan scholarship afforded, they could attend any school which accepted their application.

Tarot be damned, Rhiannon had seemed awfully sure Ali would win. This business of witchcraft put an entirely new spin on things. Bonnie had always assumed Rhiannon's and Ali's religious affiliation benign. But had she been naïve? Witches, at least in literature and the movies, weren't especially known for their forgiveness or compassion.

Play it out, Bonnie. You would have made Armen do it.

Ali gets a love-besotted Edmund to slay Stephanie. Peyton flips out when he learns of Stephanie's death. Edmund is forced to kill his friend and bury him behind the barn. Edmund is now frantic and perhaps more than a little unbalanced. Using Jesse Poole's truck, he drives to see Ali on Beltane night. For one reason or another, she sends him away, later claiming that Poole was the one driving the truck. Now despondent and angry, Edmund comes upon a stranded math teacher walking through the desert. In his *angst*, he decides to have some fun with her.

Good up to a point. However, it presupposes Edmund overcame his grief, relented on his plan to kill the world's greatest math teacher, and returned the truck. Why? The last was indisputable. After all, the truck was returned.

Then what?

Did Ali decide Edmund was unreliable and do him in to protect herself?

An image of Edmund's body lying beneath Poole's trailer sprang into Bonnie's mind—Samurai written on the sole of the right sneaker.

The writer of the nefarious e-mail had called Edmund Samurai, but Bonnie was certain that wasn't the first time she'd heard the nickname used in conjunction with Edmund Sheridan. Frame by frame she played back the minutes since Thursday morning, and a minor incident, one she would never have considered important, sprang onto center stage.

At Knowledge Bowl, before the competition started, the team had gathered around the tally board. Ali Griffith insulted Edmund, and he said, "You know you love me. Don't hide your true feelings behind this hostile façade."

Ali responded, "In your dreams, Samurai."

Samurai again, and by Ali Griffith. The Law of Parsimony demanded Bonnie connect these incidents together, especially in light of the fact that the e-mail—presumably Ali's e-mail—containing the same nickname would be fired off not three hours later.

Still, doubt nagged at Bonnie. Would Ali be so careless as to make such incredible blunders—first, the incriminating e-mail then a gaff as serious as leaving her cobra choker in Edmund's pocket? Was the girl insane as well as stupid?

Bonnie slapped the water in answer to her own question. *No, Goddamit. Unlike Edmund Sheridan, I know this child, have known her and her family for a decade. Despite circumstantial evidence, Ali Griffith is neither a fool nor a conspirator in a murder. I feel it in the pit of my stomach.*

Someone was trying to not only frame Jesse Poole, but was sizing up Ali Griffith as well.

A knock sounded on the door. "Bonnie, phone call for you."

"If it's not Jesse, tell them I'm indisposed."

"I think you might want to take this."

Why can't men take no for an answer? "Not now, please!" Then realizing she was yelling at the wrong person, she lowered her voice. "Say I'll call them back."

Armen's voice faded as he carried the phone and his conversation away from the bathroom door.

Her new-found conviction of Ali Griffith's innocence animated her. She grabbed a loofah and a bar of soap and scrubbed her knees and elbows until they glowed pink.

Another knock sounded on the door. "Me again."

Well, thank God for that. I wouldn't want a stranger knocking on the door while I'm naked as a plucked chicken. "Did you tell them I'd call back?"

Armen hesitated. "Let me go on record as declaring I told you to take the call then did as you bade me and suggested you would call them back."

Uh oh. "Armen, who was on the line?"

"Rhiannon Griffith and she had a suggestion of her own, mostly anatomical, as to what you could do with your call-back. She's on her way."

CHAPTER 15

RHIANNON GRIFFITH FILLED THE DOORWAY. Bonnie couldn't remember the woman ever looking so formidable. The witch's long red fingernails appeared positively lethal, as if they'd been filed to a point. Her black tresses framed a face dark and angry like a storm getting ready to explode on an unsuspecting mountain town.

And I'm that tiny town.

"Rhiannon, won't you come in?" Although Bonnie tried to maintain her equanimity, her voice shook.

Rhiannon pushed into the living room. Once in, she wheeled on Bonnie, finger pointing directly at her face. "You are one treacherous bitch. Do you know they took my daughter away?"

Bonnie had expected this proclamation since she learned Rhiannon was en-route. Appropriate responses had auditioned across the stage of her brain for the last forty-five minutes without a clear-cut winner. Now that Rhiannon was here in the flesh, they all seemed lame.

"I'm sorry," she offered feebly.

As if she'd never heard the word before, Rhiannon shouted, "Sorry? That doesn't cut it by half, Pinkwater. You made promises to Ali. Promises you broke the first chance you got."

Bonnie felt her anger rise with every accusing word. *No more Missus nice Pinkwater.*

"Horse pucky, Rhiannon. Short of telling lies, I did everything I could to protect Ali. Do you even have the faintest clue concerning the circumstantial evidence stacked against your daughter?"

"I know a snake in the grass when I see one." Menacingly, Rhiannon halved the distance between them.

Bonnie cast about, wondering why none of her animals were coming to her aid. *Oh, yeah, they're torqued at me, too. Well, screw this.* Bonnie swung up a crutch and jabbed it into Rhiannon's ample chest, pushing the woman back.

"Don't do anything stupid, witchy woman."

Rhiannon slapped at the impediment. "The only stupid thing I've ever done is mistake you for a friend."

"Glad to help you clear up that misunderstanding."

"Chamomile tea, anyone?" Armen emerged out of the kitchen holding a rattan serving tray. Perched atop were three cups, a small ceramic tea pot, and the honey jar.

Bonnie knew he'd been up to something in the

kitchen, but had forgotten about him in the anxiety before and the animosity after Rhiannon's arrival.

"Armen?"

If ever there was an inappropriate time for an intrusion, this was it. No way did she want this woman to stay any longer than was necessary.

For her part, Rhiannon just stared at Armen as if he'd asked her was she in the mood for a quick bikini waxing.

Armen stepped between the two women nudging Bonnie's crutch aside. "What say we have a seat and talk before we bring out the weapons of mass destruction? You two can always kill each other later, but the tea won't keep."

Bonnie coldly eyed Rhiannon, expecting the woman to shove past Armen and come after her. Much to her surprise, Rhiannon nodded.

What the hell is going on in that pagan brain of yours?

Her face still a mask of stone, Rhiannon said, "I can tell you what I think of you and drink tea at the same time." Rhiannon backed away from Armen and took a seat on the sofa behind her. She folded her hands in her lap, the knuckles white with the effort.

Somehow the woman's assertion seemed a slam against Bonnie's intelligence, as if the infernal witch was suggesting the simultaneous acts of drinking tea and arguing were somehow beyond Bonnie's capabilities.

"I can stand a cup of tea if she can."

"Well, good, it's a start."

Armen set the tea tray on the coffee table in front of Rhiannon. He returned for Bonnie and led her around the table to the far end of the sofa. Taking her crutches, he helped her sit. He turned a reasonable face toward Rhiannon. "You know, Missus Griffith, it's funny you being angry with Bonnie about your daughter."

From the look on her face, Rhiannon was having trouble finding anything funny about Bonnie, and right now wasn't in the mood to try. "What are you talking about?"

Armen knelt before the tea service and poured three cups of the pale amber tea before he spoke. He slid one to each of the two women. "Just last night she was angry with me because I was arguing for your daughter's guilt in the murder of Stephanie Templeton. Bonnie felt that Ali was far too intelligent and compassionate to do any such thing." He delivered the self-damning remarks in his oh-so-reasonable voice.

Bonnie had to stifle a laugh. *Callahan, you are a pip.*

Rhiannon looked from Armen to Bonnie and back to Armen, appearing, for all the world, like a woman stranded between opposing emotions. No doubt she was reluctant to transfer her anger from Bonnie to Armen, but she bore all the hallmarks of someone dying to learn more about the previous night's conversation. Her mouth hung open in mute testimony to her dilemma.

Armen gestured to the teacup closest to the witch. "Honey?"

Rhiannon ignored the question, turning slowly toward Bonnie. "Is that the truth, Pinkwater, or is this man just trying to save your crippled butt?"

Bonnie slapped the coffee table hard, slopping tea from all three cups. "First of all, Rhiannon, the day I need someone to protect me from you will be a hot day in Siberia, but in answer to your question, no."

"I thought as much."

"I never got mad at Armen." Bonnie knew this was a bad time to be messing with Rhiannon's mind, but she couldn't resist. The pagan maniac had it coming.

A long silence hung in the air. Rhiannon took a deep breath and exhaled it before she spoke. "You know what I mean."

"In that case, yes. I argued that your daughter didn't commit murder or even conspire to commit murder."

Rhiannon looked as if she might let her guard down. Instead, she took a sip from her tea. "Of course not, Stephanie was her friend." Staring hard at Armen, she said the words as though only an idiot would think otherwise.

Armen stirred honey into his tea, the process seemingly demanding every shred of his attention. "Ali's immediate problem isn't the death of Stephanie. There's material and circumstantial evidence linking her to two other deaths."

"What other deaths?" Rhiannon almost dropped her cup in her haste to set it down.

Bonnie peered at the woman, trying to decide if Rhiannon was being straight with her. Edmund she could understand, but how could she not know about Peyton? "You haven't seen the news or read the paper?"

Rhiannon shook her head. "We disconnect the TV during Beltane."

Armen hesitated, chewing his beard and lower lip. "Peyton Newlin and Edmund Sheridan are dead."

Rhiannon's already pale face went incrementally whiter. "My God!"

Bonnie ushered away the random thought which found this exclamation inappropriate for a member of the Wicca persuasion.

"There's more."

She walked Rhiannon through the events of the past twenty-four hours, emphasizing the damning e-mail and the cobra necklace.

Rhiannon fell back into the sofa. She blinked furiously, either keeping tears at bay or in shock. "Ali didn't write any e-mails Thursday night. She was up half the night helping me get the white-petal altar ready and pile wood for the balefire. But—"

"But what?" The question shot out of Bonnie's mouth like it had a life of its own.

Rhiannon shook her head. "Nothing. I was just thinking my baby's in real trouble."

Oh, what a tangled web we weave. Bonnie gave the woman a long look before she spoke. "Rhiannon, you've no reason to trust me, but I promise you, whatever you say here stays here."

"You have my word as well," Armen quickly added.

Rhiannon rocked forward, her elbows resting against her knees. She turned an anxious gaze toward Bonnie. "I've got to be stupid to trust you again." She took a long breath. "Before I tell you anything, you need to know that Ali would never do harm. It goes against everything she believes in."

Bonnie didn't know how to respond to Rhiannon's assertion, so she merely nodded.

Rhiannon transferred her gaze from Bonnie to Armen and back to Bonnie again. After another long pause she returned the nod. "It must've been four-thirty Friday morning . . . I'd been sleeping about an hour when, for some reason, I came fully awake. As I went down the hall, I checked Ali's room. Her bed was empty. I assumed she was just downstairs so I checked the kitchen and the altar room."

When Rhiannon hesitated again, Armen said, "But she wasn't anywhere in the house?"

Rhiannon gave Armen an annoyed glance and shook her head. "Not fifteen minutes later, the front door opened, and Ali came in. She said she was restless about Beltane and had taken a walk out to the balefire pyre. We both went back to bed."

"Naturally, you believed her." Bonnie exhaled, not sure what she believed.

Before Rhiannon could respond, Bonnie's cell phone rang in the kitchen. Armen was up and out of the room before the third ring. When he returned, he held Alice's keys in his hand. "Jesse Poole. It seems the redoubtable Sergeant Valsecci is done with our beamish boy for now."

Rhiannon gave Bonnie a questioning look.

"It's a long story." Bonnie gathered her crutches

and stood. "The short version is that we are picking up Jesse from Colorado Springs and bringing him back here. Why don't you come along?"

△

THE STRETCH OF HIGHWAY FROM BLACK FOREST TO Colorado Springs was getting to seem like an old friend. Bonnie had lost count of how many times she traveled this particular twenty miles in the last two days. She adjusted her walking boot and turned back to Rhiannon in Alice's back seat.

"Rhiannon, forgive me for asking . . . I know you were angry with me, but landing on me with both feet could have waited. Why didn't you go with your daughter to Jade Hill?"

Rhiannon looked out the side window, apparently unable to meet Bonnie's eyes. "Ali asked her Uncle Winston to go with her. He's the lawyer after all. She said I would just get angry and make things worse."

A smile crept onto Bonnie's lips. "Now why would she ever think that?"

A hint of a smile appeared on Rhiannon's face as well. "Beats me, I'm not sure where she gets these odd-ball ideas."

"What happened when the police arrived?" Armen asked without taking his eyes off the road.

Rhiannon tapped her cheek with her long red fingernails. "First of all, they wouldn't answer any of my questions. They just kept saying Officer Valsecci wanted to speak with Ali concerning a murder. I just assumed it was Stephanie's."

Bonnie studied Rhiannon's face wondering how much she could trust the woman. After all, if Ali was guilty, wouldn't Rhiannon lie to protect her daughter? Then again, she'd been forthcoming concerning Ali's disappearance Friday morning.

Armen's right. I'm not much good at this reading people business. You'd think I'd have better people skills after thirty years of teaching. She decided to test the waters by throwing Rhiannon some rope.

"I'm going to need you to resist giving in to your temper and consider the next question carefully. Did anyone besides Ali see Jesse Poole's truck Friday evening?"

Rhiannon's face clouded over. Bonnie could see Rhiannon's indignation rising to the surface as the woman understood the implications of the question. Silence hung heavy in the car. Highway Eighty-Four gave way to Platte Avenue, and they entered Colorado Springs proper.

"Ali was the only one to see the truck." Each word was spoken with measured precision, as if Rhiannon didn't trust her voice or her temper.

Strangely enough, this admission went a long way toward easing Bonnie's mind. A simple lie would have corroborated Ali's story, but Rhiannon didn't fall into that trap.

Just one more question. "Did Ali come home Thursday night still wearing the cobra necklace?"

Rhiannon frowned, looking not so much angry

as disappointed. "I see where you're going with this. Ali wore that damn cobra necklace all Thursday night while we worked on the altar and the balefire. She didn't give Edmund that necklace, Pinkwater. He must have stolen it when he broke into our house."

Bonnie and Armen exchanged glances. She remembered his assertion the break-in was a fiction. He shrugged.

Why would Edmund risk being seen in the stolen truck just to purloin a necklace whose only purpose so far has been to implicate Ali in his very own murder? From the look on Armen's face, he was thinking close to the same thing.

"Forgive me, Missus Griffith, but I need to ask," Armen said. "Was your daughter involved romantically with Edmund Sheridan?"

Rhiannon shook her head vehemently. "Absolutely not! She considered Edmund immature. The boy has had a crush on her since . . .well since forever, but she's never reciprocated. I know my daughter."

Rhiannon's last assertion seemed to beg the question. Bonnie had talked to hundreds, maybe thousands of parents in her career, and whenever she heard one claiming to definitively know their child, just the opposite often proved to be the case.

Tears welled in Rhiannon's eyes.

She's scared to death she maybe doesn't know Ali at all. Bonnie laid a hand on Rhiannon's knee. "I believe you, and what's more I believe Ali told the truth about the break-in."

Rhiannon covered Bonnie's hand with her own. Her dark eyes were full of gratitude. "Just when I think you might be the biggest queen asshole in the known universe, you go and say something like that."

"I'll take that as a compliment." She patted Rhiannon's hand. "You're not such a royal sphincter yourself."

Rhiannon chuckled and wiped her runny nose on her sleeve. "I think part of the reason I got so mad at you is because Ali chose her uncle over me."

"That makes perfect sense. No point getting mad at Warlock Winston when I'm available."

Rhiannon's smile faded. "I've got to tell you. I'm more than a little scared." She gave Bonnie an up-from-under glance.

"I know." Bonnie patted her hand again.

No one spoke as they made their way through Colorado Springs. Eventually, Armen turned Alice onto the street which fronted Jade Hill. The large concrete and pale brick edifice sprawled the entire block and towered four stories above them. "We're here, boys and girls."

$$\triangle$$

A FEMALE OFFICER CRADLED A PHONE ON FRANKLIN'S desk as Bonnie, Armen, and Rhiannon approached. Jesse Poole sat with his back to the trio, but turned at their footfalls. In his left hand he held a glazed donut, in his right a cup of coffee. He stood.

The female officer—her nametag ID'd her as Zettlemoyer—came around the desk. "Are either of you Missus Griffith?"

Rhiannon raised a hand.

"Would you come with me, ma'am?" Zettlemoyer walked off without waiting to see if Rhiannon was in her wake.

Rhiannon followed.

Bonnie leaned her crutches against the desk and plopped into a seat next to Jesse. "You don't look any worse for wear. How are you holding up?"

The boy shrugged a things-could-be-worse shrug. "Those cops, Valsecci and Keene, asked me a lot of questions, mostly about where I was last night. They also wanted to know what time you guys came by. I kept telling them I had no idea how or why Edmund ended up under my trailer. I think they believe me now." He sighed and took a monster bite from the donut.

I'm starting to believe you myself.

Armen pulled up a chair and sat to the other side of Jesse. "Of course they did. You've got one of those believable faces, or maybe it's just the bald head."

Jesse hooked his thumb at Armen. "Is he giving me sh . . . a hard time?"

It was Bonnie's turn to shrug. "I'm not always sure. Are you giving him a shahard time?"

"Absolutely not. Do I look like a shahard time-giver?"

Bonnie waggled her hand. "Around the eyes."

She slapped Jesse's knee. "You ready to go, or will you be having another donut?"

Jesse shoved the last bit into his mouth and licked his fingers. "This was the last one in the box, but we can't go yet. Valsecci wants to talk with you."

He does, does he?

She leaned past Jesse to peer at Armen. "We can spare Franklin a smidgen of our precious time, can't we?"

Armen leaned back in his chair. "I have no desires but to await upon your pleasure."

"I suspected as much."

Smiling, Jesse looked from Armen back to Bonnie. "Are you guys—"

"Don't ask, young man." Bonnie nodded past the desk in the direction Rhiannon had gone. "Did you see Ali Griffith in your travels?"

"I know she's here somewhere. Valsecci told me. I think he wanted to see my reaction."

"And what was your reaction?"

"I was surprised. Ali wouldn't hurt anyone. One of Wicca's first rules is that you never do harm."

There was something in the way Jesse said Ali's name that made Bonnie regard the boy for a long moment. She tried to get a handle on the boy who had fooled her all this time into thinking he was a throwback to a prehistoric ancestor. Evidently, he knew a thing or two about witchcraft.

"Rhiannon tells me she's spotted you once or twice hanging around her place."

"I didn't do anything wrong." Jesse stared down at his shoes, his arms folded tight across his chest.

Not if you don't count trespassing. "No one's saying you did. I'm thinking you could have just told Ali or Rhiannon you were interested in their beliefs."

"Who says I am?"

Why does everything have to be so hard? Another time she might have bandied words with Jesse, perhaps cajoled him into admitting his interest, but right now she was too tired to play games.

"Have it your way."

Bonnie looked up at the sound of approaching footfalls. Appearing decidedly less dapper than he had last night or even this morning, Franklin sat heavily at his desk. His tie was loosened, his collar open. Even the normally perfect thinning red hair was mussed.

"When do you sleep, youngster?"

As if he felt her staring at his hair, he ran a freckled hand through it. "I'll sleep when these cases are in the bag." He peered momentarily at Armen and nodded by way of greeting.

"Officer," Armen shot back.

Good God. I can't go through this testosterone nonsense again. "You wanted to see us?"

Franklin hoisted himself to his feet, fixing his gaze on Jesse. "Jess, I need to speak to these two privately. We won't be long."

Armen mugged at Bonnie as if to say, "Look who's being included."

Bonnie gathered her crutches. "Lead on, Sergeant Valsecci."

She and Armen followed Franklin into a glassed-in office.

Once in, Franklin shut the door behind them. He offered them a pair of seats, but stood himself. A yellow legal pad sat on a gray vinyl desk. Franklin flipped past the first page then extracted a pen from a shirt pocket. "What time did you visit Jesse Poole last night?"

Bonnie glanced at Armen, and he silently replied with a your-guess-is-as-good-as-mine look.

"About eight, make it eight-thirty," she said.

"You don't sound too sure."

She frowned at her former student. "Let's just say before nine."

Franklin wrote on the legal pad. "And what time did you get back to the trailer park after going to the morgue?"

Before she could answer, Armen spoke. "Some time after one in the morning."

Bonnie shot him a questioning look, and he said, "I remember because when I took the casserole out of the fridge I saw the clock on the stove. In fact, now that I think of it, it was exactly one-twelve."

A half smile made a brief appearance on Franklin's face as he wrote again on the pad. "Very precise. Did either of you, by chance, catch a glimpse of Jesse's trailer when you got back?"

Bonnie and Armen both shook their heads. The ramifications of Franklin's question sent a chill up Bonnie's spine. While she was luxuriating in Armen's canopied bed, there was a good chance, not five hundred feet away, someone was cramming Edmund Sheridan's lifeless body into the crawlspace beneath the Poole trailer.

"Do you know what time Edmund died?" she asked.

Franklin blinked, looking like a man who desperately needed a few hours sleep. "Our lab has placed the time of death around eight o'clock Saturday night."

Bonnie gave Armen a quick glance. *So much for the theory Edmund died the same night as Stephanie and Peyton.* She sorted through the hours of the previous evening realizing as Edmund breathed his last she was dancing to Van Morrison.

"Do you have any idea how long Edmund lay beneath Jesse's trailer?"

Franklin shook his head. "Not really. Jesse says he went to bed around midnight. If he's to be believed, then the body was probably hidden after that."

If he's to be believed? "Youngster, you don't really think Jesse killed Edmund then did that incredibly sloppy job of hiding the body . . . under his own trailer, no less?"

Franklin stared at her and shook his head again. "Truth be told, I have my doubts, and not just because of the body's placement."

His eyes went soft as a yawn stretched his face. "When Poole eventually murders someone, he'll probably beat them to death with his bare hands."

Bonnie studied Franklin's face, wondering if he really believed, as she once did, that Jesse was a loose cannon just waiting to explode. "That boy'll surprise you someday, youngster. Do you know he wants to be a fireman?"

"I knew his father was one. I met him a few times at the Service Olympics. Good man."

"Do you know how the father died?" Armen leaned forward.

Franklin fixed Armen with a blank gaze then nodded. "About a year and half ago, around Christmas, remember that big fire at the Salvation Army? A ten-year old girl in a wheel chair was trapped in the building. Todd Poole and another fireman went back in after her. The roof collapsed. All three died."

Bonnie sat quietly wondering, not for the first time, how much grief a young man was supposed to endure. *How would I have turned out if both my parents were taken from me while I was still in high school?* She reaffirmed her decision to move heaven and earth to help the boy.

Armen raised a tentative hand like a child who might or might not want to voice a question.

"You implied you didn't think Jesse killed Edmund because Jesse would have beaten him to death. Are we to assume that Edmund wasn't beaten to death?"

Franklin looked uncomfortable at this new question. "No, Edmund wasn't beaten to death."

He crammed his hands in his pockets and walked to the window, his back to the rest of the room. "Missus P, do you remember remarking on that snarl contorting Edmund Sheridan's face."

The image came clear in Bonnie's mind. "How can I forget?"

"Well, the coroner thought that significant as well, and confirmed what I suspected—poison. Edmund Sheridan ingested a significant amount of arsenic."

CHAPTER 16

BONNIE STRUGGLED FROM THE SUBARU, the stained-glass windows of Geraldine's Café shimmering and beckoning like a long hoped for oasis. *God, I'm so hungry I could eat vegan road kill.*

Winston's white-on-white caddy slipped into an adjacent parking spot. Rhiannon powered down the window and called, "I trust this place ain't as hoity-toity as it looks, Pinkwater." Her smiling face belied the mock hostility in her voice.

"Give it a rest, Mother." Ali Griffith emerged from the Cadillac looking like someone who'd been pulled through a strainer and stretched out to dry. Dark circles outlined the girl's eyes. She let Winston take her arm as she dragged her feet across the parking lot. "Let's just eat lunch in peace."

Rhiannon hurried to catch up with her daughter. "Sure thing, baby."

A moment of regret captured Bonnie's thoughts. *Was it really a good idea to invite the Griffiths to lunch? I definitely don't need this drama.* The timing had seemed so right. Ali had been released from questioning almost to the minute that Franklin finished with Bonnie and Armen. Now Bonnie wasn't so sure. She tried to dispel the negative thought, telling herself it had been a long morning for everyone, especially Ali and Rhiannon. Some good food would set everything to rights.

Armen and Jesse caught up with Bonnie, and Armen laid a hand on the small of her back. Funny how such a small gesture could feel so right. She wished she didn't have to contend with these damn crutches so she could take his hand in hers.

As they approached Geraldine's, the double oak and stained-glass doors swung open toward them. Molly Sheridan in her wheelchair sat squarely in the doorway. Awkward second piled upon awkward second as the girl glared first at Ali then at Bonnie. Rue and Jack Sheridan, Molly's short and solidly built parents, stood behind the chair trapped in the restaurant's foyer.

Ali had often gone toe-to-toe with goat-ropers who made the mistake of criticizing her beliefs, but right now she seemed to shrivel under Molly's hard gaze. "I'm sorry about your brother, Molly."

"I'll bet you are, witch girl, but you're going to be a whole lot sorrier." Molly spit the words out as though they tasted sour in her mouth. She grabbed the rims of her wheels and without a look at anyone else, spun past Bonnie, jumping the curb into the parking lot.

Rue Sheridan, clinging tight to her husband's arm, nodded and followed her daughter.

Bonnie turned to Armen. "Go on in, I'll be along in a second."

"Are you sure about this?"

"You kidding? I haven't been sure about anything since I woke up this morning." She rubbed his arm. "Find us a seat. I won't be long. I promise"

Armen held the door, and one by one Jesse, Ali, and Winston disappeared from view.

As she shuffled past, Rhiannon gave Bonnie a questioning look. "You're wasting your time. There'll be no changing that girl's mind. She's hurting too much right now."

"You're probably right."

Rhiannon just shook her head and patted Bonnie's face. "Knock yourself out, Pinkwater."

I must be some kind of glutton for punishment. She caught up with Rue and Jack as they neared a white Econoline van. Rue tugged on her husband's arm, and they halted.

Rue Sheridan stood a full head shorter than Bonnie, but outweighed her by at least twenty pounds. She and her equally short husband were both almost as wide as they were tall with thick limbs, ruddy faces, and short-cropped gray hair. They even dressed alike in khaki pants and shirts. A decade ago the pair had been horse people, raising and showing Arabians, but Molly's accident had changed all that. Now only a black stallion embroidered on Rue's shirt pocket hinted of that life.

Before Bonnie could offer condolences, Rue held up a silencing hand. "Edmund always spoke very highly of you, said you were the best teacher in East Plains." The woman spoke each word with a measured precision as if she needed to keep a tight rein on her emotions.

The compliment caught Bonnie off-guard. As much as she loved hearing accolades of this kind, the praise felt like a prelude to a larger statement. She didn't have long to wait.

Rue took her arm and pulled her close. "Which is why I don't for a minute believe that Edmund did this . . ." She nodded toward Bonnie's crutches. ". . . thing to you last Friday evening."

Bonnie wasn't sure how to respond. What good would it do to bring up the evidence found in Jesse's truck?

Rue must have taken her silence for agreement because the woman nodded conspiratorially. "We're not stupid people, Missus Pinkwater. We know things weren't right with Edmund . . . hadn't been right for months— the sneaking out to see his girlfriend in the middle of the night, the lying. But I know he was no murderer."

Bonnie tried to give Rue her full attention, but her eyes kept straying to Molly. The girl had rolled her chair alongside the white van. She opened the driver's door. In one fluid motion, with her left arm she pushed herself up and out of the wheelchair, then reaching a surprisingly muscled right toward the inner roof of the cab, she swung out of the chair onto the driver's seat. Twisting as she leapt, she landed facing her wheelchair. She then reached back, hoisted up the chair, and with practiced ease, collapsed it flat. The entire procedure took less than five seconds.

Jack Sheridan hastened to open the side door of the van, but it opened automatically before he reached it.

Molly, with one arm, swung the flattened chair into a recess behind the driver's seat. Jack strapped it into place.

My God, how could I have not noticed the physique on this child? That chair weighs forty pounds if an ounce. Yet, she collapsed and maneuvered it in mid-air as if it were made out of papier-mache'.

Rue must have watched at least part of the scene, because she said, "Molly's quite an athlete. She played basketball this winter and wheelchair softball the summer before."

"She looks like she lifts weights."

Smiling, Rue nodded the proud-mother-nod. "She does, and can bench press her weight."

Molly slammed shut the driver door then, with a whir, the side door slid shut. Moments later the van's engine turned over.

"She drives?" Almost as she said it, Bonnie felt foolish. Handicapped vehicles certainly weren't unknown, even in East Plains.

Rue cocked her head as if Bonnie might be mentally challenged. "Why not? After all, it's her van. We had it outfitted by a firm in Denver. I'm still getting used to her going off on her own."

Bonnie returned her gaze to Rue. "You mean without any assistance?" Again she winced at how much she sounded like someone new to this century. *Oooo, look at the tall buildings.*

"You bet." Rue leaned in conspiratorially. "I shouldn't worry, I know. She's a capable young woman. I couldn't tell you the number of times I've seen her get that wheelchair in and out by herself."

Jack Sheridan gave his wife an are-you-coming look.

"In a minute." She waved him on.

He frowned and with hands jammed in his pockets, stamped around the far side of the van. The passenger door opened then slammed shut.

Rue turned an icy stare back on Bonnie. "I don't care how it looks, Missus Pinkwater, Edmund is innocent. He had no reason to hurt that Templeton girl. As for Peyton, he and Edmund were best friends."

Yet, this best friend saw to it that Peyton got his thirteen-year-old ass kicked by Jesse Poole. Bonnie studied Rue trying to see if the woman actually believed the things she was saying. No doubt, she wanted her grief untainted by accusations of theft and murder. Bonnie wished she could help make that not-unreasonable desire a reality, but try as she might, she didn't see any way to ease the woman's pain.

"When was the last time you saw Edmund?"

"Friday morning. We let him sleep in and miss school after the late night he had Thursday."

Late night?

Not a few bells and sirens went off in Bonnie's brain. She'd dropped him off at the high school before ten o'clock. He should have been home easily by ten-thirty—not all that late for a teenager.

"What time did he get home?"

Rue must have caught the agitation in Bonnie's voice. Like an aged Mister Spock in drag, she elevated her right eyebrow. "I can't say really. Jack and I went to bed around midnight, but we knew Edmund would be late. He used your cell phone to call us from that church."

Bonnie could feel her heart beating faster in her chest. Thursday evening, Edmund had told her he hadn't been able to get hold of his parents. He'd used that argument to remain at the Interfaith Academy and cobble a ride home from her. *Why are you so surprised? You knew Peyton spent Thursday night in the Sheridan's barn. Did you think the boy genius grew wings and flew there?*

"Did Edmund tell you he hid Peyton in your barn?"

Rue hesitated then shook her head. "I didn't even know Peyton had been missing until the police found his body."

Another hesitation followed, so long in fact that Bonnie was readying another question when Rue added, "But I'm not surprised that Edmund would hide his friend from that awful man."

"You mean Colonel Newlin?"

Before Rue could answer, the white van reversed

and pulled up next to Rue and Bonnie.

Both women had to step out of the way.

With an elbow out the window, Molly frowned at Rue. "Mother, I'm tired, and I want to go home."

The statement was followed by a cold scowl aimed at Bonnie as if somehow she was keeping her mother prisoner.

Rue didn't respond to the complaint or even look at her daughter. "In answer to your question, Missus Pinkwater, yes, I definitely mean Colonel Ralph Newlin. That man is a monster. I pitied his poor wife and son. I worried for Edmund every time he went to that house."

Bonnie peered at Molly. *How much of what you know have you shared with your mother?* "Had he been doing much of that of late?"

"Going to the Newlin house? Quite a bit, actually, why do you ask?"

"Do you want to tell her or should I?" Bonnie laid a hand on Molly's arm.

The girl yanked her arm out of reach. "I knew I should never have talked to you. This is none of your business."

Rue stared first at Bonnie then Molly. "Does this have to do with the e-mails Sergeant Valsecci asked about?"

Bonnie folded her arms across her chest. "Molly?"

The girl exhaled in exasperation. "I told you a dozen times, Mother, it's that Griffith bitch. She's the one Edmund had been sneaking out to see." Molly glared an I-hope-you're-satisfied-glare at Bonnie.

As for Rue, her already ruddy face turned two

shades darker. Like a shot, she slapped her daughter. "I won't have you using language like that."

Rue approached the driver's window as if she meant to pull her daughter through it. "And I told you time and again, I don't believe Edmund was seeing Ali Griffith."

Rue slammed a callused hand against the van door. "The same thing I told the police."

Oh my, now this is getting interesting. "If you don't mind my asking, why don't you believe your son was involved with Ali Griffith?"

"Because he told me he wasn't, when I asked."

That's a tough one to refute.

Still rubbing her now-flushed face, Molly snorted and pointed an accusing finger at Bonnie. "But you know it's true, and now you're breaking bread with the . . ."

Rue shot her daughter a threatening glance.

"Witch!" Molly's voice broke and her features contorted. Folding her arms across the steering wheel, she buried her face in them. Her body shook with her sobs.

A pang of guilt swept over Bonnie. *I should leave this grieving family in peace.* She stood mute for a moment then approached the van. This time when she laid a hand on the girl, she didn't pull away. "You're wrong, Molly. I don't think Ali was seeing your brother. And I don't think she murdered him."

"Liar," Molly said, but her accusation carried no conviction as if the girl had lost the energy to argue.

"I'm not lying, Molly. Ali has been busy all weekend with a witch's celebration called Beltane. She simply hasn't had the time." Bonnie ignored the voice in her head that spoke of the missing time early Friday morning. After all, Edmund died Saturday night.

Molly sniffled and raised her head. Her eyes were no longer accusing. "What about the e-mails? What about Your Wicked Little Witch?"

Bonnie shrugged. "I haven't worked all that out yet, but my gut tells me there's another explanation for that *Nom De Plume*."

She rubbed a soothing hand across the girl's back. "The police will catch your brother's killer, Molly. I promise."

How in hell am I going to keep that vow?

BONNIE PLOPPED DOWN INTO THE CHAIR AS SOON AS Armen slid it out. "*Merci,* Mister Callahan."

The rest of the troop sat arrayed around a large circular table. On her left sat Winston then Rhiannon. Ali was directly across. To Bonnie's right, Armen resumed his seat. Jesse completed the scene, looking more than a little nervous next to Ali.

Bonnie shook out her napkin. "Did you all order?"

She offered a convivial smile and noticed the tight faces on her companions, particularly Rhiannon and Ali. Red blotches mottled the girl's cheeks.

Wonderful. Someone's pissed, and I think I know

at whom.

For a long moment no one spoke. Ali and Rhiannon exchanged glances, both apparently uncomfortable.

"That girl thinks I murdered her brother?" Although Ali asked it as a question, the words carried the finality of a statement.

Bonnie held Ali's gaze with hers. She saw no point in lying to the girl. "I believe so."

Lips pursed, Ali nodded a resigned nod. "She thinks I'm this Wicked Little Witch?"

Bonnie matched her nod, waiting for the inevitable question. Still, neither she nor the girl relinquished eye contact.

"How about you? Is that what you think?" Although barely above a whisper, Ali's voice was hard, just shy of accusatory.

Bonnie had to admire the girl's forthrightness.

Let's get right to it. "I don't buy it, but I couldn't tell you why. Truth be told, my dear, if I didn't know you, I'd think you were as guilty as sin."

Ali held Bonnie's gaze for a moment longer then looked down at her lap. "Thanks for being honest. I know me, too, and I think I look guilty." She blinked furiously, her lower lip trembling.

Rhiannon put an arm around her daughter. "Everything's going to be fine, baby."

Ali shook her head. "No, it's not, Mother. Three of my friends have been killed, including my best friend. This is East Plains, remember? By tomorrow morning everyone will be talking about how I did it."

A great tear spilled out of her eye and rolled down her cheek. "My friends are dead and all I can think about is how it makes me look."

Bonnie wanted to tell her to stop beating herself up, but didn't trust herself not to sound like a teacher on a scold.

"Not everyone thinks you did it." Jesse's voice seemed to emerge disembodied from the ether. All heads turned in his direction.

"The people in my trailer park have got me pegged for Edmund."

Momentarily, Ali regarded Jesse like an unwelcome intruder, and then her stony face softened. "At least you won't have them thinking you're already evil because you're a witch."

"Nope." Jesse rubbed a paw across his bald dome. "They just think I'm a skinhead hood."

A well-aren't-you? look made a brief appearance on Ali's face, and then fled leaving behind a mix of curiosity and sympathy.

"You kind of do look the part." Ali offered a not unkind half-smile.

Jesse reddened, clearly pleased at any show of affection from Ali. "You ain't exactly hiding who you are either."

Bonnie wondered if these two children might be good for one another. *Get a grip, Pinkwater. This isn't the Dating Game. Either one of them could be a cold-blooded killer.*

Ali regarded Jesse for a long moment. "Why

should I?"

The boy held up both his hands and pulled back. "No one's saying you should."

She gave him one more glance before turning back to Bonnie. "Mother told you about me going out to the balefire pyre Thursday night."

And now we get to it. "Yes, she did."

"So you're thinking, maybe the little witch drove over to Edmund's. Maybe she snatched him up and throttled him with her broom."

Bonnie and Armen exchanged glances. *Did Franklin inform Ali how Edmund died?* Bonnie didn't think so. "Young lady, you're either innocent or trickier than you look."

Rhiannon gave Bonnie a quizzical look. "That's a left-handed compliment, Pinkwater. Sounds as if Ali has to be either stupid or guilty."

Bonnie was saved from having to respond by the sudden appearance of a thin-as-a-rail waitress. Like all the employees at Geraldine's, the young woman had the raw-boned look of someone training for a marathon. For the next few minutes, while everyone ordered, Bonnie gathered her thoughts.

As soon as the waitress left, Bonnie said, "I think it's time we all laid our cards on the table, so to speak."

She turned to Jesse. "You implied Edmund was the one who put you wise to Peyton's insults Thursday morning."

Jesse reddened. "That's right."

Ali was shaking her head. She looked suspiciously

at Jesse. "This is about the fight? I can't believe Edmund would do that. He and Peyton were friends."

From the expression on Jesse's face, Ali may as well have driven her fork into his sternum. The boy knotted his napkin in a meaty fist.

"I'm not lying," he whispered hoarsely.

Ali inhaled deeply then let it loose. Her features softened as she regarded Jesse. "You're not, are you?"

She inched a hand toward Jesse's but stopped just short. "Why would Edmund do such a thing?"

"Why, indeed?" Bonnie laced her fingers beneath her chin. "I think, at the very least, we can all agree there was more to Edmund than we knew."

Ali nodded. "He stole my necklace."

Jolted by Ali's statement, Bonnie's mind raced to retrieve a recent memory. "Do you recall the exchange you had with Edmund at the Academy, when you called him Samurai?"

Pursing her lips, Ali was silent for a moment then her eyes went wide. "He teased me about something."

"He said you were hiding your true feelings, that you really loved him."

Rhiannon looked up sharply.

"Relax, Mother." Ali returned her attention to Bonnie. "Edmund was always saying things like that. I remember. I came back with, 'In your dreams, Samurai'."

"Did you call him that often?"

"Samurai? Sure, all the time. He'd call me witch girl."

The same thing Molly called you. "This is important. Do you know if anyone else called him by that nickname?"

Ali shrugged. "Not that I know of. Why is that important?"

"Because that's the pet name Wicked Little Witch used in the e-mail."

Ali's hand came to her lips. "I didn't write Edmund any e-mail on Thursday evening."

Bonnie wished she could reach across the wide table and grasp the girl's hands in hers. "But someone did. Someone who either called him by that name, or knew that you did."

"They're trying to make my baby look guilty." Rhiannon almost growled out the words.

Bonnie ignored Rhiannon. "Did you know Edmund had Samurai printed across the bottom of his sneakers?" she asked Ali.

"His new white Sketchers? It wasn't there Thursday night."

"How can you be so sure?"

Ali jabbed a fingertip down at the table. "I saw the bottoms of both his shoes when we were sitting on the van's bumper. Edmund is . . . was always . . . crossing and uncrossing his legs. Besides, he wouldn't write Samurai on his shoes. That's a Junior High thing to do." She wrinkled her nose.

Bonnie considered the statement. "Then there are only three possibilities." She held up her index finger. "One, you're mistaken about what you saw."

"I'm not."

Bonnie waved away the denial and lifted a second finger. "Two, Edmund wrote the word on his shoe in the interim between Thursday night and Saturday." Although she didn't say it, "the night of his murder" hung heavy in the air.

"Keep in mind that Edmund has been acting out of character lately, even his mother thinks so. There's that whole business of breaking into your house and stealing your necklace. Would you a week ago have suspected him of doing such a thing?"

Ali shook her head.

"Neither would I, but all the evidence points to his doing precisely just that." Bonnie ticked off a third finger. "Then there's only one possibility remaining."

"Someone else wrote the word on the shoe," Rhiannon offered.

Bonnie slowly nodded. "If they did, and Ali is correct about what she saw, then they wrote it between Thursday and Saturday. And since Samurai shows up in the e-mail it seems likely the person who wrote the e-mail also wrote on the shoe."

"The Wicked Little Witch," Ali said.

"A very Wicked Witch, I would imagine."

CHAPTER 17

W<small>ITH A GRUNT</small>, B<small>ONNIE SHOVED OPEN HER</small> front door. "I'm going to nail my feet to the carpet and not budge from this house until morning."

Staring up like an ebony Egyptian god, Euclid sat motionless as Bonnie, Armen, and Jesse filed past him. The cat growled and sniffed suspiciously at Jesse.

Jesse reached out a hand, and Euclid pulled away. "I don't think your kitty likes me."

Bonnie frowned at the small Burmese. "Most days, I'm not sure if he likes me."

Arching his back, the cat permitted her to stroke him once before he sauntered off. For the second time that day he presented all assembled with a view of a raised tail and a puckered rear end.

"I've got to get a cat that doesn't do that." Bonnie

pointed with her chin toward the back of the house. "Come with me, youngster."

Leading him right, away from the kitchen and toward the back hall, Bonnie could hear the trio of dogs whining to be let in.

"In a minute, ladies," she shouted.

Instead of turning left to the laundry room/dog kennel, she turned right again, advancing on the two guest bedrooms adjacent to her garage. The first, where Armen had slept, looked as neat as if maid service had straightened the room. *I think I'm in love. Callahan, your mother should be alive and give lessons on how to train a son.*

Using her crutch, Bonnie pushed open the second door. A compact little room with a twin bed and a student desk came into view. Posters of Michael Jordan and Scotty Pippin adorned two of the walls.

"I'm assuming since you've been on your own for the past month, you can make a bed."

"I can make a bed."

"Good. Because, between the two of us, you're in better shape for housework." She nodded for him to slide open the closet door. "Grab a set of sheets and do the manly thing. There's also a comforter at the back of the closet."

She stepped out of the way. "Well, I'll leave you to it."

As he reached up to retrieve the sheets, he whispered, almost too faint to be heard, "Thank you, Missus Pinkwater."

Something in the way he spoke told Bonnie he'd had precious little to be thankful for in the past few months.

"You're welcome, Jesse."

She studied the bald head and wide shoulders of the teenage enigma, thinking just how much their relationship had changed since Thursday morning.

Hell, four days ago, I was sure he meant to punch my lights out.

When he turned around, he caught her staring. Their eyes locked for a long moment. "I'm not complaining or anything, but how long you think I'll be staying here?"

She shrugged, trying to make light of the question. "A couple of days, until things settle down."

Truth be told, it could be a lot longer. If the killer struck again, and suspicion fell on Jesse, it might be a considerable time before he would be safe going back to his trailer.

Jesse nodded, and Bonnie saw understanding written in his rugged face.

He dropped the sheets on the small bed. "Then I have another favor to ask you."

"Fire away."

He drew a deep breath and released a sigh that went on for a week and a half. "It's my mom."

Of course, you've got a funeral to plan. "Do you want some help with the arrangements?" She cringed, thinking of Ben's funeral just eighteen months previous. That day seemed a lifetime ago.

Jesse shook his head. "I got most of it worked out, the service and all. Mama wanted to be cremated. The funeral home was going to pick up . . ." He swallowed, wiping a beefy hand across one eye. ". . . her body today. Except now, with my truck impounded, I got no wheels to get to the funeral."

Bonnie leaned heavily on her crutches. She remembered her own mother's death. There'd been a ton of decisions to make, and she had Ben to help her make them. This boy was alone in the world.

"Would it be all right if I went to the funeral with you?"

Jesse's blinked back tears. "You don't really need to go. You could just drop me off."

"Don't be silly, Jesse. I would be honored to attend your mother's funeral. I wish fate had permitted me to know her. I'm sure she was a great lady."

Jesse sniffed, a shy smile brightening his face. "You should have seen her before she got sick, before my dad died. The two of them were terrific together, always laughing, getting me to laugh."

But I never knew them, or you then. The Jesse Poole I came to know was the bald-headed Neanderthal who whupped up on thirteen-year olds. She dispelled the errant thought, allocating it to that sector of her brain she'd lately come to call the I-don't-know-shit-about-Jesse-Poole-region.

"You've had a rough time of it this last year."

Jesse shrugged an I'm-no-different-from-anybody-else shrug. "Mom was already real sick when Dad died, and me, I didn't help things. I went a little nuts, drugging, and getting in stupid trouble, fights at school, you name it."

He rubbed his bald pate, like his scalp was a sort of an exclamation point on the choices he had made. "Changed the way I look about then."

She sat down heavily on the bed and indicated for him to do the same. "I didn't want to say anything, but I was wondering what makes a guy with hair shave his head."

Jesse sat down heavily atop of the pile of sheets then hunched forward, his elbows resting on his knees. He turned and offered her a shy smile. "You don't like it?"

"I didn't say that, but I'm thinking your mother must not have liked it much."

"Not much." He licked his fingertips like he was planning to deal out a hand of cards. "We made a bargain. I got to keep the shaved head, but I had to quit the other stuff."

"And did you?"

Jesse nodded slowly. The folds of his face bunched into the palm of his hand. "Gave up drugging, drinking. Hadn't been in a fight since Christmas."

"Yet, you always seemed so angry in the halls, like you were getting ready for a fight, getting ready to punch someone."

Jesse broke eye contact with her, staring down at the floor. "I was mostly pissed off at the kind of folks you hung out with . . . that Newlin and that Stephanie Templeton chick." He reddened, obviously aware he was speaking ill of the dead.

He sat up, his face hard as if he needed to say more or explode. "You know what made me mad the most?"

She shook her head and kept silent, knowing she wasn't really being asked for an answer.

"They'd walk right by me like they didn't see me at all, like I wasn't really there."

"Peyton and Stephanie?" She asked the question and held her breath, dreading what he might say next.

"Not just them," he whispered.

I was guilty as any of them. A long quiet moment passed, Bonnie remembering last Thursday evening. She'd reveled in the company of her Knowledge Bowl team, enjoying their wit and their intelligence. Had she subconsciously, or maybe not so subconsciously, discounted children like Jesse as not worth her time, not worth knowing?

"I'm sorry, Jesse."

His eyes wide, Jesse waved away the apology. "No, no, you don't understand. You got nothin' to be sorry about. You came and got me at the cop shop. Look at me here in your house, sittin' on your bed."

He bounced ever so slightly, as if acknowledging it was now his bed if only for a little while. "It's like I was angry all that time, so we never got to know one another. Maybe I didn't need to be mad at Stephanie either."

"And Peyton?"

"Peyton Newlin was a little piss ant." He reddened again. "Every beating I gave that creep, he deserved."

She locked eyes with Jesse. "Maybe not the last

one. There's a good chance Peyton never said the things Edmund accused him of."

Jesse waved his hands beside his head, the same gesture he'd used Thursday morning, as if clearing the air of a swarm of bees. "Isn't that just a screwy bunch of crap? Why would Edmund do that?"

"I keep asking myself the same thing. Supposedly, they were best friends." She let her voice trail off, a far away thought trying to leapfrog into her consciousness. *God damn it, they were best friends. I'm not wrong about that. I may not be able to read Armen, but I damn well knew my students.* Another more distant, more nebulous memory tried to elbow its way to the forefront. It seemed nestled in that library that Edmund had called his bedroom.

Jesse's insistent voice sent both thoughts packing. "Missus Pinkwater?"

She realized he'd been talking to her for the better part of a minute. "Sorry, I went visiting another time zone. What were you saying?"

"You can't drive." He pointed to her walking boot. "You think Mister Callahan will want to go to Mom's funeral?"

"We'll have to ask him. What about Ali Griffith?"

Jesse shook his head. "She's already got too many funerals to go to. Besides, she didn't even know my mom."

You're right about that crop of funerals. My God, Stephanie, Peyton, and now Edmund. My beautiful, beautiful children. She shook off the melancholia which threatened to drag her down.

"But now Ali knows you. Jesse, we don't go to funerals for the sake of the deceased. We go to comfort the living."

Again he shook his bald head, even more insistently this time. "Please, Missus Pinkwater, I just want to say goodbye to my mama. I don't care how many people come."

"Just for my own curiosity, how many do you expect?"

He shrugged, looked embarrassed and raised three fingers. "If Mister Callahan comes." His face and eyes went hard. "Like I said, I don't care."

Me thinks you protest too much. She remembered the antagonism of the crowd at the East Plains trailer park, and the way painter-man and the others had already made up their minds about Jesse's guilt. *Surely, some of those people had been friends of the Pooles.* Anger and frustration welled in her. Collateral damage from these murders was beginning to spread.

As if he read her mind, Jesse said, "Rough times, huh?"

"You can say that again."

A smile crept onto Jesse's face. "Rough times, huh?"

Bonnie stared at him then mirrored his smile with one of her own. *Who knew you had a sense of humor, you bald-headed joker.* "You just keep surprising me, Jesse Poole."

"That's not too hard. Up until a day ago, you didn't know me from Davy Crockett."

On impulse, she extended a hand in his direction. "Bonnie Pinkwater."

He regarded the hand then engulfed it in his larger one. "Jesse Poole, nice to know ya."

"Same here."

$$\triangle$$

TRADITIONALLY, MONDAY MORNINGS HAD NEVER been easy for Bonnie. If she did a statistical analysis, she'd more than likely find she'd been late for class on Monday more than any other day. However, this particular Monday she'd had good reason to get to school early. She had to present Jesse Poole to Principal Lloyd Whittaker for summary justice. She came out on the side of the boy, testifying she thought righteousness would be better served if leniency were the order of the day. And that was how she'd left it. There'd be no telling what Lloyd would do, but she could hope her long time friend might listen to his better, his kinder angels.

She whistled as she hurried down the long hallway to her class with ten minutes to spare.

Freddy Davenport poked his head out of his office. "Bon, do you have a minute?"

As per usual, the room was in disarray with candy wrappers filling the trash cans and spilling out onto the floor. Also typical, the man had the stick of a lollipop protruding from his mouth. Freddy plopped down at his lunch table/desk, a number of manila folders strewn across it surface.

Freddy licked his thick lips. "I have a quandary."

He collected the top three folders and swung around in his desk chair to face her. His eyes looked haunted.

Stephanie Templeton's name was printed on the top folder. It was no great leap of logic for Bonnie to deduce the names on the other two.

Freddy's hands shook as he clutched the three folders. He offered a rueful half-smile. "I haven't informed J. T. Sullivan of the circumstances complicating the outcome of his scholarship. Truth is, Bon, I don't know how all this will play out. A part of me wants to throw up my hands and hope somebody else will sort it all out."

She could see his problem. Not only were three of the remaining candidates for the scholarship dead, the sole finalist still drawing breath had a good chance of being arrested for their murders.

"What are you going to do?"

Without even seeming to notice he was doing it, he handed her the three folders then scooped up the rest. "I'm going back over the original thirteen, now ten of course. Before I call J. T., I want to tell him we at least have candidates for his *largesse*."

Bonnie gave Freddy a cursory nod. Her attention was drawn to the folders that lay in her hands. She gave a quick peek at Stephanie's then Edmund's. For reasons she couldn't have explained, she ruffled through Peyton Newlin's pages with more scrutiny, as if she expected answers to the recent tragedies to reveal themselves in the official documents and printed records. Bonnie also half expected Freddy to snatch the folders away claiming confidentiality was being compromised. When he didn't, she surmised confidentiality might be a moot point at this juncture of events.

She noted that Peyton would have been fourteen in a few days.

I think I knew that.

The young genius's grades, also enclosed, were certainly no surprise. He'd garnered nothing but A's in all four of the schools he'd attended. He'd skipped second, fifth, and sixth grades shooting from fourth into seventh at a Kennedy Junior High in Norfolk, Virginia.

As she read through this stark biography, a deep melancholy came to rest on her. Was there anything in this bare-bones outline which would help her remember the essence of the troubled child, or the even more troubled family that brought him into the world? If there was, she didn't see it. She shut the folder and handed it and the other two back to Freddy.

He took them without comment.

As Bonnie exited his office, they grunted their farewells. She turned the corner leading to her room. Carlita Sanchez, her books clutched to her breast, strode in from the gym hallway. They met at the door.

"Good morning, Missus P." The girl sing-sang the words, smiling like the proverbial canary-eating cat.

Bonnie had a sinking feeling what was coming. "Good morning to you, too, Carlita."

"Hanging with Mister Callahan is doing you good. You're five minutes early." She tapped her imaginary watch. Her sly smile widened.

Bonnie didn't need to ask how her weekend with Armen had become common knowledge, or at least Carlita Sanchez knowledge. Bonnie had worked in East Plains long enough to know that nothing remained a secret for long. By noon there would be alumni from ten years back who would know she spent the night at Armen's.

"Put a sock in it, Carlita."

"Whatever you say, Missus P." Carlita held the door so Bonnie could maneuver through on her crutches.

Bonnie had more on her mind than small town gossip. In the early meeting, Lloyd told her he'd considered closing school for a day or two, but the Divine Pain in the Ass made the executive decision that life must go on even if, for some, it had ended abruptly. For once Bonnie agreed with Mr. Potato Head. A day or even a week wouldn't put a dent in the horror this community had experienced. The students might as well be here at school where they could at least commiserate with their friends.

Bonnie hobbled to her desk and draped her fanny pack on the chair. "Get out Friday's homework."

Several students groaned, including Salvador, who normally was a hard worker. A quick scan of the room made it clear a significant fraction of her students was missing. Ali Griffith was in that number. *I suppose that's to be expected.*

"And do we have an alternate suggestion to the perusal of Friday's homework?"

Rebecca Weber, a slim black girl with a penchant for goofing off, raised her hand. "How about The Witch of Agnesi story?"

Bonnie's initial reaction was to perversely deny the request because acquiescing would mean relinquishing control. The random thought struck her as petty and mean-spirited. Her saner self prevailed. *You're going to have to re-teach today's lesson no matter what. There's just too damn many of them gone.* Besides, hadn't Bonnie herself asked for an alternative suggestion? A psychiatrist would probably point out she had been looking for an out.

Truth was she really hadn't the heart or the energy to push the children through the next unit. "All right, Rebecca, here comes the story of The Witch of Agnesi right smack at your face. But first, in order to understand how The Witch of Agnesi curve got its name, you need to know a little about an extraordinary woman Mathematician. Maria Gaetana Agnesi was born in 1718 in Milan, Italy. A child prodigy, she could speak fluent French by the age of five and had mastered Latin, Hebrew, and Greek along with several modern languages by the time she'd reached nine."

Salvador, who could speak three languages, raised his hand. "Missus Pinkwater, I thought women weren't educated at that time."

Sally, you have a great career ahead of you as a straight man. "Right you are, Salvador, but Maria was an exception for two reasons. First of all, sections of Italy, particularly Bologna, were emerging as intellectual centers where traditional ideas about women were being challenged. More importantly, her father was the Professor of Mathematics at the University of Bologna, and unlike many scholars of his time, believed women, especially his daughter, the intellectual equals of men."

Her foot and the palms of her hands made protestations concerning her damned crutches. "Salvador, bring me my desk chair, please."

The boy rolled the chair from the back of the room. She handed him the crutches and sat. "Thank you, my fine young gentleman."

He made an exaggerated bow and returned to his seat.

She settled into the chair, mentally restringing the threads of her tale. "So precocious was Maria, her father insisted she hostess and participate in round-table discussions with some of the great minds of Enlightenment Italy. Even though Maria was shy by nature, she held her own with these heavyweights."

Bonnie nodded to Rebecca. "Keep in mind, while all of this was happening, Maria Agnesi was younger than you are right now. For the next decade and a half this would be the reality in which Maria Agnesi resided."

Bonnie paused for dramatic effect and noted with satisfaction that several students actually leaned forward.

Gotcha.

"By thirty, Maria had published one of the most important mathematical treatises of her day, Analytical

Institutions, a two-volume work on Integral and Differential Calculus and Real Analysis."

Bonnie put her hands together and slowly spread them apart. When the space had grown to about ten inches, she said, "We're talking huge math books here. Be grateful you don't have to carry those monsters around in your backpacks."

A few students laughed, albeit weakly.

What the hell. At least some of them think you're witty. "The book ranged over much of the mathematical topics of the day, but for the most part the hundreds of pages have been forgotten. What is remembered is a tiny section on parametrically defined curves."

"The Witch of Agnesi," Salvador said.

Right on time, Salvador. Bonnie nodded. "The Witch of Agnesi." She signaled for him to help her stand and hand her the crutches. Once at the blackboard, she wrote the Cartesian equation

$$XY^2 = a^2(a - X).$$

Bonnie underlined the equation. "Maria wasn't the first person to study this curve and its parametric relatives. A century before, the famous French Mathematician Pierre de Fermat, in his posthumously published treatise, *Isogoge ad Locus Planos et Solidos*, had given the curve the Italian name *versiera*, which simply means a curve that turns."

She swung round to face the class. "And here's where the story takes an excursion into the bizarre."

She rubbed her hands together and retook her seat.

"Maria used the same name that Fermat had used, *versiera*, when she spoke of the curve in her Analytic Institutions. She embellished and extended Fermat's ideas, making large portions of the Mathematics her own."

Again, Bonnie paused, relishing the hold she now had on the children. When she thought she'd tortured them long enough, she went on. "Now the scene shifts some fifty years hence. Maria Agnesi is dead. John Colson, a British Mathematician and linguist at Cambridge University, decides to translate Analytic Institutions into English."

Bonnie wrote the word *versiera* on the blackboard and underlined it. "He did an admirable job except for this one word."

Next to *versiera* she wrote *aversiera* and underlined the new word as well. "He mistook *versiera* for this almost identical cousin . . . with disastrous results. For, you see, this second word, although it differs from the first by only one letter, has an entirely different meaning. The word *aversiera* means bride of the devil."

"A witch," Rebecca said.

Bonnie nodded with satisfaction. "You betcha. And Maria, being dead, isn't around to correct the mistake. Thus, this innocent turning curve is dubbed . . ." She spread wide her hands, inviting her class to finish the sentence.

Almost to a child, they called out, "The Witch of Agnesi."

"The infamous Witch of Agnesi. Over the years, this appellation has become so intertwined with Maria Agnesi herself that many later thought Maria was a witch who named the curve because of some perversity in her nature. That was the unkindest cut of all."

Bonnie let her last statement hang in the air, hoping for a response.

Moments later Salvador raised his hand. "Why?"

Bless you, dear boy.

"Because Maria's fondest wish, one which her scholarly father denied her, was to become a nun. As it was, she spent a goodly portion of her life in the service of Bologna's poor and sick. Maria would have been appalled to learn her curve had been so named."

In no mood to redirect the energy back to classwork, Bonnie spent the remaining time answering questions about Maria Agnesi and Colson's unfortunate translation of her work. When the bell finally rang, she rationalized the wasted time by telling herself the story would help her students remember the curve and how to graph it.

When the last student exited the room, she realized that another day had passed where she failed to give homework.

And so it goes.

She forgave herself the lapse. Fortunately, Friday's homework was still on tap to go over Tuesday morning. Besides, the entire business of homework and parametric curves seemed to pale in comparison to the tragedies of the past few days. She knew this attitude, so unlike her, would pass, but it also served to point out just one more bit of collateral damage the murders had thrust upon her world.

A selfish way to think of it, but what the hell, I suppose most of us believe the world revolves around ourselves. Irrationally, she cast the blame for her wasted Math Analysis Class on Edmund's Wicked Little Witch.

It was with this mind set, eraser in hand, she turned back to her blackboard and prepared to expunge both *versiera* and *aversiera* in one broad stroke. Her hand froze just inches from its target. Bonnie studied the pair of words, and a grin spread across her face.

"Of course." She chuckled. "I know you now, my Wicked Little Witch."

CHAPTER
18

ARMEN SHOT BONNIE AN UNEASY GLANCE. "All right, here we are, my Robin to your Batman. Now I want that explanation. I don't even know where we're going. And I hope to God you're right about someone covering my class." He slowed Alice for the stop sign at East Plains and Belleview.

Bonnie waved an impatient hand urging him to turn left. "Stop worrying and convince this ancient jalopy to give us just a little more speed." She bit back a sudden urge to tell him to turn around and head back to school. In the classroom her reasoning seemed flawless; now she wasn't so sure.

Armen must have seen the look of uncertainty on her face. "Bonnie?"

No, dammit. I'm right.

"All right, hang on. First of all, the key to unlocking

this string of murders resides in the person of the Wicked Little Witch. If she didn't actually commit murder, she certainly urged Edmund to do his worst."

"You'll get no argument from me there. I just don't see—"

Splaying her fingers, she cut him off. "Bear with me, Mister Mouse. Our problem all along was that we couldn't see the forest for the witches. We're lousy with them—Ali, Rhiannon, not to mention Winston and the rest of the Beltane bunch. You couldn't swing a black cat for the past couple of days and not smack a witch upside the head." She hesitated, hoping Armen would at least acknowledge her witticism with a grunt.

A smile played at the corner of his mouth, but he extinguished it. "I'm listening."

"The waters got further muddied when this Wicked Little Witch started electronically penning missives to Edmund urging him to hang tough and promising him the moon." Feeling she was on a roll, Bonnie hurried on before Armen could interrupt. "I went round and round trying to dope out who this female Iago might be."

She held up the thumb of her left hand. "Of course, Ali came to mind, but I just didn't buy it."

"What about the missing time Thursday night?"

"Ali did what she claimed. She didn't have time for anything else. She walked out to the bale pyre, maybe stood looking at the night sky, then came back to the house." Bonnie laid a hand on Armen's knee. "It's too damn far, Armen! Ali wasn't gone long enough to trek to either Fulton Hill or the Sheridan barn, not if she participated in any meaningful way in the murders of Stephanie or Peyton. A round trip to and from either one of those places would take an hour at least, and that's just for the driving."

Armen presented her with a skeptical face. "*If* we believe Rhiannon's estimation of how long the girl was absent from the house."

"Which I do. I mean, why tell us at all about Ali's nocturnal sojourn then lie about the details? All she needed to do is keep the whole story to herself."

"Uh huh." Armen didn't sound entirely convinced, but he didn't argue.

I guess that's as good as I'm going to get. "Next, I fixated on Molly, Edmund's sister. Did the girl just create the persona of Your Wicked Little Witch, write those e-mails herself? Edmund's poisoning certainly seems to point to Molly. Poisoning is an intimate method of murder. The probability is Edmund knew his murderer, took the lethal drink or food right from his killer's hand. Edmund trusted this person—much as he trusted his sister."

"How could she get Edmund's body—?"

"Under the trailer? That's not my problem. I think that girl is as resourceful as she is strong. On top of that, did I mention she played wheelchair softball?"

The car started to fishtail on the rutted country road, and Armen swerved into the skid. By the time he'd finished with the maneuver, his hands were shaking.

"Settle down, Mister Mouse. We need speed, but above all get us there in one piece."

Armen drew a deep breath and muttered, "Of course, I still don't know where in creation *there* is."

"I'm getting to that. Just take Belleview to hell and gone, as if you're going to Edmund's house." She waved toward the road ahead.

He laughed ruefully. "Your wish is my command, Princess Bonita. Don't worry, I won't wrap us around a tree, mainly because there are blessed few trees out here on the great American desert." He gave her a sidelong glance as if to say, "How long do you think I'm going to put up with being treated like one of your students?"

Bonnie rubbed his shoulder. "I remember this handsome gentleman whose mother told fortunes in Armenia. He made me guess at his origins rather than tell me outright. Said it would feel better in the end."

A smile flickered at the corner of Armen's lips. "*Touché*. Fair enough, I'll play. So this Molly is strong enough to do serious damage with a baseball bat?"

"Plenty strong. Hell, she could probably take out the both of us without working up a sweat. But none of that matters. The real problem with Molly as a suspect is that she's another one telling the truth, this time about the girlfriend—Your Wicked Little Witch again. Her mother all but verified that. She didn't disagree with Molly's assertion of a love interest, just who that love interest might be."

"And you know who the love of Edmund's life was?"

"Stay with me." When he continued looking skeptical, she said, "In the middle of all this witchcraft there were two more witches—one the product of a medieval mistranslation, the other a comic book character." She retold the story of Marie Agnesi and how a simple turning curve became the bride of the devil.

Armen squinted at her. "That is peculiar, but I still don't see the connection to these murders."

"Neither did I." Bonnie kept one eye on Armen and the other on the unpredictable rutted road. She didn't relish the ignominy of ending up in a ditch. "Something had been nagging at me, something I'd heard, but for one reason or another it never registered. Then, just as I was about to erase *versiera* and *aversiera* from my blackboard, I saw it. Once again, one word had been substituted for another and that simple substitution changed everything."

"You've lost me again."

Bonnie slowed her breathing trying to force her mind into teacher mode. As was always the case, it wasn't enough for the good teacher to understand a process. The good teacher had to select the perfect pedagogy to make the process plain to the listener as well.

"Go back with me to Edmund's bedroom. Remember all that comic book talk that began with Herbie Popsicle?"

"Herbie Popnecker."

She waved away the correction. "Whatever. Before long you and Molly were discussing the ins and outs of Edmund's collection."

Armen nodded. "Uh huh. She mentioned Overstreet, the comic book register, and Edmund's primo collection he kept in a dehumidifying safe."

Good man! Cut right to the chase. "Exactly. Do you remember Molly claiming Edmund would sell everything if the price was right?"

This time Armen shook his head, taking on the smug look of someone who remembered a choice bit the teacher had forgotten. "I remember her saying he'd sell almost everything. There was a run of five mint condition Harvey comic books she said he would never part with."

"Right again." She slapped his arm and immediately regretted it. *Don't distract the man while he's driving.*

For his part, Armen just smiled. "Thank you, Missus Pinkwater." He adopted the sing-song voice of a kindergarten child.

"You're welcome, Master Callahan." *My God, in the space of four days this man has got you all turned inside out. You're not a schoolgirl, Pinkwater. Get a grip.*

Her hand made its way back to his shoulder like it belonged there. "Correct me if I'm wrong, but I think the comics in question were the first five issues of *Casper the Friendly Ghost*. As I recall, Molly was incredulous he would put any stock in these books beyond their worth and the fact he'd made a great deal on them."

"Considering the other more important pieces in his collection, I could see her point."

"Yes, important."

She swallowed a sarcastic remark concerning comic

books and their relative significance in the world. Besides, there was something endearing in a man who wore a white goatee and yet still held on to a few childish values.

"And it was at that juncture we both missed the real reason why Edmund cherished these particular books."

"The real reason?" He said the words like she was about to spring the punch line of a joke on him.

"Yes, the real reason." She stuck out her tongue at him. "You missed it because you were focused on the other books in this magical vault of Edmund's, and I missed it because I was being lulled into a fugue state by a barrage of comic book talk."

"I have to presume Edmund being enamored with *Casper the Friendly Ghost* falls short of this so-called real reason."

Bonnie resisted the temptation to pinch the shoulder she was caressing. "And I'll presume you're being deliberately obtuse. The subject is witches, Callahan, witches. Here's where our one-word-can-make-all-the-difference confusion raises its less than beautiful head. In the phrase Wicked Little Witch change Wicked to Good."

She watched his face as the realization dawned on him. She had to admit, it was a face she could get used to.

"The poster above the computer," he said, letting each word fall slowly from his mouth. "It pictured not only Casper the Friendly Ghost but also Casper's best friend, a Good Little Witch. The same Good Little Witch who was introduced in those mint condition

Harvey comics."

She nodded. "Indeed. A Good Little Witch named Wendy."

ALICE TOOK THE TURN AT COYOTE ROAD LIKE SHE WAS made for poorly maintained country roads. *Good girl. Just get us to that misplaced hacienda, and I'll buy you all the oil you can drink.*

"If I'm right, all of the children's deaths have nothing to do with the scholarship or Thursday morning's fight, or even Peyton's apparent abduction."

"Was Peyton abducted? From all indications, he went willingly to Edmund's barn."

"If we add Wendy to the equation, the explanation of how he got to that barn is simplified."

Again, the light of comprehension shone in Armen's face. "Peyton was in her car when she drove away."

She nodded the slow nod of the righteous. "It's entirely possible he was somewhere on the Evangelical Academy's grounds, but it makes more sense he simply snuck around into her SUV, climbed in, and stayed hidden. Wendy and Peyton planned his disappearance before she arrived at the Academy, which explains why he became so distracted when she showed up."

Armen raised both hands as if to make a point then, much to Bonnie's relief, put them back on the wheel. "Why hide Peyton at all? Why fake his running away?"

Why, indeed?

As they sped down Coyote Road, Bonnie's stomach tightened. She dreaded what she might find at Wendy's house. Suddenly, a very large portion of her psyche hoped her reasoning was a pile of cow manure. Still, the momentum of her argument pushed her on.

"Let me answer your pair of questions with a pair of my own. Who's been the villain in this Passion Play from the very beginning? Who also seems to have fallen off the face of the earth even though both the military and civilian police are diligently searching for him?"

A tight knowing smile formed on Armen's lips. "The good Colonel."

"I don't know about the good part, but yes, Colonel Ralph Newlin. If I'm right, all this death and misery can be traced back to that sphincter in Air Force blue, and a plan to put a permanent end to a nightmare marriage."

"With Edmund Sheridan's help?"

"You betcha." Bonnie resisted the urge to punctuate her remark with a punch to his arm. "In a misguided effort to comfort Stephanie, Edmund said something incriminating to Stephanie. Wendy had to get rid of her."

Armen chewed his lower lip and beard, his head nodding. "And that very night Stephanie Templeton would die on Fulton Hill. Shoot, you don't have to play baseball to get your hands easily on a baseball bat. Not if your husband plays softball."

"Let's take it from the beginning. From early Thursday morning, things start to go wrong." Bonnie tugged at her ear, sorting through the events of that not-so-long-ago morning. "Edmund tries unsuccessfully to get Peyton in a fight."

"Yeah, why do that? Edmund was Peyton's best friend."

"Because he *was* Peyton's best friend. I'm sure in Edmund's mind he was doing Peyton a favor." She turned to face Armen. "The deal was to get Peyton out of the way."

When Armen looked like he might interrupt again, Bonnie said, "I got a theory about that, too. For now, just hang with me. If Peyton gets in a fight, he gets his thin ass suspended. His father would be pissed, so Edmund could suggest, with Wendy's approval, he lay low in the Sheridan barn. The boy is gone for any homicide that would take place."

Open-mouthed, Armen nodded in agreement. "That would be a lot simpler than spiriting Peyton away from a Knowledge Bowl competition. But Peyton refused to fight back."

The double row of poplars lining the Newlin driveway loomed in the distance like dark mountains against the morning sky. Bonnie took a long shuddering breath to still her voice. "If it wasn't for that unplanned-for choice, Stephanie Templeton would still be alive and by consequence Peyton, when he learned of Stephanie's death."

"All right, let's say I buy it. That still doesn't explain why Peyton was secreted off to the Sheridan's barn in the first place."

"Do you remember much from child psychology classes about dysfunctional families, particularly ones where one or both of the parents are physically or sexually abusive."

Armen pursed his lips in concentration. "I remember the secrecy, the one parent who becomes the enabler, the good child who masks the troubled family by being exemplary."

"I'm thinking more of the relationships within the family rather than the family's structure *per se*, especially, the child's relationship to the abuser."

Armen sighed deeply. "Often, the child will be closer to the abusive parent than he is to the non-abusive parent."

"Closer to the abusive parent," she echoed. "And what if that parent is a hero, a larger than life Adonis twice decorated by the President of the United States, no less?"

"You got the makings of one screwed up kid."

"You betcha. Now suppose this kid's mother and this kid's best friend in the whole world get it into their homicidal craniums they need to put an end to the monster who is making all their lives a living hell?"

"They'd have to get Peyton out of the way, at least temporarily." Armen turned his mouth down in distaste. "I still have trouble picturing Wendy Newlin with Edmund."

Bonnie spread wide her hands, signaling she was none too sure of the nature of the pair's relationship. "It may be nothing more than Wendy utilizing a willing foil. She's certainly every horny nerd's wet dream. It wouldn't take much to wrap the boy around her scheme and make him agree to help her get rid of an abusive husband, especially if that husband was the father of his best friend."

Armen licked his lips, obviously getting into the spirit of the give-and-take. His eyes went wide. "When you called Wendy from your classroom, the male voice you heard—."

"Was probably Edmund."

"And Ralph Newlin himself?"

"By Saturday morning? If it was anybody else, I'd say he was singing in the heavenly choir. Given that we're talking about Ralph Newlin, I seriously doubt it."

Armen turned into the tree-lined drive. "Hold it! We both saw Wendy's face in the wee hours of Sunday morning. Someone broke the woman's nose."

Bonnie nodded her agreement. "I considered that. I think Edmund did it."

"Edmund?"

"Imagine how you would feel if you realized you'd been poisoned. Wouldn't you lash out?"

Armen looked dubious. "I suppose."

"It all ties together. And Edmund would hardly suspect Wendy would poison him, especially if she was his lover."

She meant to explain more but all thought was driven from her mind. At the end of the horseshoe drive sat Ralph Newlin's yellow Stingray. The trunk was open.

Not a sound came from within the sprawling adobe structure. No light escaped either since a series of pleated curtains made it impossible to see through the long stained-glass window.

A woman's scream sounded from within the house.

The expression on Armen's face told Bonnie he was thinking precisely what she was. What if they were wrong? What if Ralph Newlin was at that very moment throttling his wife?

Armen reached beneath the dash and popped the trunk. "I'll go."

"Not without me, you won't," she whispered. *You idiot, the time for whispering is long past. Whoever's in that house probably watched you come up the drive.* She fully expected Armen to give her a hard time about accompanying him, but he only offered a tight smile and nodded.

While Bonnie fumbled in the back seat for her crutches, Armen disappeared to the rear of the car, appearing a moment later with a tire iron. He smacked it once in the palm of his hand.

Bonnie's heart felt like it had grown too large for her chest. It pounded for release against her ribs. "Let's do it."

The door wasn't locked. Bonnie swung it open, and they peered into the semi-darkness of the front room. Armen squinted as he led the way, the tire iron in front of him like a dousing rod. A sickly sweet smell became apparent.

Blood?

Bonnie's suspicions were confirmed a moment later when her eyes grew accustomed to the gloom. The body of Ralph Newlin lay face up and spread-eagled not ten feet from the open door. From the single rutted depression on the carpet, he'd been dragged by the feet. A streak of dried blood leading back toward the kitchen discolored the carpet.

A grunt came from behind the open door. Something thin and metallic struck Armen in the upper chest. The tire iron flew from his hands. It dropped with a thud into the thick carpet. The metal rod struck again, this time catching Armen full in the face. He fell to his knees and toppled.

Before Bonnie could react, the door slammed shut.

"I knew you'd come flying in here if I screamed." Her shoulder pressed against the door, Wendy Newlin held a metal-headed golf club in both hands. Her misshapen face was flushed. A streak of blood stained the front of her cashmere sweater.

Wendy sighed and fixed Bonnie with a one-eyed stare. "Ten more minutes and I would have had Ralph safely tucked into the trunk of his beloved Stingray."

Wendy lifted a corner of the curtain and squinted into the morning light. "Good girl. You didn't bring the police."

"Wendy, you can't get away with this." Bonnie pointed with her crutch. "There'll be no hiding that blood stain."

Wendy advanced a step. She clasped the club in one hand. Instead of brandishing it, however, she stroked her swollen and discolored cheek. "You're wrong. That nice Sergeant Valsecci will bear witness to my husband's brutal attack of Saturday night. Tearfully,

I'll explain how he returned. This time, he intended to kill me. A woman has a right to defend herself."

Bonnie took a step back, shaking her head as she went. She knew she should just shut her mouth, play for time, but her Imp of the Perverse prodded her to speak. "I don't think so. From the looks of your husband, I'd say he's been dead for several days. How are you going to explain how a dead man attacked you on Saturday?"

When Wendy didn't respond, Bonnie went on. "Edmund get in a few licks before he shuffled off his mortal coil?"

Wendy sighed again and nodded, as if Bonnie had caught her filching the last piece of pumpkin pie rather than how a dying young man had broken her nose. "He surprised me. I really thought he'd succumb quicker."

She stroked her swollen nose. "No matter—one thing I've learned over the years is how to take a punch."

Again, Bonnie's saner self demanded she shut her mouth, and again her Imp of the Perverse prevailed.

"Three children are dead because of you. One of them is your own child."

She took another backward step and felt a panel of drapery brush against her arm. She didn't dare take her eyes off Wendy.

"Shut up," Wendy hissed.

She raised the club as if she meant to swing it. "That maniac Edmund killed Stephanie and my son. That's why I had to kill him."

Bonnie pursed her lips and offered a sympathetic

smile. In a moment of crystal clarity Bonnie knew the woman was lying. "I don't think so, Wendy. Your last Wicked Little Witch e-mail says otherwise."

Wendy squinted at Bonnie with her one good eye. "I don't know what you're talking about."

In for a penny.

"Cut the crap. You never intended for Edmund to read that e-mail. You'd been calling the boy Casper up until that last letter."

Wendy's lopsided face blushed. "And I was his Wicked Little Witch." She shrugged. "He was always over here, hanging out with Peyton, playing video games. One day he came when Peyton was out with his dad. We played a different game."

Edmund, you poor nebesh. You never had a chance with this woman. She meant to kill you from the moment she seduced you.

"In the last letter you called Edmund Samurai, Ali's pet name for him. You wrote that letter for the same reason a magician gets you staring at the hand that doesn't hold the coin—misdirection. All along you've been casting suspicion away from yourself—first Jesse Poole then Ali Griffith, but the cleverest stroke of all was how you used Edmund."

Wendy shook her red mane, her face hard, her eyes chips of flint. "You don't know how close you came to dying Friday night. Edmund talked me out of going into that ravine and finishing you off."

Bonnie could swear she saw a flicker of a smile touch Wendy's lips. Bonnie's heart sank. The woman was a family-sized loaf of banana bread.

Still, Bonnie had to reason with her. "Why did you listen?"

Wendy shrugged again. This time a capricious shrug that said "Maybe I shouldn't have." "When you cursed Jesse, we knew you thought he was the driver. Edmund pointed that out to me, and it made sense to let you report Jesse was driving the truck."

Thank you, Edmund.

Bonnie risked a momentary glance at Armen. He seemed to be breathing, but that didn't mean his skull wasn't filling with blood. Whatever she meant to do she'd better do it quickly. When she looked back at Wendy, the woman was once more staring at her.

A sad smile pulled back one corner of Wendy's swollen lips. She cocked her head. "You know, I meant it when I told you I wanted to be your friend. I had hoped . . ." She drew a long breath and sighed. ". . . when this was all over we could get to know one another."

Yet, you tried to kill me an hour after you told me that. Bonnie adopted the frozen smile she normally reserved for students she wanted to throttle. "I would have liked that, too."

The corners of Wendy mouth turned down—a look of disappointment rather than anger. "Who's the liar now? You think me a monster. You have no idea what I've sacrificed for that warped little genius: the beatings, the humiliations. The least he could do is support me after I was forced to do away with the Templeton girl."

Time to get smart, Pinkwater. You need to get on this strudel's good side. Bonnie shook her head. "I don't think you're a monster at all. I saw Peyton's records. He would have been fourteen in a few days. You told me you've been married for less than fourteen. How pregnant were you when you got married?"

Wendy laughed, high-pitched and staccato. "Not pregnant at all. I had just given birth. It was a difficult delivery because of my age and the damage Ralph did to my spine in the rape."

Bonnie wasn't sure how to respond. She was spared the effort.

"I was twelve. Ralph and his brother held me down and took turns with me." A tear leaked from Wendy's good eye. "I was too young, too fucked up . . ."

She laughed again. "In more ways than the obvious ones. Anyway, a deal was struck between my parents and Ralph's."

"A deal?" Against her will, Bonnie felt herself being sucked into the tragedy that was Wendy Newlin.

Wendy nodded and swiped at the tear. "Ralph's brother was already into politics, being groomed to be the governor or senator or something. My parents threatened to make trouble. They'd always been white trash. Still are. Money and a respectable marriage to a respectable family smoothed everything over. Ralph was chosen to do the honorable thing."

An almost animal snarl issued from her swollen lips. "The honorable thing. Every day of my life, he reminded me what a favor he'd done me."

Her fingers played over the swollen half of her face. "Some days a little more forceful than others."

Armen groaned.

The dreamy look that had taken over Wendy's face evaporated. "I wish things had turned out differently for all of us, but life goes on." She advanced another step.

Bonnie's heart raced. She backed up while casting about for anything to give her a little more time. "Franklin knows you poisoned Edmund."

Wendy raised the club. "Nice try, but obviously, he doesn't. If he did, he'd be here, not you."

She advanced another step. "I'm sorry, Bonnie. I wish things didn't have to be this way."

Screw this.

Bonnie grabbed a panel of the drapery and yanked. The curtain rod tore free from the wall. With a yell, she hurled the dislodged curtain at Wendy.

Wendy swung and entangled the club.

As Bonnie wheeled on her crutches, she heard Wendy spit curses at her. *That'll keep her busy for all of ten seconds, then what?* The tips of the crutches sank deep in the carpet, slowing her down.

Before she'd taken three steps, Wendy was on her. The metal club struck her in the right hand, sending her sprawling. *Jesus Christ, that hurts like a son of a bitch.* She fell onto her *derrière* and toppled backward.

Wendy Newlin bore down on her, the club high over her head.

Bonnie deflected the blow with her crutch. Her injured hand shrieked in protest.

Damn you, bitch. She hurled the crutch at Wendy's face.

Wendy batted it aside.

Ignoring the pain that sang an aria from every bone in her body, Bonnie hoisted herself to her feet. There was nowhere to run. She turned to face her attacker.

Come and get me, you twisted asshole.

Wendy swung the club like a bat and Bonnie's head was the ball.

Hell, they call it a walking boot.

Jamming her injured foot into the carpet for stability, Bonnie swung her remaining crutch at the club and the hand that held it. The golf club clattered against the ribs of the crutch. The next instant the crutch's tip connected with Wendy's wrist.

The woman howled in pain and dropped the club. She stooped hurriedly to retrieve it.

Not in this lifetime, sister.

Bonnie pulled back on her crutch and flipped the tip end into her hand. As Wendy rose holding the golf club, Bonnie swung the crutch, putting every foot-pound of force she could muster into the swing.

The metal bracing struck Wendy full in the side of the head. The blow launched her toward the stained-glass mural. Wendy exploded through the glass in a shower of frosted reds and purples.

The late morning sun reflected off the broken shards and the blood pooling around Wendy Newlin's lacerated throat.

EPILOGUE

NEXT SATURDAY EVENING FOUND BONNIE staring past a massive ceramic bowl of potato salad at a ten-foot multicolored maypole. The late spring sun had yet to set and lent a surreal aura to the rainbow of colors woven about the monolith.

Armen sat next to her, holding court about their harrowing escape from the clutches of Wendy Newlin. If Bonnie had to estimate, she'd be forced to say she was reserving less than twelve percent of her attention for Armen. The rest she gave over to the impressive maypole which towered over them all in the Griffith's front yard.

Here she sat at a long picnic table sharing corn bread and watermelon with a slew of witches, and truth be told she felt right at home. She'd had very little to do with the maypole's creation. That was the work of Rhiannon, Ali, Jesse, Winston, and those witches whose names she knew she could bring to the forefront of her brain if she cared enough to try. Still, something magical had transpired in the weaving of the long ribbons. Then there'd been the singing, welcoming the goddess back from her long winter's repose, asking for her blessing on the coming year.

Who'd have thought I'd be so moved by a bunch of rummy pagans. But what the hell, Beltane is supposed to be a time of renewal. I guess that's what we all need right about now. She turned back to Armen. He seemed to be winding down on his tale of adventure.

"My mother always said I had a hard head."

Armen's swollen nose bore a contraption of aluminum, sponge, and surgical tape, which did nothing to hide the fact that both his eyes were blackened and his poor proboscis was too obviously broken.

"Truth is, Wendy laid a pretty convincing concussion on me. We were lucky Franklin showed up when he did."

Bonnie could feel the hint of the smile that had been trying to work its way onto her face evaporate. "Not in time to save Wendy Newlin, though."

Rhiannon shoved aside the large ceramic bowl, engulfing Bonnie's uninjured hand in her larger one. "Bonnie, don't beat yourself up over this. You did all you could."

Rhiannon chucked Bonnie on the shoulder. "You know, I've been thinking about Wendy Newlin myself, and what the Tarot had to say about her."

"How so?"

"Well, two of the cards specifically indicated Wendy Newlin's situation. The Nine of Swords spoke to Wendy's darkening mind—her despair, the hopelessness of her marriage."

Bonnie recalled the card—a woman sitting up in bed, her face buried in her hands, a black wall behind her. *Damn it, woman, you murdered your child. Why can't I just assign you to the fires of hell and be done with you?* An image swirled in the mists of Bonnie's depression—a twelve-year old girl being raped again and again by two grown men.

"Then the Two of Swords," Rhiannon said.

Bonnie didn't need any reminder of this card—The Hoodwinked Woman, a woman living a lie. Sold by her own parents to a man who hated and abused her for more than a decade. Bonnie also remembered the alternative interpretation of the card—a woman desperately needing a friend.

Tears pooled in Bonnie's eyes before she swiped them away. *I would have saved you, Wendy. God damn it, I tried.* Bonnie had attempted to staunch the flow of blood that insisted on escaping from Wendy's throat at an alarming rate. In the end, the woman's life simply poured out crimson onto her flagstone patio.

"If she lived, she'd have spent the rest of her life in prison, or a mental institution," Rhiannon said.

"I know." *And I'll spend the rest of mine living with the decision I made staring down at Wendy Newlin's lifeless corpse.*

The idea had come to Bonnie the instant Wendy breathed her last. What if Wendy hadn't died without regaining consciousness? What if she'd confessed to the murder of her husband and completely exonerated Edmund?

Hell, it could even be true, but even if it wasn't, it should be. The entire Newlin family was gone. Not one of them would be hurt if the guilt for all these deaths shifted away from Edmund. Forget the fact that Edmund was, at the very least, an accomplice. This wasn't about Edmund and what he did, or didn't do, during the final days of his mixed up life. The Sheridans would be spared a horrific ordeal. The decision was made almost as quickly as the idea was formulated.

The police and the East Plains paramedics were called. A still unconscious Armen was taken into Colorado Springs. Wendy Newlin was pronounced dead on the scene. Both she and Armen were taken in the same van into Colorado Springs. Franklin Valsecci showed up forty minutes later.

Bonnie fed Franklin the revised tale of Wendy's Newlin's final minutes of life. She wove it around Wendy's story of a long ago rape and a lifetime of abuse.

She couldn't remember where she'd heard the aphorism, but someone once said that if you wanted a lie to be believed, it should be manufactured of nineteen parts truth to one part fantasy. Bonnie couldn't swear to a ninety-five percent ratio, but the mixture did the job. If Franklin suspected she was lying, he evinced no hint. He nodded at the appropriate junctures and said it tied in with facts he'd already discovered. Besides, what good would it do to pin blame on Edmund? The boy was dead.

With any luck, the story would bring long delayed justice down on Ralph Newlin's politician brother.

As Bonnie stared across the picnic table at Rhiannon, she searched her conscience. *I can live with my decision. Everything may not be as I would have chosen it, but it's close enough.*

"I'll be okay."

"I know you will. I threw your Tarot last night." Rhiannon patted Bonnie's uninjured hand. "You're going to come through this just fine."

"You're all right, Rhiannon Griffith."

"Who said I wasn't?"

This time Bonnie found it easier to smile. "We've got to be going." She grabbed a flowered cane leaning against the picnic table.

Armen rose to join her.

"So soon?" Ali asked.

Bonnie hooked her arm into Armen's. "I promised this handsome gentleman we'd watch The Best Movie Ever Made tonight."

"*Casablanca*," Rhiannon said, matter of factly.

Bonnie squinted up at Armen suspiciously. "Did you tell her?"

Armen shook his head. His black eyes and swollen nose made him seem like a little boy dodging the blame for a broken window.

"Don't go picking on the poor man." Rhiannon

wrapped an arm around each of their shoulders. "He didn't need to tell me. I'm a witch, remember."

Rhiannon winked at Bonnie. "Besides, didn't A & E proclaim *Casablanca* the best movie ever made?"

Bonnie shook her head. "That was *Citizen Kane*."

"Well, it should have been *Casablanca*."

Armen and Rhiannon exchanged glances then almost simultaneously they slurred, " 'Of all the gin joints, in all the world, she comes walking into mine'."

Earlier in the week Bonnie had traded in her crutches for the cane. She was glad she had a lock on Armen's elbow as they walked back to the Subaru. She felt definitely proprietary with regard to one middle-school Science teacher, and was more than a little happy Rhiannon didn't follow them all the way to the car.

When they reached Alice, Bonnie turned to wave and noted with satisfaction at how close Ali was sitting to Jesse. The two had become inseparable. They'd attended not only Mrs. Poole's funeral together, but also those of each of their deceased classmates. They'd even celebrated together when Ali was awarded the Sullivan Scholarship.

"Take care, everyone," Bonnie yelled. "We'll see you soon."

Rhiannon mouthed something and held up three fingers. Bonnie chuckled.

"What did she say?" Armen asked as he held the door.

"I'm not really sure. I think it was a line from *Casablanca*." *I'm getting pretty good at this lying stuff.*

Of course, the message had nothing to do with The Best Movie Ever Made. Rhiannon had prescribed the optimal dosage for her patented love potion.

As Armen started up the Subaru, Bonnie snuggled close to him. She fully intended to sit through the entire showing of *Casablanca,* but afterward, who knew? Bonnie didn't think she'd need the love potion. Yes, they were a couple of fifty-year-olds, and certainly they bore multiple contusions, lacerations, and broken bones. Yet, if she had anything to say about it, the evening would end with them creating a little magic of their own.

And the morning after, maybe French toast?

GHOSTLY LIAISONS

TERRY LEE WILDE

The Ghost Appeaser . . .

Sixteen-year-old Emily Rundle's curious nature causes her big problems when she moves with her family to Florida. First of all, Emily's different. Really different. Then the nightmares begin. The kind she can't escape. The kind that make her sweat in terror, and are forcing her to solve a dangerous mystery.

The Knight in Jeans . . .

Michael Shipley just moved to town too, and realizes immediately Emily is trouble with a capital T. If he becomes involved with her his life will change forever. But premonitions that Emily's life will be in danger force him to protect the girl who's gifted with extraordinary abilities like his.

The Danger . . .

Both Michael and Emily have painful histories, memories they'd rather forget. But faced with dangerous new challenges, they must overcome their pasts, threats at school, bullies in the flesh, and ghostly apparitions bent on a deadly game of revenge. What began as a seemingly simple matter of ghostly appeasement ends in a race against time as Michael and Emily fight the evil that threatens to overwhelm them.

ISBN#1932815376
ISBN#9781932815375
Bronze Imprint
US $9.99 / CDN $13.95
Paranormal
October 2006
http://terryspear.tripod.com/terrywildeauthorofyoungadultbooks/

Secrets
F.M. McPherson

Mike Jaeger is a typical teenager. Well, sort of. He's got some problems, mental problems specifically. Maybe a few more than most. But at least he's human.

Or not.

At the ripe old age of sixteen, Mike begins to awaken to a new self. A self that remembers forty thousand years of war with humans.

Mike and his father are clones, as was every ancestor back to the First Brother, the homonid who saw his Pack-sister, his future mate, raped and tortured by humans. Sharing empathically in her fate, First Brother vows revenge on humans, and for that is cast out of the Pack. Every descendant since remembers the events vividly, for emotional memories are inscribed in their very DNA.

But Mike doesn't know his hallucinations are memories, or that the shadows in his mind are Pack-brothers. And his father can't bring himself to tell Mike what's happening to him. Mike only knows he has one good, true friend, Dave.

And Dave, too, has a secret.

ISBN#1932815309
ISBN #9781932815306
Bronze Imprint
US $9.99 / CDN $13.95
Available Now
www.fmmcpherson.com

STONES OF ABRAXAS

K. OSBORN SULLIVAN

David Stanhope is an average twelve-year-old. His two best friends are geeks. Both his older sister and his dodge ball obsessed gym coach seem to despise him. And his parents are dragging him to a broken down old cabin in the woods for summer vacation.

But there's a secret lurking in David's attic. It takes David and his sister Amanda to the magical world of Abraxas where a centuries-old Black Magician is bent on destroying them. Will David and Amanda be able to survive and return to their own world?

And why is the dragon afraid of a compass? Can a centaur wear a tool belt? What about the huge talking frogs, hungry vampires, a harpy who cheats at cards and Lucy the Moat Monster?

Maybe David isn't so average after all.

ISBN#1932815767
ISBN#9781932815764
Bronze Imprint
US $9.99 / CDN $13.95
Fantasy
Available Now
www.kosbornsullivan.com

The Secret of
SHABAZ

JENNIFER MACAIRE

ONCE UPON A TIME, there was a brave and noble unicorn whose name was Shabaz. So wondrous was this beast, so loyal and devoted to his mistress, that he gave up his horn to a powerful magic to save her and her infant daughter from the evil and terrible Dark Lord, a necromancer. He travels through time with his precious cargo, and Birchspring, a warrior elf, to a place they believe will be safe.

TWO HUNDRED YEARS have passed. Tania, a servant lass, toils in the stable of the once mighty Castle Storm. An orphan, Tania has only her Grandfather Birchspring, and the tired old war horse she tends. Her life is hard and dull with drudgery.

Until Tania hears that a new Dark Lord has risen, and threatens the centuries of peace the countryside has enjoyed. It is not all she learns. "Grandfather" Birchspring can no longer contain the secret of Tania's heritage. The tired old war horse can no longer maintain his masquerade. Together, the three cannot sit idly by while the evil force that destroyed Tania's mother returns to finish what he once started. Ill equipped, with only great heart and noble purpose, they ride to war. BUT IT IS MORE than battle they encounter. And it is only the force of love that will endure. Love, and the unicorn's final, precious gift. . . .

ISBN#1932815090

ISBN#9781932815092

Bronze Imprint

US $12.99 / CDN $17.99

Available Now

www.jennifermacaire.com

HORSE PASSAGES
JENNIFER MACAIRE

Voyagers from earth have not only found haven on a far-away planet, but vast herds of horses that seem to vanish as if by magic. In reality the horses are able to open passages through time and travel from planet to planet. Settlers on the Home Planet learn to tame these horses and accompany them on their journeys, following the herds through the universe. Their life, their existence, is idyllic but for the scourge of the alien Raiders, who stalk and capture the herders and their horses.

Twins Carl and Meagan Cadet are the youngest herders in the Federation. Though they savor their privacy and the bond with their horses, they eventually join forces with the rowdy Jeffries brothers. Just as they are learning to live and travel together, however, tragedy strikes.

No one has ever escaped the Raiders. But when Luke Jeffries and Meagan, long ago orphaned by the cruel and barbaric aliens, find themselves slaves on a mining planet, they know they must try. Yet to do so, they must first discover the key to unlock the mystery of the marvelous Horse Passages.

ISBN#1932815120
ISBN#9781932815122
Bronze Imprint
US $9.99 / CDN $13.95
Available Now
www.jennifermacaire.com

THE LONG HUNTER

A NOVEL BY
DON MCNAIR

ILLUSTRATIONS BY JAMES TAMPA

Matt was only a boy when Indians killed his parents and kidnapped his three-year-old sister. Blaming himself for the tragedy, Matt sets out on a journey of the heart to find little Mandy. He doesn't get far, however, before he's "bound" to a cruel and brutal inn keeper. Sick and barely alive, he's rescued by a kindly old man who takes him in and teaches him the rudiments of survival in the wilderness.

But Matt's time with Noah is too short-lived. When the vengeful inn keeper guns Noah down, Matt commits murder as well. On the run now, and still seeking his sister, Matt heads into Can-tuc-kee and the Cherokee Indian Territory. His plan, as a long hunter, is to amass enough skins to buy some land and make a home for him and Mandy. Once again, however, Matt's plans go awry.

Captured by Indians, the young man once again finds himself "bound". He watches his best friend die a hideous death at the stake. And he learns a great deal more about survival. Escaping the Indians at last, he helps fellow Virginians settle the rugged, majestic land he has come to love. Ultimately, he learns what "home" really is . . . and where it resides.

ISBN#1932815511
ISBN#9781932815511
Palladium Imprint
US $19.95 / CDN $26.95
Available Now

RhiANNON
GODDESS IN TRAINING
TRACI HALL

Rhiannon Godfrey is a teen with a twist. She's psychic. Of course, that's not too unusual seeing both her parents are Wiccan. They are also wicked, Rhiannon believes, when they move from trendy, super cool Vegas to Washington state just so she can have a "normal" high school experience. Hah.

Beyond mad, Rhiannon neglects to inform her parents the farmhouse they just purchased is haunted. To prove that she doesn't belong in a "normal" high school but in Dr. Richard's Institute of Parapsychology which she's attended since first grade, she decides to send the ghost to the Other Side. Not that dispelling ghosts is her area of expertise, but really, how hard can it be? Well . . .

And then there's Jared Roberts. Totally hot. For a cowboy, that is. Things seem to be looking up until his twin, the shallow and popular Janet, shows up. When she turns mean on Rhee's new friends, it seems a little payback is in order. Things are getting a bit tricky balancing really scary ghosts, old secrets, serious trust issues, and her very first kiss. But she can handle it, can't she? After all, she's

RHIANNON, G0DDESS IN TRAINING

ISBN#1932815589
ISBN#9781932815580
Bronze Imprint
US $9.99 / CDN $13.95
December 2006
www.tracihall.com

*For more information
about other great titles from
Medallion Press, visit*

www.medallionpress.com